THE PERENNIAL MISS WILDTHYME

Edited by Dale Smith

Obverse Books
Cover Art © Paul Hanley
Cover Design © Cody Schell
First published September 2015

Printed and bound in Great Britain by
TJ International Ltd, Padstow, Cornwall

Death of the Author © Jay Eales
Right vs Left vs Wrong © Paul Vayro
Wildthyme and the Wolf © Graham Tedesco-Blair
Dolores Smith and the Birthday Bear © Kara Dennison
The Girl Who Went Up In Smoke © Greg Maughan
Onesies © Steve Palace
The Opera of Samhain © Donald McCarthy
A Grove Invisible © Juliet Kemp
Michael Drake © Dale Smith/Ian Potter
The Midnight Empire © Julio Angel Ortiz
Self Possessed © Ian Potter
Closure © Paul Castle

Iris Wildthyme and Panda © Paul Magrs

The moral rights of the author have been asserted.
All characters in this book are fictional. Any resemblance to persons, living or dead, is co-incidental.
All rights reserved. No part of this publication may be reproduced, stored in a retrieval system, or in any form or by any means, without the prior permission in writing of the publisher, nor be otherwise circulated in any form of binding, cover or e-book other than which it is published and without a similar condition including this condition being imposed on the subsequent publisher.

Obverse, never obvious

For Aunty Iris

More Iris Wildthyme from Obverse Books

1. Iris Wildthyme & the Celestial Omnibus
2. The Panda Book of Horror
3. Miss Wildthyme & Friends Investigate
4. Iris: Abroad
5. Wildthyme in Purple
6. Lady Stardust
7. Fifteen
8. Iris Wildthyme of Mars

CONTENTS

Death of the Author - Jay Eales	7
Right vs Left vs Wrong - Paul Vayro	29
Wildthyme and the Wolf - Graham Tedesco-Blair	46
Dolores Smith and the Birthday Bear - Kara Dennison	60
The Girl Who Went Up In Smoke - Greg Maughan	74
Onesies - Steve Palace	88
The Opera of Samhain - Donald McCarthy	102
A Grove Invisible - Juliet Kemp	114
Michael Drake - Dale Smith, With Ian Potter	126
The Midnight Empire - Julio Angel Ortiz	147
Self Possessed - Ian Potter	161
Closure - Paul Castle	183

DEATH OF THE AUTHOR
JAY EALES

"It's times like this," Panda gasped as he and Brenda Soobie fled through the corridors of the Flamingo Hotel in Las Vegas, "that I feel I should reconsider my life choices."

"How so?" Brenda said as she tried another locked door, and squinted behind them into the basement gloom, strewn with show props and lighting rigs, for signs of their pursuer. They could hear the tinny refrain of Mariachi horns, punctuated with a keening baritone wail growing ever nearer: "Whiiiiiiii-haiiiiii-iiiiiii…"

Brenda still wore the striking feathered dress she'd worn on stage during her set just a couple of hours earlier. She had abandoned her shoes. Stilettos were only really useful as weapons during a scrap. Not so good when one had to beat a hasty retreat in cramped conditions.

"Deeeliiiiiiilahhh!" The trumpets chorused once again, as the Tomdroid rounded the last corner into view. His hips gyrated hypnotically, and Brenda warded against their evil intent by only looking through her fingers at the advancing android. Even so, her knicker elastic struggled to retain integrity under the Tomslaught. The Tomdroid was a sight all right; trousers so tight they might have been sprayed on; frilled shirt worn at half-mast; the illusion of pure Tomness spoiled only by his red eyes shining from the gloom, and the unnerving way his sideburns fanned in and out like gills to reveal speakers whenever musical accompaniment was required.

Panda gestured towards their robotic foe, "Come to Vegas, baby, you said. It'll be fun, you said. I was expecting swimming pools … booze … celebrity parties … knock out a few reviews by the poolside while you climb the bill."

"Panda, you can be an ingrate sometimes! Why, only today, you've met Elvis and Priscilla, backstage with Tom Jones over there …"

"Not the real Tom Jones," Panda said.

"Granted, but a decent facsimile. None of your Tussauds' rubbish."

"You've missed the important bit, Brenda."

"Okay, so 'Tom' turned out to be part of an alien conspiracy to abduct the Presleys, and not best pleased when we spangled their masterplan, but you have to admire the handiwork." Brenda and Panda continued to slowly back along the corridor, trying not to be too obvious about it.

"Call me old-fashioned, but I find it difficult to appreciate anyone that's actively trying to knock the stuffing out of me." Rapidly running out of corridor, there was one last door to try.

With an unspoken plea to the God of Gamblers or any other entities that might currently inhabit the casino capital, Brenda gave the door handle a confident twist. She and Panda practically fell inside.

There's a room, with a door. Windows, one, two three, four. Ready to play?

Wait a minute. Windows? In a basement? That's a bit rum, thought Brenda, but lacking any other obvious exits, beggars could not be choosers. But which one? The arch, the square or the round window? Panda stood with his back braced against the door, in a vain attempt to hold back the Tomdroid. Brenda could not think of herself as a square – that was for certain. The circular one? Well, she'd certainly been around. But there was really only one choice – the 'arch' window it was. Clambering through in a most unladylike manner, Brenda scrabbled about one leg at a time, and then reached back at full stretch to take Panda's own grasping paw, yanking him towards her as the Tomdroid burst into their refuge. Panda had just enough wits to wave farewell to their pursuer as he closed the window behind them, and then they fell headlong from the frying pan into …

"Jings!" exclaimed the Shopkeeper, as Brenda and her furry little friend tumbled through the mirror, deposited in an ungainly heap on his changing room floor. You could tell he was surprised by the way his fez huddled right at the crown of his head, as though in fear for its life. Surprised by the way he'd gone exponentially more Scots in all the excitement, he blamed an early life furnished in Oor Wullie comic strips. Almost as surprised as his unexpected arrivals, who had climbed through a window and fallen out of a mirror.

He did the gentlemanly thing, by extending a helping hand while turning his face away as Brenda straightened her peacock dress, turning it from practically pornographic into merely outrageous.

When the Shopkeeper finally decided it was safe to risk another look, and his fez had just about recovered from the shock, his eyebrows shot up so fast, they nearly knocked it right off his head.

"Iris Wildthyme, as I live and breathe!"

Brenda fixed him with an appraising eye. This younger body didn't quite generate the same withering intensity that some of her older/younger incarnations managed.

"I haven't gone by that name in quite a while, honey," she chuckled, and lowered her sunglasses conspiratorially. "I'm travelling incognito," her honeyed voice purred, "Sorry, but have I had the pleasure?"

The shopkeeper met her gaze with a gentle smile, his head tilted to the side just so. After an uncomfortably long pause, he responded: "No. I don't suppose you have."

Brenda clocked the Shopkeeper's fez, and rolled her eyes. "What are you trying to say with this?" She jabbed the headwear with an accusatory finger, and felt it shrink away from her touch.

"Fezzes are …"

Brenda shushed him with a raised finger.

"Whatever you're about to say, stop right there. They most definitely are not."

"Comfy."

Brenda sucked air through her teeth disapprovingly.

Before Brenda could say another word, the Shopkeeper waved her down, and sighed, "Buses."

"Beg pardon?" Brenda said, thinking wistfully about Putney Common as the Shopkeeper attempted to hustle them out of his changing room. He kept glancing over at the mirror, rocking gently against its catch, before urging them into the corridor.

"Customers. Like buses. You don't get a sniff of one for hours and then two come along at once. I need to get an assistant."

"I should probably warn you," Brenda said, "When we were dumped unceremoniously in your changing room, we were being pursued …"

"You don't say." The Shopkeeper did not seem fazed by the possibility, but instead, he slipped into the next changing room, reappearing a few moments later dragging an identical full length mirror into the corridor. Brenda found herself lending a hand as he manoeuvred the heavy furniture into the room they'd just vacated. He pivoted the mirror on the spot until it stood facing its opposite number in the room, and stood back, with a contented expression.

"Pursued by a homicidal robot disguised as Tom Jones." Brenda watched for the Shopkeeper's reaction. The point at which his credulity was bound to snap. When the reaction came, it was not quite what she was expecting.

"This happens to you a lot, doesn't it? I can tell." Utterly calm, and charming with it. You want to watch this one, old girl, or before you know it, you'll be offering to take him away from all this. Wherever all this was.

Panda looked at Iris. One of them had to say it, and it might as well be him. "Well, it's not unusual."

The Tomdroid burst through the arched window frame, landing precisely on the ground on the other side. He was in a desert, but this was not Las Vegas. His sensors detected tell-tale traces of intra-dimensional transit technology at work.

There was substantial lag between entry and exit points – almost four seconds. Behind him, the window had become a full length mirror, and aside from the occasional cactus to break up the landscape, it was the only feature. He scanned for life signs and found none within range.

The club singer and her tiny pet had prevented him from fulfilling his primary directive. All that remained now was vengeance. His eyes sparkled, like the red, red lasers of home. He stepped through glass that was not glass, and this time, he noticed a spike in the middle of transit, as though his progress was being diverted mid-jump. His internal chronometer span as it attempted to adjust to local time. Still no life sign indicators. He strode on. It took him twenty-eight crossings, each time to a fresh location, before his learning algorithms cottoned on to the truth of his situation. There was no way to retrace his footsteps. His mission had failed. Vengeance was denied him. The Tomdroid ground to a stop, out of options.

With no other course of action open to him, and his power cells dwindling, he powered down into standby mode, where he would conserve his remaining energy until such time that a new possibility presented itself. Although it was a waste of his resources, he sang softly to himself. It made him feel a little better.

The Shopkeeper couldn't tempt Brenda to a costume change, though she did agree to the loan of a delightful pair of elfin boots and a winter coat. If they were to explore their new surroundings, on the snowy cobbles of Samhain, barefoot was not advised.

Panda balked at tea being the only refreshment on offer, but he choked a cup down for the sake of politeness.

"What about the Tomdroid?" Brenda asked.

"Let him get his own Oolong," the Shopkeeper joked. "Don't you worry about him. Give him enough time in the changing room and he'll be right as ninepence."

"If you say so. Are you sure you can't give us a guided tour of Samhain, being new in town and everything?"

"Would if I could, lovely lady. Best if I don't leave the shop unattended right now, though. Just in case Tom the Tin Man does anything unexpected, eh? In any case, Samhain's the sort of place best discovered for yourself, I've always found."

Before they knew it, the Shopkeeper – somehow, they did not catch his name – was giving them a cheery wave as the door bell jangled, and Brenda and Panda found themselves in Festive Road, among the streets and houses of Samhain; most British of villages.

"Where is this place, Brenda?" Panda asked.

Brenda stuck her index finger in her mouth and held it aloft for a few moments, before reaching a conclusion: "Yorkshire."

"Yorkshire?" Panda wailed, "How on Earth are we going to get home without the bus?"

"One thing at a time," Brenda said cheerily, before striding out towards wherever her nose was pointing her. Panda had to jog along to keep up.

Whatever bit of Yorkshire they found themselves in, it was a decidedly cosmopolitan little corner, if Brenda was any judge. Literally the first person they happened across was a city gent, complete with bowler and brolly, taking his carnivorous plant for a walk. Or the other way round. Samhain's architecture, like its citizens, was a patchwork. Cobbles and tarmac co-existing side by side. Aerials of all shapes and sizes nested on many a roof. Even the thatched ones.

"Shky!"

"Guy!"

"How many more timesh? It's kissh the shky, I'm telling you!"

Brenda turned down a side street, and into the midst of a full-on barney in the middle of the lane, between two elderly gentlemen of indeterminate origins.

'Guy' wore a samite robe of Byzantine fashion, and just the one sandal; his hairline long since retreated beneath the follicle horizon. 'Sky' had the full complement of footwear – in his case that was eight in total – one for each of his arachnoid limbs. 'Sky' skittered over the cobbles, circling his opponent. Neither of them seemed prepared to give ground to the other. Panda tugged at Brenda's coat sleeve, encouraging her to get a shift on, before …

Too late, as the one with the most legs spotted their movement out of the corner of an eye.

"Shcuse me, Missh … Would you be at all familiar with the worksh of Hendrixsh?" The arachnoid's jaw struggled with the human words, but he persevered. He and 'Guy' turned to look expectantly at Brenda.

"Know him? Honey, Jimi and I were more than familiar." Brenda's eyes lit up at the memory, warming her more than the Shopkeeper's coat ever could.

'Sky' bounced up and down on his leg joints.

"Pleashe … Would you be able to shettle our dishpute? My learned colleague knowsh a thing or two, but when it comesh to mushical legendsh …"

"Oh, come on!" the Byzantine protested, "Hendrix is all right, but he's no Sidebottom."

The arachnoid gasped as though wounded, momentarily lost for words, and unused to the sensation. He macerated loudly, juices frothing from his mouth in his distress.

"Well," Brenda said, leaning in, "Jimi kissed a guy or two in his time – who hasn't, right? But this time, it was the sky he was into. And what a sky it was …"

'Guy' threw his hands high and turned his back on the assemblage, limping off up the road on his uni-sandal. He affected not to hear the arachnoid snickering behind him.

"Thanksh ever sho!" 'Sky' said to Brenda. "Love the old bugger to bitsh, but when he getsh an idea in hish noggin, he won't let it go. You know the Byzshantinesh ..." He shrugged, which was a complicated manoeuvre for an arachnoid, involving his entire upper body and both front-facing limbs."

"My pleasure," Brenda said, but by then, Panda was pulling her away.

Walking on, as they drew closer to the village centre, they encountered more folks, all with a cheery greeting, as thought they were old friends. Some appeared to have mistaken Brenda for someone called Jo-Ella, and Panda for someone called Smallbear.

"Pass on my regards to BigBear, if you would!" called a young lady, dressed in a nun's habit, and somehow maintaining dignity while cycling by on a penny farthing. Panda grunted loudly at the fourth case of mistaken identity in a row. Brenda rapped him on the head for his rudeness.

"Don't you think this place is a bit ... weird, Brenda? Like they're trying too hard to be surreal? I mean, come on! A nun on a penny farthing? What's that all about? I half expect to bump into a man dressed as a daffodil next." He stopped walking and looked around, an eyebrow cocked and loaded, just in case. When said phantasm failed to materialise, they continued on their way.

Once they were some distance away, one of the doors facing onto the street quietly closed, and with a disappointed sigh, Derek turned and went inside. He adjusted the seat of his green spandex suit where his undercrackers had ridden up. The petals that framed his face drooped, matching the forlorn expression he wore.

Just as Panda stepped out to cross the road – mesmerised by the neon mirage of an off-licence further down the high street – he totally failed to spot the van hurtling round a blind bend and heading right at him.

There were monkeys in the cab, sharing the steering duties between them as they bounced about with mad abandon.

Brenda saw them first, though Panda would later recall the clockwork keys spinning at their backs. As Brenda called his name, she gave an almighty yank, and pulled Panda back from the road, feeling the impact as he was clipped by the speeding vehicle.

The van showed no sign of stopping, and sped off down the road, zig-zagging from side to side as it went. Brenda squeezed Panda's paw tightly, committing the name painted on the side of the van to memory. Master Maker, it said.

"Brenda ..." Panda's voice was a hoarse quaver, "Brenda, I can't feel my legs!" He looked down and was relieved to see that his legs were perfectly fine.

"Oh, Panda!" Brenda gasped, seeing just a moment before he did, the loose stuffing spilling from Panda's shoulder, and the missing limb, abandoned in the gutter.

Panda fainted.

Drifting through layers of consciousness, Panda felt himself gently lifted up, buffeted by clouds and carried over the streets and houses of Samhain. Everything was bright, his sight like an overexposed Polaroid. His procession was underscored by a keening sound, something choral, hovering on the knife-edge between tear-inducing beauty and just bloody annoying. Was that singing, he could almost hear? Could he almost hear it, or was it almost singing?

And then he was going down, down into the darkness. Panda glimpsed cobbles, heard the discordant jangle of bells, and then he was lost.

When Panda next came up for air, it was as though he was being jabbed by a succession of sharp little knives, wielded by devils. Even worse, they were still singing, the pitch grating over his nerves. From the heights of Elysium to the depths of Hades in one swift manoeuvre. Do not pass go, do not collect a bucket of gin and tonic. He felt it was time to babble: "Mater? Shall I ever play the pee-ah-no again?" He whimpered, feeling phantom twitches from his missing limb. Back into the abyss he went.

"I must have some booze!" Panda stared at the concerned faces of the strangers crowding around him, and then saw Brenda among them.

He relaxed at the sight of her, even as he wondered what he was doing on some sort of workbench. A glass was swiftly produced, which Panda grabbed eagerly with both paws – yes, both – and downed the contents in one go. It was a toss-up as to whether he was more shocked to find his arm as good as new, or that he had just gulped down lemonade when expecting the heavenly nectar of alcohol.

After Brenda had talked Panda down from his hysterical rant at such a dirty trick being played on a fellow when he was under the weather, introductions were given. The eldest among the company was Wise Old Mog. For a stuffed cat doll, she had seen better days. Her seams were looser than she might have preferred, and her colours had faded over years spent lying curled up in the shop window. Her legs were randomly sized, giving her an uneven gait, but this did not seem to trouble her.

"If Mister Rifkind had wanted me to have all my legs the same length, then that's what he would have given me." Mog shuffled around the workshop, introducing Pristeen the ballerina, who pirouetted for the newcomers. Her smile was painted on, but it fitted her perfectly. Pushing in were Pinch and Punch, twin bundles of energy, half kitten and half pom-pom by the looks of them. Always moving, their excited squealing voices Panda now identified as the mysterious singers that haunted his dream. They playfully nipped and nudged Panda, to his annoyance, calling out their names as part of the game. It was obviously their thing.

"Pinch!" Pinch cried as she took a little nip at Panda's leg.

"Punch!" said Punch as he barrelled into Panda's side.

"First of the month, and no returns!" they chorused. Panda gave Punch a little sideswipe, knocking him into his sister.

"Hey!" he complained, "we said no returns!"

"It's not the first," Panda replied. This satisfied Pinch and Punch, who went back to wrestling with each other and climbing the shelves.

Next was Derek the Drummer Boy, a military styled marionette. Unable to shake hands as a drumstick was carved at the end of each arm, by way of apology, Derek beat out a brief tattoo on his drum for them. Only Rasher the piggy bank seemed less enthusiastic than the others at meeting Brenda and Panda. His glazed skin was cracked and while someone had done a splendid repair job on him, you could see that he'd once been broken. He clinked as he walked around them, though his guts echoed, so Brenda popped a couple of coins in his slot. That seemed to improve his disposition. Fortunate for her that the coat she'd borrowed from the Shopkeeper had a few pennies stashed in its many pockets.

"We are the RifKind," Wise Old Mog said, "This shop, Rifkind's, has been our home for as long as anyone remembers." Mog made her lopsided way to her cushion, and circled three times upon it before sitting down to continue her story.

"Mister Rifkind made us, and together we made things better." The others nodded in agreement. "We would find things in the streets of Samhain – abandoned things – things that were once loved, but had seen better days. And we would bring them here to the shop. Mister Rifkind would put the loved thing up on the table here, just as with you, and we would bring them back."

"And we would sing!" chorused the kittens.

"We would all do our part," Mog continued, "When the loved things were good as new, Mister Rifkind would put them over there in the window display, and someone would pass by and love them again."

Brenda looked over at the window onto the street. There was a translucent orange plastic sheet across the glass, to prevent fading in the sunlight. It gave the shop a sepia quality, a warm and old-fashioned glow. From outside, she imagined that it looked as though the shop was frozen in amber.

"Could we thank Mister Rifkind for all your kindness?" Brenda asked, but Mog's head fell sadly.

"I'm afraid Mister Rifkind is no longer with us. He has travelled over the bridge."

"Over the bridge," the RifKind said in unison.

"It was so very sad, but you can't mend people. We go on. We find the things and make them loved again, just as he would have wanted."

"Not like the monkey man …" Rasher said. Mog's brows furrowed.

"Do you mean those monkeys that ran over poor Panda?" Brenda said.

"That's right, dear. Master Maker and his Helpers," Mog said, "They're monsters!"

"They take things what ain't even broke … an' then … then they breaks 'em!" Rasher said, barely able to spit the words out.

"That sounds awful," said Brenda.

"That ain't the worst of it, Missus. Then …" Rasher waddled nearer, his voice deeper and more serious, "… then they sticks 'em to other things. All wrong!"

Derek the Drummer Boy expressed his displeasure through the medium of beating his drum skin to within an inch of its life.

Pristeen bounded over to Rasher, giving him a comforting ear scratching to calm him down.

"That's why we don't talk about him. Not among the RifKind." Mog said, "In any case, we have new friends! We must be better hosts."

"You could show them what we made!" Punch said, skidding to a halt in front of Mog's bed.

"The memorial? Why not indeed." She turned to Brenda and asked if they would like to visit the churchyard, and see what they had produced to honour their creator. Brenda did not feel she could decline.

At the highest point in Samhain stood the church. It dominated the landscape, and some of the oldest buildings in the village huddled around it for warmth.

The pub stood in its shadow, and Panda made a mental note to investigate further on the way back down the hill. As they skirted the church, they passed through a section deep in shadow, and they all involuntarily shuddered. Brenda caught a glimpse of a plaque dedicated to Michael Drake, "who kept the war from Samhain", before hurrying into the next patch of sunlight.

The churchyard itself was quite plain. For the most part, it was a series of rows of grassy graves with simple memorials. Some had floral tributes, while others were tended only by the council appointed gardener when the grass was due a haircut, something that was a little overdue, if the unruly tufts of greenery were any indicator.

Wise Old Mog pointed out a few graves of particular interest: "This is Olivia Price's stone."

"The poet?" Panda asked.

"Indeed. She went over the bridge some time ago, but she loved Samhain so much, she wanted a permanent memorial here." Mog ambled along the line, "And this is for Will Owen, and this for Peter Wilde, who I'm sure you'll have heard of."

"Quite a few creative types for a small village," Panda commented.

"And here is our tribute, for our dear Mister Rifkind." Mog stopped before one of the most flamboyant of grave markers. Bursting up from the ground like a bunch of flowers from a magician's hat, the stone featured a diorama of Mister Rifkind – younger than Brenda has imagined – as he crossed a rainbow bridge towards his reward, visualised as a bright light, presumably to represent some sort of heaven, she thought. The stone was capped with the name Rifkind's curving over it, a direct copy of the logo outside the shop. The only other words engraved were simple enough. No dates, merely this: 'Over the Bridge' and below that: 'And far away'. It was beautiful and heartfelt. Even Panda felt his heart strings tug, such as they were.

"Sorry for your loss." Panda said, for which Mog thanked him. "It's a lovely stone you've chosen. What is it?"

"It's Bridge-stone. Made from purest Hebdenite, it is. Only the finest for Mister Rifkind, after all." Mog said.

"How long has it been since he died?" Panda continued.

"Died? I don't follow you." Mog seemed confused.

"When did you … lose him?" Panda rephrased his question carefully.

"He went over the bridge twelve years ago and more, now. Over the bridge, where everything is factory-fresh and nothing less than nearly-new."

Panda chose not to press the issue any further, but Brenda kept looking at the words on the memorial. She put her finger in her mouth and held it up in the wind, puzzling something through.

"Let me see if I have this right," Brenda said. "This stone is Hebdenite?" She pointed to the memorial, "And Mister Rifkind isn't dead?"

"Dead?" Mog looked confused again.

"Broken, but not fixable," Brenda explained.

"He went over the bridge."

"And the bridge is made of Hebdenite. We're definitely in Yorkshire."

"This is Samhain," Mog said.

"I think I know where Mister Rifkind is, Panda."

"He's over the bridge," Mog repeated.

"How did he get there," Brenda asked.

"He walked." Mog said, matter-of-factly.

"I think we need to find this Hebden Bridge." said Brenda.

"Though it saddens me to lose new friends, I'll show you," Mog said.

The track that led down the hill and out of Samhain was narrow and wound round on itself. From the top, Brenda could see glimpses of it through the mist. It was not the smoothest of surfaces, with deep ruts gouging the hillside, made long ago by carts, caravans or both.

Panda took Brenda by the hand and they set off into the mist, while Wise Old Mog gathered together the RifKind to wave them on their way. Rasher shook his head and snorted to himself, plainly not in favour of their journey, but Mog brooked no dissent. Within the first couple of minutes, they had reached the first bend, and became lost from view. The chill air gave Brenda goosebumps, despite the marvellous Shopkeeper's coat. Panda's fur took on a frosty sheen as they walked.

The track changed underfoot as they travelled, moving from dirt and frozen muddy ruts into sections of brick, quilted with tarmac patches. They could see less and less in front and behind, enclosed by soft grey fog. Although they had only been walking for ten minutes at most, their limbs were growing heavy with fatigue. Each step required more effort than the last. Panda struggled more than Brenda, and eventually Brenda scooped him up without protest. As they moved further, the fog grew brighter, and the soft mist gave way to sleet, seemingly aimed to push them back up the track.

The icy sleet stung Brenda's cheeks, and the glare caused pinpricks of light to dance over her retinas when she attempted to blink it away. She shifted her grip on Panda, whose back was rimed with ice as he held onto Brenda's shoulder to shield himself from the worst of the weather. Brenda could go no further. To an observer, had there been one, it would have looked as though she was a mime artist walking against the wind. She resisted the urge to sit down, knowing that if she did, she might never stand up again.

Admitting defeat, they trudged back up the track, and the going was immediately much easier. The weather at their backs encouraged them back into Samhain. Given the steep incline and their bone (and stuffing) deep exhaustion, it should have been hard work. Brenda was immediately suspicious. Panda was more hopeful for an intervention by a St Bernard with a warming nip or two of something glorious, but he was disappointed.

There was indeed a four-legged friend at the top of the rise waiting for Brenda and Panda, at Samhain's official boundary. But it was not a rescue dog with a barrel of brandy. It was Rasher, and he was attempting to savage a clockwork monkey, whose shrill cries of alarm were as insistent as a car alarm.

As if on cue, Master Maker's van pulled up sharply to the kerb in front of them. This time, it was driven by the organ-grinder himself and not his monkeys. Even so, he had to divide his concentration by fending off his over-excited Helpers, who jabbed at the horn to display their displeasure.

While Rasher and the monkey fought, the other RifKind were in a stand-off with yet more clockwork primates. Mog did her best to hold back her friends while the monkeys capered before them, baring their teeth unpleasantly.

Rasher's opponent kicked and flailed at the porcelain pig, its arm trapped in the porcine beast's chops. The clockwork key in its back struggled, turning jerkily over its cogs as the motor ran down. As the thrashing lessened, Rasher finally chose to listen to Mog's pleas, and deigned to release his grip. The Helper whimpered, and loped away to the ranks of its fellows, who parted to let it inside the huddle.

"Caught 'im, I did!" Rasher said, "Sneakin' about."

The Helpers took up a chorus of protest howls. Derek beat his drum in reply, matching racket with racket.

"Up to no good, I reckons," Rasher continued.

"Are you sure?" Mog asked. "What exactly was it doing?"

"Lickin' our windows. Spyin' on Miss Pristeen too, I 'spect, the filthy animule."

"I sent him." Master Maker spoke up for the first time. His voice was calm and soothing. He wore vivid white dungarees, decorated with a multitude of patchwork pockets randomly distributed across the fabric, each with a stylised MM logo.

"I merely wished to apologise for the behaviour of my little friends earlier on in the street. They know better than to drive the van without me, but sometimes, when I'm distracted in my Makeatorium, they wind themselves up. The young, you know!" As he spoke, Master Maker's hands were always in motion, as though he was invisibly making something at all times.

Rasher harrumphed, and Mog looked doubtful, but said nothing.

"I sent Laddo with a note of apology," the Maker said, looking into the mass of Helpers, who moved aside to reveal Laddo, who was rummaging through his fur, suddenly discovering a crumpled note, previously forgotten. He edged forward and handed it to Mog, an embarrassed grin plastered over his face as he withdrew, half bowing, half curtseying, with his key chattering away to itself.

"We're here to help," said Master Maker, looking at the exhausted forms of Brenda and Panda, still puffed out from their walk.

"We don't need your 'elp!" Rasher said before Mog could shush him.

"I wasn't necessarily talking about you," the Maker said, with just a hint of annoyance, before turning his attention fully to Brenda. "I see you've been trying to go out. I can see that Samhain had other plans. It does that sometimes." He drew nearer to them before continuing, "If you'll let us, I think we can help."

This time, Mog rapped Rasher on his porcelain head before he could protest.

"You could give us a lift," Panda said, patting the side of the van, which gave a hollow thud.

Master Maker apologised profusely, and explained that the dimensions of his van exceeded the width of the track in places, something that Panda had suspected in any case.

"I had something else in mind." He turned to Mog, "With your permission?" Master Maker asked. The elder RifKind considered for a time, her paws air-typing to aid the process, before nodding her assent.

The word given, Master Maker sprang into action, winding his Helpers' keys with abandon, and directing them like a master conductor. The monkeys capered, they loped and they swung. A metal dustbin lid was procured, scrutinised and accepted. From the innards of Master Maker's van came the tools of his trade: the hammers, the angle grinder and an oxyacetylene torch. With a practiced air and a shower of sparks, snip-snap, the bin handle came away and was discarded.

"That wan't even broken!" Rasher gasped, but the others were entranced by watching Master Maker and his Helpers at work. Pinch and Punch grew so excited, if Mog had not nudged them, they would have launched into their fixing song.

"Not now," she whispered.

The hammers beat out a melody almost as well as one of Derek's own, and his drumstick hands twitched in time with them, as the Helpers reshaped the bin lid, flattening, smoothing and repurposing it. Some stood by, with loaded paintbrushes at the ready, awaiting any opportunity to add a flourish here and a go-faster stripe there.

Professionals would have waited until the hammering was concluded, but the wind-up monkeys were the epitome of the overenthusiastic amateur. They were at least fast …

Within minutes, the bin lid was unrecognisable, which was just as well if the original owner had stepped out of their house to wonder why their dustbin was open to the elements. A gleaming (in places) sledge (of sorts) had taken its place. The handle had been reattached to the front of the sledge, for Brenda to grip for safety.

"What about that poor devil's bin, eh?" Rasher grumbled, once again the sole voice of dissent.

"We can just make them a new one! Give us twenty minutes and …" Master Maker looked around the street, "… and a length of that guttering up there. Piece of cake!" He caught Rasher's horrified look, and winked at him.

Farewells were made again, and this time seemed more final. Master Maker managed to wrangle his Helpers back into the van – he still had the ignition key, so there would be no repeat of the earlier incident – but he hung back to help get them moving, as the only one big enough to give them a proper push start. Brenda knelt down on the sledge, and took hold of the handle. Panda sat on Brenda's knees, and wore a pair of swimming goggles thoughtfully scrounged from the shop by Pinch.

As Master Maker did some exercise lunges to warm up and took up position behind Brenda, ready to get the sledge underway, Mog tugged at his trouser.

"I shall come too," she said.

"No!" Pinch and Punch chorused, and Pristeen stood aghast.

"I've made up my mind, dears. It's always been my job to believe in things, and such a long, long time since I had anything new to believe in. Do you see?"

Brenda patted the sledge behind her, "Hop aboard, honey. Any more for any more?"

The RifKind shuffled uneasily. Even those that could speak remained silent. Just as well really, as there was only so much sledge one could make from an old bin lid.

At a word from Brenda, Master Maker started to push. Slowly at first, but as they reached the first bend, their speed began to pick up. Derek drummed along with them. It was all he could do.

"Lean into the bends," the Master said, as they began to outpace him, and he had to let them go.

When the sledge rounded the corner and out of sight from Samhain, the RifKind waited solemnly for Master Maker as he walked back into the village.

"Over the bridge," Pristeen said.

"And far away," said Rasher.

Brenda could still hear the distant drums as their speed increased. They lost a little momentum with each rutted bend, but once they reached smoother ground, it was all she could do to hang on and lean out at the appropriate time.

Panda and Mog had to clutch onto her and follow her lead. The mist enveloped them as before, and the intensity of the light made it nigh on impossible to see to steer. Brenda was relying on her memory of the earlier, slower descent.

The stinging sleet helped Brenda to focus, even as it acted as a brake on their progress. They were still travelling at a clip, just enough to force their way further into the white.

"What if you're wrong?" Panda shrieked into the wind.

"Bugs on a windscreen, I should think."

The sledge had slowed tremendously, but kept on, just.

"I believe in you, Brenda," said Wise Old Mog, and she should know. It was her job.

Just as it seemed that the white could grow no brighter, the sledge punched through what felt like a plate glass window, and it was suddenly dark.

Once they had blinked away the fireworks dancing in front of their eyes, they found themselves in an ordinary street in an ordinary town. The weather was better too; almost Spring-like. Behind them was the Hebdenite bridge that had been immortalised on Mister Rifkind's memorial. Looking down at them was an ordinary fellow with an extraordinary beard, which gave him a slightly untamed look. He stuck out a hand, to shake or to help them up, and ended up doing both.

"I'm Ned," he said.

"We made it!" Panda cried, and hugged Brenda, but as they turned to congratulate Mog on their grand adventure, they found her lying face down in an undignified manner on the back of the sledge. Her fur was more faded than it had appeared in Samhain. In the warm light of day, she was quite, quite stuffed.

"You'll be after Rifkind, I suppose?" Ned said.
"How on earth did you know that?" said Brenda.
"I'm a Netherwarden. It comes with the job." He waggled a finger towards Mog, who Brenda was clutching tightly to her breast. "Also ... Bit of a giveaway."
Ned stuck his hand into the front pocket of his cardigan and pulled out a fob watch. Flipping open the case, he gave the glass a sharp tap. "Thought so. I don't want to rush you, but if you nip down to that supermarket a bit sharpish, you'll find him arguing with someone over a parking spot."
"He keeps to a regular routine, does he? Like clockwork." Panda asked.
"Oh no," Ned said with a distracted air, patting the pocket where he kept his fob watch, "It's a Dramatic Device™. One of the perks of the job. Now, off you go. And good luck." Ned returned to his post at the border of Samhain and Hebden Bridge, like some sort of Yorkshire Heimdall.
Brenda hoiked Mog up onto her back, with her mismatched limbs draped over her shoulders like a rucksack. Panda jogged along beside her.
They arrived in the car park just in time to see a man in his late sixties struggle to his feet beside one of the vehicles. He had a plastic bag full of charity shop books; dusty old tomes full of social realism, and 'important messages'. When he saw that he was being observed, he quickly pocketed a handful of tyre valve dust caps and pulled out a hankie to wipe off the worst of the muck from his fingers. Caught black-handed.
"Mister Rifkind?" Brenda asked.
"Who says?" he replied defensively, before clocking the faded Mog toy on Brenda's back. "Oh. Fans, is it?" He sighed. "I'd hoped I could get past that after all these years. What d'you want signing? Give it here, then."
He looked again at his dirty fingers, and gave them another quick scrub with his handkerchief, but if anything, he put more back on than

he got off.

Panda stepped forward, but Rifkind cut him off, "You're not one of mine, are you?"

"I'm not one of anybody's, I assure you," Panda said.

"We're not fans," Brenda assured him, "I don't even watch TV. We're here to solve a mystery for some friends in Samhain."

"Samhain, you say? I used to live there, but I had to go. Had to get away, so I could write summat … important. Summat without puppets." Rifkind bent down to address Panda, "No offence."

"None taken, I'm sure."

"Those stories I made when I were practically a kid – they follow me everywhere – Whatever I want to pitch, they just ask me whether there's toys in it. Why won't they let me write about – I don't know – a boy and his bloody goshawk or summat?"

Brenda rounded on him, "Don't take this the wrong way, but isn't that just a bit ungrateful?"

"Ungrateful?" Rifkind spat, "The hours I put in, bringing things to life for the kiddies? It takes it out of you, you know. I did everything I could for them, but all the time, they just went through their paces. If anything, I were holding them back. And as long as I were there, nothing would ever change. My leaving were as much for them as for me. No matter what I did, I could never escape."

"Be fair," Panda said, "You didn't go very far. Just down the lane."

"Samhain's further than you might think," Rifkind said, "but point taken. If it had been about money, I'd have signed contracts – let them make toys and all sorts." He noticed Mog, still hanging off Brenda's back, "You've done well with Old Mog there, though."

He took Mog's threadbare old paw in his hand, and it was as though he was struck by a thought, "Oh my lord! She's my Old Mog, isn't she?" Rifkind's demeanour immediately softened, and he insisted on dragging them into a nearby teashop. He explained that his knees were feeling the cold, despite the warm weather, but he had also spotted the owner of the car he had nobbled heading towards them.

Rifkind cleared the plastic gingham tablecloth of excess menus and condiments, and Brenda placed Mog in the centre.

Rifkind kept stroking at her battered old fur, lost in sepia-tinged memories. They squeezed their teacups around the edges of the table, ignoring the clucking of the teashop staff.

"Missed you, old girl," he said. "I had such hopes for her – for all of them, really. But most of all, my Wise Old Mog. I thought she'd encourage them to follow their own dreams. Not just keep on doing what this silly old sod thought up one night after too many ales."

"It's all they know," Brenda said.

"I take it they're no better, then?"

"We've only just met them," Panda said, "but they do seem a bit set in their ways."

"But well-meaning," Brenda chimed in.

Rifkind blew on his too-hot tea.

"My own fault. I just gave them one characteristic. They were never meant to go on forever."

Brenda pushed the unasked for biscotti in its little wrapper around her saucer, unable to think of anything to say. She unwrapped it, but then put it down again.

"Every day the same. If it weren't a ballet shoe they brung me, it'd be a ship in a bottle or summat, over and over again. It were simpler back then. Dream up a bunch of cheese-eating moon-men, spin a few yarns and move on. You try to put a bit of yourself in them, but not too much, you know? Not for what you got back for it."

The more he spoke, the more familiar Rifkind seemed to Brenda. He had put much more of himself into his characters than he knew. Parcelled out among the RifKind, but they all spoke with his voice.

"Even when I knew I had to get out, I couldn't just stick them back in a box and move on. Midnight flit in the end. Thought it were for the best at the time, but now? I don't know. I've tried not to think about it." A haunted expression fell over his face, "I left them. They just did what I made them to do, and I left them."

"You could come back with us. Tell them, not us." Brenda said, though she knew before he spoke what his answer would be.

Shaking his head sadly, Rifkind drained the rest of his tea. "Wouldn't do any good for any of us. Anyroad, I've got my career to think about. Such as it is." He patted his plastic bag of worthy reference books. "I really think I'm making headway. My agent keeps talking Baftas." He sounded as though he was trying to convince himself as much as them.

Panda and Brenda finished their own teas and scraped back their chairs on the tea shop tiles. Brenda reached out to reclaim Mog, but Rifkind got there first.

"Before you go, do you think I could give Mog one last hug?"

"Help yourself, honey," said Brenda.

Rifkind lifted Mog from the gingham very gently, her legs swinging in random directions. Years fell away for both of them as they shared a moment, ignoring the stares of other customers. Mog did not look quite so pigmentally-challenged – a trick of the light, perhaps. Rifkind felt her stirring next to him, as though waking from a lovely dream. He fancied that he heard a soft yawn, but he had always had a good imagination.

The author was back in his workshop, waiting to see what his creations had brought for him this time. The excitement was real, despite him already knowing, as he had written them all. The ballet shoe, the ship in a bottle, the flag. He remembered them all, and the memories washed over him. Grumpy old Rasher, always the first to question anything, but always for the best of reasons; Pristeen, who only loved to dance; The kitten twins, with their inexhaustible enthusiasm for whatever they were doing right here and right now. And looking after them all was Mog, wisest of the wise. Rifkind found his cheeks moisten, the soppy old sod.

Reluctantly, he broke the embrace, and passed Mog over the table to Brenda. "Get her back safely," he said, his voice cracked with emotion.

As Brenda and Panda crossed the road that led up the hill, Rifkind was able to watch them through the window. They waved. He waved. Ned waved.

His eyesight was not what it had been, but as Brenda and Panda headed up the track towards Samhain, and the air grew bright around them, painting them in silhouette, Rifkind swore that he saw the larger of the two figures bend down momentarily, and then there were three of them walking up the hill. One of the smaller figures walked on all fours, with an unmistakeable rolling gait.

"More tea?" the waitress asked.

Rifkind put his hand over his cup, "No ta, love. I think I'm about done." He got to his feet and headed for the door.

"Mister R? Your books!" She waved the charity bag at him.

He turned at the doorway, the bell jangling as he opened the stiff door, "Bin 'em. I've got more important things to write."

RIGHT VS LEFT VS WRONG
PAUL VAYRO

"Just open the door."

"That's what I'm trying to do." Panda continued to heave on the changing room handle, flicking a threatening grimace at Iris as he did.

"Maybe you should try pushing." Iris tired of the charade and pushed instead. Panda was still attached to the handle as the changing room door swung gently upon its hinge. He released his grip and fell to the ground.

"Why would it have a handle if it needed to be pushed?"

"Why would we be gifted common sense and then choose so often not to use it?" Panda couldn't be sure if this was a personal dig. By the time he'd decided, Iris was half way towards the door of the fancy dress shop they'd returned to, back in 1862. He followed.

"Would sir like to return his outfit now?" The shopkeeper stepped out from behind a giant duck suit, the fez atop his head unsure if it was missing the rest of a costume.

"How long is left on the rental?" Panda looked down at his cavalier uniform. It had served him well back in 1643, as the duo crashed a three day party celebrating Michael Drake: the saviour of Samhain, although why and how he was such a thing had remained as big a secret as the ingredients of the dip named in his honour. Panda suspected it was jam, although that could have been days old remnants upon his paw.

"You signed up for a week." The shopkeeper was intentionally vague. He just wanted it back before the mead and ketchup stains could be added to.

"But how long is left? Time travel makes a mockery of such contracts."

"Three days." He winced as he spoke. There were a lot of easily spilled liquids in Samhain.

"Then I shall return in three days." Panda tried to un-sheath his sword triumphantly. It got stuck in the flap of his pants and made him look like he was having a stroke.

"Come along, Panda. If I remember rightly there's an inn nearby."

Iris beckoned her sidekick nearer the natural daylight.

"There is, Iris. Just follow the well-worn path." The shopkeeper took one last soulful look at his cavalier costume, fearing what would return.

Iris turned, suspicious of the personal nature of the response. She moved closer. "Have we? No? Maybe?" She headed back to the door, unsure of anything other than Panda would be following, even if he had to limp.

"Gin? Do you have gin? What year is this?" Iris sat at the bar, her hat drooping across her eyes. The barman was younger than his moustache suggested, and devoid of the confidence to challenge such a forthright woman.

"1862." He hoped his calendar was up to date.

"Good. Then there shouldn't be a problem. A big glass, but not too ostentatious, and a whisky for my friend; make it fierce."

Panda clambered onto the stool next to her. His cavalier outfit had stirred the attention of the roundheads in the corner, but with a fancy dress shop on the edge of town they had grown numb to assuming anything from appearance alone.

Panda and Iris had frequented the inn before, or after, depending on your theory on time and the chronological order it plays out in. In its current guise the furniture was mainly wooden in nature; metal had been woven via brute force to add decoration and strength. The lighting came predominantly from the sun, oil filled lamps awaiting the onset of the dark. The whole room sat somewhere between the Wild West and a gentleman's library, it was unclear which was winning the battle.

The barman poured the gin and retrieved the whisky from the cupboard; it was the bottle they used to get the barbecue going on Rib Sunday.

"I think we've been spotted." Panda nodded towards the roundheads as he whispered to Iris, a difficult task without any discernible lips.

"Of course we've been spotted. I'm dressed like a walking charity shop and you're a soft toy." She glanced at Panda's outfit. "Who's wearing the uniform of their political nemesis." She toasted the group with an imaginary glass, as hers still hadn't arrived.

All nine roundheads offered an awkward, tooth driven grin in unison, before eight of them whispered towards their leader: Simon Fleece.

"It'll be fine, these things always are. We may have to pass through a sticky situation, but narrative justice will ultimately prevail and we'll leave as heroes at best, mere survivors at worst."

The barman placed the drinks on the bar, nodding his pleasure at having done his job. He backed away as the sound of new footsteps entered the air.

"My darling." Another cavalier, Roger Daltrey, stood in the doorway, hands on hips, chin pointing to the sky. The feather atop his hat blew in to his eyes; he ignored it, he was professional like that.

The roundheads collectively spat out their warm beer, its temperature had no bearing on their action. The sight of a second soldier was bordering on an invasion, or a stag do; both were saddening. The whispering towards Simon Fleece became a concerned murmur as Roger strode across to Iris.

"Did you shut the changing room door behind us?" Iris berated Panda.

"You were last out."

"This is not the time to start using that common sense we discussed." Iris downed her gin and whispered to Panda. "Although this may be the time for that sticky situation I mentioned."

"My cherub from a perfectly fluffed cloud, my petal from the queen of all roses, you make my eyes even more grateful for the gift of sight." Roger flourished as Iris signalled for another gin, a bigger one.

"Have we met?" Iris quickly recounted the last three days of partying. Some of those cupboards were very dark. It could have been anyone in there.

"Have we met?! Hahahahahahahaha ..." Roger laughed towards the pub. The pub wondered if it had missed a punch-line and resolved to pay more attention in the future. "Oh I do love our humorous ... somebody really should come up with a word for mockery based interplay."

Iris turned to Panda as her gin was replaced. "Have the roundheads noticed the cavalier? Maybe we can get him out of here before this escalates."

Panda grimaced at his shot of whisky. "Have the roundheads

noticed a brazen, six foot cavalier, come through the door they're all facing?" Iris refused to take sarcasm as an answer and waited for a proper reply. "Why don't you ask me if the cavalier's noticed the roundheads?"

"Brutes!" The answer was yes. Roger unsheathed his sword and pointed it to the corner. Panda wondered if he had time to shave his head. The corner stood as one and shuffled across, just out of reach of Roger's blade.

"Hold on there ... Cavalier?" Simon Fleece spoke. The other roundheads stayed behind him, their faces circling like satellites; except for one seven foot beast who appeared stuck in conversation with the very air.

"Roger Daltrey is my name, if your filthy tongues must address me."

"Who?"
"Who?"
"Who?"
"Who?"

"Barman, are we sure we can't chill the beer somehow?" Oliver felt the 'who' question had been fully covered.

"Roger Daltrey, King's Guard, and I'd gladly die for the honour." He swiped the air between them and lowered his eyes in vacant honour of his leader.

"Well that's silly. Why die for some bloke you barely know?" Simon spoke. The collective whispered in his ear. "Oh, good question. Has he ever even bought you a birthday card?"

"The King need not lower himself to such indignities."

"That's a no then. You mean you'll give your life and he won't even give you a birthday card." The roundheads laughed in unison.

"Do not make me sully my blade upon such debates." The twitch of Roger's moustache suggested he was serious.

"Okay lads, calm yourselves down." The group hushed, except for the giant. "Look, Roger, there's no need for anyone to get stabbed. Even with one and a half of you −" He motioned towards Panda. Panda's instinct was to attack. Iris held him back suggesting 'not now' with her eyes; her nose wiggled 'maybe later', "− you'll never get us all before we overwhelm you." The whispering interrupted once more. "That's a good point actually. You might get us if we stand in a row, but

Gerald doesn't even know he's awake until he's been stabbed." Everyone looked up to Gerald. He was wittering.

"I'm yet to meet the biscuit I can't at least tolerate; even the fig …"

"Took a few cannonballs to the head." Simon offered a vague explanation. "The thing is, Roger, those days are behind us. We haven't run a spear through someone's face for …" The collective offered information again. "No, the thing with the juggler doesn't count. That long!" Fleece turned back to Roger. "Nigh on two hundred years. There is no King of Samhain to defend, so you can lower your honour and come and enjoy a beer."

Roger winced in false pain. Panda downed another whisky. Iris sighed. She was hoping somebody would get punched. She wasn't overtly for violence, but if it was going to happen she didn't see why she shouldn't watch.

"No … No king!" Roger could barely believe the words he was uttering. "Then who dictates the rules?"

The roundheads turned back from the journey to their table. "Nobody dictates anything. We all come together and discuss things, once a week. We work out what's best for everyone and vote on it. Then the council announces the fairest way to achieve it."

"Blasphemy." Roger appeared to be having a seizure. "Who lives in the biggest building? Wears the most opulent clothes? Displays the royal jewels on royal days?"

"If you mean the Town Hall, nobody lives in it, although we think Errol sleeps there when his wife's annoyed at him, which is most of the time. And if we had any jewels we'd sell them. Buy us one of those big slides for the new pool we're building. You'd like that, wouldn't you Gerald? Get a big slide for the price of a ruby."

"Once came down with flu, couldn't stop shivering. Once got trapped in a suit of armour for the whole summer, boiled like an apple. Today I'm just right."

"See."

"You're all cursed with the madness. This is insanity. One person should rule, only that way lies purity of thought and a vision for us all."

The roundheads huddled together. Iris and Panda prepared to run, just in case they were putting together a rudimentary cannon. They emerged with a thought. "It seems fairly clear you're not going to accept our ways without some form of fight, so why don't we let the town decide? Would that make you happy?"

"Decide what?"

"Whether to have a King. We can hold an election. Are you free on Friday? Gives you a day to explain your alternative to the people of Samhain."

"A day?"

"How much longer do you need? You only have to inform the town of what they could have instead."

"What about a campaign? Tactics? Balloons?"

"All we're doing is asking people how they would prefer to live. Why would you need tactics for such a thing? Surely the truth is the only tactic?"

"Such a naïve town."

Gerald followed a fly with his eyes as he commented. "There's a certain poetic irony to placing the question of dictatorial rule through the democratic process. Like two islands destined never to reunite, guided together by the pull of contradiction. I like it when me belly rumbles. Like a funny tummy cavern."

"Thanks for that Gerald. Roger, there's a council meeting tonight –"

"Nice narrative coincidence." Iris was happy to be a mere gin filled commentator.

"– I'll pose it to everyone. Shouldn't be a problem. We're very democratic like that."

"I sense a trap." Roger didn't, but thought it best to say it to avoid future embarrassment.

"You either go with the election offer or we put you in a cupboard with Gerald, see who comes out."

"I agree to your offer." Roger managed to sound like he was the one being helpful. "But first I must insist on a glass of port with the fairest damsel ever to catch the nostrils of a dragon."

"You do whatever you need to. We should set off and arrange the chairs." The whispering intruded once more. "And grate the cheese. Cheesy chips have made the town meetings a far more popular affair."

"Cheesy chips. In 18 ... whatever the year is." Iris was perplexed, and a little peckish at the thought of such a treat."

"Indeed. A lady of fair mirth accompanied by a dog that walked on two legs, funny little chap: angry and with giant rings around his eyes. They passed through here on their way to nowhere, enlightening us to the magical combination we now cherish as our own."

Iris and Panda looked at each other. Neither one's memory could help. They assumed it had either been such a good night they'd erased it, or it was yet to happen.

The roundheads left as Roger adopted the stool by Iris' side. He signalled for two ports with a waft of his hand. The barman resented the inherent arrogance within the cavalier's gesture. It pleased him greatly when Iris picked up both drinks and downed them.

"There you go. Drink shared. Shall we go?" Iris stood as Panda realised the roundheads thought he was a dog. He let it simmer along with his other resentment about being small. Its outlet would come. "Barman, a bottle of gin to take out."

Iris received the bottle and stumbled towards the door. Panda jumped down and followed. Roger joined the pair, wondering why his wooing wasn't working. Iris hoped at least one of them knew where they were going.

The town had agreed to the election, as expected. They'd also agreed that anyone caught weeing in the pool would have to clean the public toilets for a month. As the toilet brush was down to its last bristle, it was a punishment nobody wished to suffer. Roger had spent the night celebrating. Iris and Panda didn't need a reason to join in.

As the night ended, drunken wisdom had seen the trio head to the centre of town rather than their beds. It seemed a better idea than trying to wake up early. Having been given a platform from which to spread his message, Roger, Iris and Panda had blearily set up the campaign table and chairs, and proceeded to pass out. By the time they awoke, Samhain was sauntering towards activity

Election fever was barely the sniffles. Nobody wanted change, but the cavalier didn't intend to let something as simple as public opinion get in the way of revamping the entire political landscape.

Wiping the dribble from his cheek, Roger grinned. He'd been struck by an idea, and after straightening his feather, he set out to test it on the first person to cross his path.

"Wish to see a king, Sir? You could become a real Sir, if there was one." Roger tried to entice Harold Tatterton, the local fish soother, in to debate.

"I'm happy with the council, although they could do with emptying the bins more often; which they could do if they didn't have so many. I mean, what do I do with a bottle covered in paper? Is it the green bin or the brown one?"

"It surprises me that you think like that. You look so clean." Roger's eye glistened with mischief as his idea was unleashed.

"What's that got to do with anything?" Harold stopped walking.

"You mean you don't know. Oh, nothing ... It's just that, statistics show that over ninety percent of democrats smell. Don't wash you see. Not like a king and his followers. Pride themselves on being sparkly fresh."

"I did not know that." Harold tried to smell his armpits without being spotted.

"Come to think of it –" Roger sniffed gently. "– maybe you are a democrat."

"I bid you good day sir." Harold scuttled away with an air of self-consciousness he hadn't previously owned, engaging the next person he met, in concern.

As word spread of the personal hygiene of democracy, more and more people visited Roger, curious as to what else this stranger knew. By five pm, he had a crowd bordering on a hundred, nearly half the town. Simon Fleece and the roundheads had equally been enticed.

"... and their ancestors used to be monkeys, whereas kings are a product of the love of angels and gods ..."

"What is this?" Simon Fleece interrupted Roger, who had the crowd tied to his whim as he strode across the table. Simon and the other roundheads joined him on the temporary stage. Iris and Panda moved away before it could collapse under such a burden.

"I'm just educating the town on the truth behind democracy." Roger twizzled his moustache, it felt essential.

"Why didn't you tell us you punch squirrels in the face for fun? The red ones too, not even the smelly, democratic grey ones." Questions began emerging from the crowd, all aimed at Fleece.

"And that you make your grandma live in a box outside your back door?"

"And that you can't do jigsaws for any age above three?"

"Yeh."

"Yeh."

"Booooooo. Smelly democrats."

"Yeh, stinky 'let's vote on everything' losers."

"Is that what Roger has been telling you?"

"Yes." The answer was the same, wherever it came from.

"You were only supposed to lay out the facts and differences between the two systems. Let people decide which they'd prefer. Not taint it with games and irrelevancies."

"So I may have embellished a few statistics here and there." Roger wished he'd practiced his evil laugh more. It was the perfect time for a sinister cackle.

"This is outrageous." Simon turned to the crowd. "Well, good people; did he also tell you that kings chop peoples' heads off for looking at them funny? Or that one would use the money a town had saved for a local swimming pool to build their wife a walk-in wardrobe? Or that they could make it illegal for anyone to say the word hat, just because they wanted to?"

"How would I refer to the thing on me head?"

"Exactly."

"Well he would say that. He's a smelly democrat." Roger stepped forward once more, to the righteous cheers of the crowd.

"This is silly …"

"Democrats are silly." Roger played to the crowd. They revelled in his verbal mischief.

"Come on, men." Simon Fleece abandoned the impromptu debate. He followed the rest of the roundheads through the ensemble. The crowd held their noses and made trumping sounds, in mockery. Roger bent down and turned to Iris.

"I will see you in your rightful place as a queen. Do not fear of that my love ladle."

"Please never call me that again. Stick to the endless gin; far more chance of getting what you want. And just because you've found a few people more gullible than a teenage boy that's been told to close his eyes and wait for a surprise, doesn't mean you're going to win this election."

"No, but my master plan will." Roger tapped the side of his nose. His right eye suggested he was up to something, his left eye was still wondering what had happened to 1643. Roger stood back up on the table and orchestrated the audience. Iris turned towards Panda.

"He's going to get us in trouble."

"But he does keep giving us free booze." Panda's hat was a disgrace to everything that sat straight.

"We can have one toast over the free booze, but we must do it with concerned faces."

The wooden cups thumped together as an air of seriousness was maintained. What was Roger's plan, and why were the fish of Samhain so stressed they required their own soother?

Roger's meeting had gone on into the night. Those that had stayed were treated to the fineries they could count on once the king was installed, which were essentially a bath of lethal punch and as many potatoes dipped in hot butter as you could handle. The record was seven, but nobody could be sure how long they'd officially stayed down. Iris and Panda had left when the followers began chasing pigeons in order to stick feathers in their hair/hats, as tribute to Roger's own display.

Having woken up without a bottle to hand, they searched for the cavalier and access to his bar tab. They spotted him coming out of the Stationers, with a box under his arm and a coy look upon his face.

"There you are." Iris was pleased with her recognition skills.

"Did you miss the quickened beat of your heart when in my presence, the fluttering of hope …"

"Not really. We've run out of booze."

"Then we shall rectify such a thing, for what is a queen without her crown?" Everybody paused, unsure if this had actually strayed into an insult.

The trio stopped briefly at the inn before continuing their journey. Roger was on his way to the town hall for polling day, which meant Iris and Panda were on their way there, too. The lady of the group offered a query.

"What have you been buying?" Iris cared little for the answer, but felt it a better topic than poetic whimsy.

"Erm … things … stuff … quill tops."

"Quill tops?"

"Yes, you know. Those funny little statues you put on the end of your quill. Hilarious things."

The questioning ceased as a passer-by spoke to Roger. Mr Daltrey had become the main topic of conversation for Samhain, usurping the rumours about Joseph Fandango and what he'd really been up to with Cynthia Hairnet in the cemetery.

"The thing with democracy, Roger, is that nearly half the people don't get what they want. At least with a king, pretty much nobody gets what they want. Get the smelly ones out of office and into the bath, eh, eh."

Carlos strode away, fist in the air.

"Undeniable logic my good fellow." Roger tried to mirror the fist action. It only made his box wobble, dislodging its bounty inside.

"You and your nonsense are ruining this town, Daltrey. Why would you have a king guiding the town by his whim? We're happy with the council's whim. At least it's a democratic whim."

Jenny Deniable shook her fist in his direction, equally walking away.

"Well you've divided opinion." Iris commented as the town hall came ever closer.

"Democracy has divided opinion; I am merely the alarm clock of truth."

Roger reached for his moustache, in order to twizzle it's end and accentuate his smug tone. It loosened his grip on the box, allowing a bottle of dark liquid to escape and career towards Panda, striking his whisky, mid swig. Thankful for his woollen jaw, Panda was less pleased to see the lid leave the neck of the container, allowing its contents to pour freely across his outfit.

With the empty bottle rattling on the floor, he stood, stained and unimpressed.

"That's your deposit well and truly gone." Iris could only stick to the facts as Roger's moustache twitched an apology.

After several seconds pause, Panda wiped a few spots of ink from his face and took a hearty gulp of his drink. Realising he wouldn't have to clean the stain helped his mood remain balanced. The trio continued walking, only one of which had widened his gate.

"So, box of quill tops, you say?" Iris couldn't resist.

"And a little ink of course. What's a quill and it's top without ink?" As they reached the door to the town hall, Roger ignored the discussion and grew noticeably twitchy. "I'll just be a moment."

Roger ran around the corner. A shuffling noise could be heard followed by the sounds of expended energy, before a thump and silence. The duo couldn't deny their curiosity and peered after him. He was gone.

No sooner had they swapped confused glances, and Iris had a poke and a smirk at Panda's stain, than the cavalier re-appeared through the window, still with the box.

"It's nigh on impossible not to ask what you're up to?" Iris reverted to the obvious question.

"Suddenly my mystery intrigues you. My air of …"

"Considering we either talk about what's going on or you start comparing me to a waterfall in moonlight, I'd rather talk about what's going on."

"The master plan."

Roger continued to use the action of tapping his nose as some form of answer. He strode away, laughter fuelled by a joke only he knew. Iris and Panda both suspected it wasn't as funny as he was making out.

The polling day ambled by, punctuated by messages of both support and derision for Roger. Iris and Panda couldn't be sure if they were equally a target of emotion, so chose not to be affected by any of it. Panda had fascinated Edwin Rorschach, the town thinker, with his stained outfit, to the point of growing uncomfortable. Everybody else used it for the basis of mockery.

As the bell rang out for the end of voting, the counting began and the population of Samhain headed to the town hall for results night. The Indoor Lacrosse Society was outraged: Friday night was their night in the hall. They'd have to share with The Marble Thwackers on Monday. Last time that happened they lost an entire defence for over a month with sprained ankles.

Roger took his place on the stage. He stood proudly, feet together, hands behind his back. Simon Fleece looked out at the crowd. He shook his head at the numerous pigeon feathers that greeted him. The democrats had made an extra effort to have a bath before arriving.

Iris and Panda bumbled on to the stage. They were inextricably linked with Roger, irrelevant of their mild protests. The ink stain that had caused so much mirth had gone from the bear's tunic. Simon was about to comment when he was called over by the Head Counter.

Words were passed back and forth, Fleece slowly adopting the flummoxed expression of the adjudicator. A handful of voting papers were shaken in disbelief before being handed over. The Samhain official raised his hands in resignation and walked away. Simon wandered back to the centre of the stage, in deep thought. He looked at the papers, then to Panda's uniform, then back at the papers. He was clearly still pondering as he began to speak.

"It would appear, and I have no idea how this can be right, that the Monarchists have won the vote, one-nil."

Roger raised his arms in expected triumph. The crowd paused to take in what had been said. Anyone with a pigeon feather equally raised their arms. Some continued making smelly gestures toward their peers. The democrats responded with protests about how they'd only had a bath an hour ago, before murmuring their discontent and disbelief about how an election could finish one-nil. Simon continued to think, maintaining his varying glance at the soft toy and Roger, as the crowd thought out loud.

"I don't understand. I definitely voted."

"Me too."

"And me."

"Smelly and liars. Boo the democrats."

"Did you vote?"

"I did. And my vote won it."

"Actually, it was mine."

"I think you'll find it was due to me."

Common sense waited for everyone to start doing the most basic of maths in their heads, as Roger stepped forward.

"I have pandered to your system, and your system has returned a clear verdict. We could always double check and ask the new king what he'd prefer?"

"Ask a king if he wants to be king …" Simon was interrupted by his own curiosity as he turned to Panda. "… Have you changed?"

"I may have parted my hair slightly differently this morning, but nothing major."

"No, your clothes. Where's that ink stain?"

"Oh yeah. It's gone. See, belief does work better than two in one tablets."

"Where did it come from in the first place?" Simon was transfixed on Roger. Panda shuffled, unsure how best to answer. He didn't want to risk the free whisky. "It doesn't matter. I think I know."

Panda sighed with relief.

"People of Samhain. All of these slips were returned as blank. Only one contained a vote." Simon thrust Panda to the front of the stage. "And we all saw yesterday how Roger's funny little dog had an ink stain covering nigh on his entirety; and yet now, nothing."

Everyone stopped, waiting for all the pieces to fall into place. Panda wondered how many more times his rage would accept being called a dog.

"You." Simon Fleece pointed at Roger. "You switched the voting ink for invisible ink." A sigh of realisation came from the audience. They were glad someone had worked it out for them.

"I ... well ... outrageous." Roger unsheathed his sword. "This is treason."

He swiped at the air, backing away to the side of the stage. The audience went from realisation to mumbled outrage. Pigeon feathers were removed in disgust, some were stamped on, others thrown poorly at the stage. For all his bravado, Roger knew when he'd lost a room, and ran.

Iris and Panda saw the fleeing cavalier and looked at Simon, he looked back. They agreed it was best the duo went with him.

Simon turned to the crowd.

"Are we going to let this fiend get away with such mischief? Initiate council directive 1436." The crowd didn't know what he meant. "The Angry Mob procedure."

"Oh that."

"Oh goody. I love a good mob."

"It's been so long. Think I've forgotten how."

Everybody stood, some practiced waving an angry fist and cursing the air. The emergency glass boxes that ran down the side of the hall were smashed, torches emerging from them. Roundheads passed through the hall, offering the flames to get them going. After a good few minutes, Simon spoke once more.

"Is everybody ready?"

"Nearly."

"This pitchfork isn't very sharp."

"Bit like the guy holding it."

"That's entirely unfair. I'd better not find out who said that."

"I said it. And just remember, blunt fork, unruly mobs can be a haven for accidents."

"Is that a threat? He threatened me. Did everyone hear that?"

"Don't forget, torches high, keep the murmurs and general shouts and insults flowing, wave those pitchforks; do Samhain proud."

Simon picked up his own personal flame and watched the room slowly empty. He knew they should have done mob drills.

The perfect narrative spot for a siege was the old abandoned church at the heart of the village; everybody in town knew it and had no hesitation heading there. Iris, Roger and Panda had already entered and begun barricading the door with all the easily moveable furniture they could find. They knew it would offer little resistance, but would give a good visual indication of how close to breaking through the mob were.

"Now what?" Panda realised they'd trapped themselves in as much as the townsfolk out.

"We fight until our lungs will no longer breathe the breath of virtue, until our hearts have beaten their last glorious thump ..." Roger wished a camera was rolling. Iris interrupted the blurb.

"Don't be silly. There'll be a secret passage or something equally tenuous. Always is in places like this."

No sooner was the sentence finished than a giant of a man who could easily be mistaken for a boulder, emerged. It was Delaware Tubthump, caretaker of the church and origami hobbyist.

"Shall we flee from the fleeing?" Panda realised no amount of fighting was going to stop Delaware eating anyone he wanted.

"Not yet. I think he may be the solution."

"Of course he is. This fine fellow looks like a King's Guard if ever I've seen one."

"I'm the caretaker. Didn't you read the sign? This is an abandoned church. That means that other than pigeons and poetic shafts of light it should be empty. You lot are in breach of the sign, and I expect have something to do with the whole village being on the path; another breach of the sign."

"So, you're one of them." Roger raised his sword.

"If you stab me with that I'll get very annoyed, and I won't die, so I'll be able to take out my fury on the person that annoyed me." The warning was calm enough to make Roger meek.

Iris remained focused, or as focused as she can ever be on a Friday. "We have no intention of hanging around. What are the chances there's a secret tunnel?"

"Of course there's a secret tunnel. Has a secret staircase, too, but I didn't tell you that." Voices could be heard through the door.

"Shall we knock?"

"Knock? We're an angry mob; start thumping the door down."

"Seems a bit impolite."

"I think you're mistaking us for the polite and ruly mob that pop round and offer tea and biscuits."

"They sound good. Do you think they're free on Thursday? Mother's coming round for brunch."

"Will you stop trying to make brunch a thing. Just wait for dinner."

"You mean lunch?"

"I know what I mean."

"It is lunch."

"Then why do you have dinner ladies? And school dinners?"

"Good point."

"I'm just going to start thumping the door. Feel free to join in." The door bulged inwards, knocking the looser items of furniture from the pile, as planned.

"Roger, are you coming?" Iris beckoned to Roger as Delaware lifted the altar upon its secret hinge, exposing the entrance to the tunnel.

"I must stay and defend the King."

"There is no king."

"A king is a state of mind, not a man."

"I have no argument against nonsense. We're going though, just so you know."

"It is a burden of my own making, one I must defend …" Delaware dropped the altar before any more of the sentence could be heard. The caretaker flipped open the secret staircase and headed to his haven of tranquillity, which was an old organ chamber filled with posters of doves and sunsets. The last sound he heard was that of the front door caving in, followed by an honourable yelp.

Crawling out from under a fake bush, half a mile outside the town, Iris and Panda looked back towards Samhain. The torches could still be seen burning, the roars of a captured prey littered the air, although their hearts didn't sound fully in it. Iris and Panda dusted themselves down and headed back to the fancy dress shop. It seemed the only option.

The owner looked at Panda's outfit and dreamt of only having to deal with the stains from three days ago. The tunnel had taken its toll on the golden stitching, the hat would have to be rebuilt from the rim inwards.

"Would it be possible to use your portal? I think this time is done with us." Iris asked as politely as she could muster.

"Of course, Iris." The familiarity confused Iris again as Panda stripped, revealing a new layer of filth with every item of clothing.

"Are you sure we didn't … hmmmm." Iris openly pondered as the shopkeeper debated burning everything he was handed. Eventually her companion was ready, and with minimal offerings of goodbye, the pair passed through the changing room door, unsure where destiny would take them, but hoping it served gin.

As for Roger, he spent three weeks in Gerald's wardrobe before apologising. Once outside, he began to see the merits in democracy, especially when invited to crop his wig and become the town judge. Over time he grew into a valuable member of Samhain society, and lived in mild contentment, with an underlying bitterness, for ever more.

WILDTHYME AND THE WOLF
GRAHAM TEDESCO-BLAIR

The time stream on the other side of the glass was ever changing, depending on its mood. Sometimes it looked like the interior of a lava lamp, sometimes like multi-coloured paint swirled from below, sometimes like a stormy tunnel made of clouds, sometimes like the gears of a clock ... today it was flashing green neon whenever Iris looked between her silver booted feet, kicked up on the Bus' steering wheel, making minute adjustments with her ankles when necessary. The Bus knew where to go, and her attention was mostly focused elsewhere. Abba played from the Bus' 8-track at a slightly less than reasonable volume.

"I still think it's a cop out," said Panda, perched behind the driver's seat. "If you're going to go through all the trouble of getting through the whole novel, only to have the whole thing pulled out from under you in the last chapter ..."

"But getting there's the whole point," said Iris. Her honey-blonde hair was huge, and one wondered how she'd managed to fit it into the bubble helmet that went with the now-sleeveless silver space suit she wore. "Otherwise why not just flip right to the last chapter and read that? It's like I was telling Jacques the other day: if the mystery story contains the solution inside of it, it's hardly a mystery at all, is it? You should just cross the word right out."

"Oh, don't bring him into this. You know I can't stand that man."

"I know what this is. You're just jealous that I read faster than you."

"Just because you can finish a novel with a flick of your fingers, while some of us have to read each page, doesn't mean my opinion is any less valid. If anything, it makes mine all the more important. I have to commit. All that dialogue that might be important later, all the red herrings, all the digressions about fruit vendors in the 19th century or the economics of a fishing boat. All the inside jokes. It takes a lot of effort. Take that one you found the other day ..."

"*Tea Time for the Vicar of Stropworth-on-Hamble Brook?*"

"Yes, that's the one. The ending didn't work at all. How could

Vicar French have known that Inspector Croft was going to arrest Miss Tobias right at the same time that Dr. Television was going to steal the jewels from Lord Tilbury?"

"Because the Vicar is a master detective, and a student of personalities. I'll admit it's a little improbable, but hardly impossible. You'd rather she didn't catch the criminal at the end and Miss Tobias went to jail for a murder she didn't commit?"

"The next thing you'll be telling me is that because she's a woman of the cloth, it'd be just fine if she called down a man with wings from a pulley system in the ceiling who'd sort out the whole mess after assembling everyone in the drawing room."

"You really don't believe it? After all we've been through?"

"Well –" Panda started.

A look came on to Iris's face. She suddenly shook her self up to a sitting position, hair flying into her face as she whipped the wheel around with a few big twists and a couple pumps of the brake. The contents of the bus shifted, the internal inertial dampeners begged to be repaired with a deep groan and wheeze, and the various items formally strewn about the seats wished they'd been roped down, judging from their protesting bangs and crashes. Panda held onto the railing with his two little paws like his life depended on it.

"A little warning! Goodness! What are you doing now?"

"I know just the place to solve this little argument."

The bell on the fancy dress shop door jingled pleasantly as Iris pushed it open. As if by magic, the Shopkeeper appeared, smiling brightly. He wore a smart red fez, glasses, and a well fitted shirt and vest with bowtie.

"Miss Iris, Panda, a pleasure to see you again," he said, shaking hands. A pleasant Scots burr rrrrrrolled on his Rs. "What can we do for you today?"

"A bit of a dispute between this little rascal and myself," said Iris. "Over mystery stories, of all things."

"Well, I'm not sure I can help there. My tastes run a little more modern, I'm afraid. Woolf, Mansfield, Sackville-West, Naoko Takeuchi …"

"Oh no, my good man," said Panda. "She means with the, uh …"

"Ah, yes! Of course. I've got just the thing. If you'll come right this way."

He lead the pair through a beaded curtain to a larger back room where all the walls were lined with clothes, the garment bars double stacked one above the other, and each one carefully covered with a plastic lining to protect it from the dust, a different sort of cramped than the dummy stuffed front room. A lava lamp flowed pleasantly under a poster of The Kinks. A sewing machine and various spools of thread, fabric tomatoes stuck through with needles, and loose scraps of cloth covered a long table with a ruler tacked to the edge. Today's newspaper, dated 3 October 1977, sat on an end table. At the end of the room were the changing rooms, with heavy velvet curtains for privacy.

"You've changed the place since we were last here," Iris said.

"Which time was that?" the Shopkeeper replied, flipping through a section marked "Rogues, Ne'er Do Wells, and Blackguards". He passed a tan jacket with an enormous, multicoloured scarf and fedora, a leopard print coat and bright red hat with a purple band, and a red sport coat with blue shirt and yellow tie, before finally settling on a tweed overcoat with a deerstalker cap.

"You know, I don't remember. I like it, though. It's hip. The carpet, the lava lamp, the beads. You could have a pretty groovy thing here."

"If people in small towns went to 'things', rather than the pub, when they wanted a drink," said Panda.

"And for the gentleman," said the Shopkeeper, handing Panda a smart black suit from the turn of the century, along with a bowler hat and black doctor's bag, conveniently scaled down.

"Oh. Now, we're getting a little cliche here, aren't we?" Panda crossed his arms, and frowned as best as his stuffing would allow.

"If you want to solve a mystery, you return to the source," said Iris.

"So we'll be dressing up as Dupin, then? Or Ja'far ibn Yahya, perhaps?"

"Neither of them had sidekicks," said Iris.

"Zadig and Cador, then?"

"Do you remember the last time we went to Babylon? All those nasty folks were convinced you and I were trying to steal the tablets of destiny, and we nearly got maced to death by that one burly fellow, Ninurta?"

"Oh dear, yes. Confusing Siris for Iris, thanks to all those feathers on your hat. Icky place, Babylon."

"This will be much more fun, I promise."

"Do remember how it works?" chimed in the Shopkeeper.

"Well ..." said Panda, looking at Iris. She looked back with a grin.

"Why don't you give us a refresher, just in case I don't remember all the details," replied Iris.

"Certainly!" He clapped his hands together, and held them together with the tips just under his bowtie, as if in prayer. "You enter the dressing room," he gestured towards the draped velvet curtains, "and then don your costume." He mimed removing his hat and held up the tweed coat in front of his body.

"After you've done so, the mirror will begin to shine," the Shopkeeper continued. "Step right through, and soon you'll find yourself transported through time and space and off to adventure! And once it's over, you'll head back through the portal and find yourself back here, ready to change back into your old self."

"So, the costumes come right back, then?" Panda asked.

"That's right."

"You never sell them?"

"Oh no."

"And you're not charging us?"

"How could I charge for a service like this?"

"So how exactly do you stay in business then?"

"Panda! Now don't be mean," said Iris. "He's doing us a favour, after all."

"And this is safe?" asked Panda.

"Well," said the Shopkeeper. "We had one unfortunate incident with a gentleman who wanted to dress up like a colonial space marine, but even he returned safely. Your adventure is what you make of it."

"We're sure to arrive in the same spot?" asked Iris.

"Of course. Those two costumes are keyed to one another. Couldn't have Sherlock Holmes without Dr. Watson, could we?"

Iris and Panda entered the dressing room and tugged the curtain shut behind them. Almost as soon as she'd gotten the hat on her head, Iris found herself dressed. Panda had slightly more trouble, lacking any digits to do his buttons or tie, but she soon had him kitted up nicely. The mirror began to shimmer with a watery vibration before breaking into a solid rectangle of white light.

They stepped through the portal together, hand in hand.

There was a great commotion in front of the shop. Well, as great a commotion as a small town like Samhain could manage. Deputy Saxon was doing his very best to keep the crowd of fifteen or twenty people at bay while Constable Wallace performed his investigation.

According to the copy of the Samhain Morningstar someone had left on a cafe table outside the nearby public house, it was the week of 15 June 1906. "It seems the mirror's left us in Samhain. That's a bit odd, isn't it?" said Panda.

"Yes, quite," replied Iris. She fished about in her coat's pocket, located a pipe and tobacco, and was soon puffing away. "Though I'm sure you noticed the all the noise across the street. Shall we?"

They made their way over, and Iris slid through the press of people, using her walking stick as a wedge when necessary.

"Morning officer," she said, doffing her cap. "Herlock Sholmes, consulting detective, and this is my partner, Wilson. What seems to be the trouble here?"

"Well ma'am, it seems someone's robbed the fancy dress shop. Real puzzler, too. Doors was locked, no one broke any windows. Wallace is in with the shopkeep right now."

"Mind if I step inside? The proprietor is an old friend."

Without waiting for a reply, Iris slid past him into the shop. The layout was mostly the same, with the changing rooms in the back, but no wall had been built to divide the two rooms yet, so you could easily see the rows of costumes hung along the walls: some faced out for display, others hung side by side to make room. There were obvious gaps. The wooden floor creaked under her boots, and the thatch roof looked like it could use a little patching up. The shopkeeper sat in a comfortable chair by the fireplace, head in his hands, fez miraculously staying on, while the constable sat opposite and kept asking the same few questions. Constable Wallace was a large, ruddy cheeked man with a well curated moustache and a obvious flask bulge in his uniform breast pocket. They both seemed absorbed with an engraved card, about the size of an invitation or telegram, which they passed back and forth. Both looked up as Iris and Panda entered.

"Iris! Panda!" exclaimed the Shopkeeper, jumping to his feet and crossing to hug her. "Oh, thank goodness someone's here."

"Yes, the deputy outside explained the situation. Seems rather baffling," said Iris.

"It gets worse, Miss," said Constable Wallace. He handed her the card. On it, in elegant and tasteful Garamond print, was the following:

Greetings. You have just had the pleasure of being burgled by Arsene Lupin, the famous thief. You may display this card as proof that your residence or place of business was worthy of my attention.
Best Regards
A. Lupin

To the left of the text was a cameo of a man with a monocle and top hat. Beneath, in red ink, in the distinctive scrolled writing of one using a quill pen, was written: "You'll see me again, sooner than you'll think!" The back was blank. Iris held it up to the window, smelled it, looked real close, but no secret messages revealed themselves.

"What a curious thing. That Lupin, he's a story character, right?" asked Panda.

"He is, yes. But this card is even more curious. It was made on a very old printing press. And they haven't made paper like this in, well … In quite some time." Iris nodded. "Alright, I want you to walk me through all the events that have occurred up to this point."

Iris pulled a chair close to the other two, while Panda perched on her arm rest, and the shopkeeper began his tale.

"Yesterday was a normal day, no premonitions in my dreams or men in dark cloaks peaking in the windows or anything. I rented a suit of armour to Lord Tilsby, a Robin Hood to his son Gregory, and a Queen Elizabeth I to Lady Tilsby, for the fancy dress ball they've got this Saturday, so most of the morning was the fitting for the three of them.

"Lovely folks, really. Their valet came to pick up the costumes after tea. I then went around the pub for dinner and a pint to close out the evening. I sleep upstairs. Didn't hear anything out of the ordinary. Slept pretty soundly. Come morning, I find a bunch of gaps in my stock, and this little note leaned up against the cash box."

"And the costumes were the only things missing?"

"Oddly enough, yes. No money, nothing else valuable."

"Which costumes were they?"

The Shopkeeper's hand went to his chin, he crossed his ankle to his knee, and his eyes rolled back and to the left. "Let's see ... An Aladdin, two future men, a Roman centurion, the red knight, a hunter, a cook, a caveman, a Phileas Fogg, a zookeeper, a diving suit, a magician, a Wild Bill Hickok, a clown, a pirate ... um, three different princesses, a Widow Twanky ..."

Iris cut him off. "So substantially more than one man could carry off alone?"

"Definitely."

"No sign of forced entry?"

"None. Door was locked, front and back. No open windows or anything, either."

"And while I'm sure it'll be difficult, given the crowd of people outside, were there any tire tracks outside the shop? From a cart or a motorcar, perhaps? Can you remember?"

"I ..." The Shopkeeper removed his fez and spun it between both hands, the tassel slapping against his palm. "I don't think so. It wasn't rainy. The milk had been delivered. I'm sorry."

"No, no, that's alright. If you can't remember, you can't remember. Does anyone other than yourself have a copy of the key?"

"Mrs. Zakalwe from the tea shop up the road, in case mine was lost, but I hardly think she's a suspect. She's sixty six years old."

Iris nodded, stood, and spun on her heel, the tail of her hunting coat flaring out as she took in the shop. There were doors on the changing rooms rather than the velvet curtains, the Kinks poster was now an ukiyo-e print of sunflowers that looked Van Gogh-esque to her eyes, the lava lamp had been swapped for a paraffin one ... It was rather like there were holes in a cut out book, with a wheel at the top you'd spin to replace what was in the windows, changing what period the characters in the scene were in.

"Have you dusted for fingerprints yet?" Iris asked.

It took the Constable a moment to realize she was speaking to him. "Well, with all due respect ma'am, we're not exactly in London out here ..."

"No, of course. And a thief of Lupin's expertise would be sure to wear gloves ..."

"You don't really believe it's this Lupin? I mean, he's a story ... not real ... um ..."

"Fiction?" said the Shopkeeper.

"That's the word," said Constable Wallace.

"What other explanation could there be?" said Iris. "If you were a master thief and looking to evade capture, what better escape than into a novel? A men's magazine? Our imaginations?"

"A nearby barn with the gentleman's merchandise, is more likely," said Constable Wallace with a grin. "All due respect, ma'am. The card is just some foolery trying of throw us off the trail, or cast undue aspersions on our Gallic cousins. I think myself and Deputy Saxon will be following up with Mrs. Zakalwe, to make sure she still has that key. We'll let you know soon as we find anything."

He and the Shopkeeper shook hands, tipped caps, and the constable left.

Panda dug around in his doctor's bag, and found a flask of medicinal gin inside. "Well. However are you going to solve this one?" He took a sip, and smiled. "Locked room, no clues, suspect out of a men's adventure rag …"

"It is a bit of a puzzler," said Iris, sitting down. "Is there anything you feel comfortable telling me now that he's gone? Perhaps an unhappy customer looking for revenge? Someone hooked on a fantasy?"

"Oh no," said the Shopkeeper. "Nothing like that. Everyone in this time is quite friendly and mundane. We get the occasional mysterious stranger on a train with a dark secret, or young person visiting their widowed aunt who needs to get their confidence back, but otherwise mostly folks who need a break from the workaday life of being a barrister or a farmer or," he paused, with a grin, "a shopkeeper."

"A lot of those in town?" said Panda.

"More and more every day, yes. Progress marches forward. From farm to mill. Life gets easier and harder. New problems replace the old, while the same old ones put on new costumes, and people pretend that they've never seen the like before. Of course, if you ask the elderly, it's the worst the world's ever been, but then that's always the case. But some definite improvement discernible today. Hi-yo, hi-yo, as the poet Anderson would say."

Panda sighed. "What shall you do, then?"

"I honestly don't know. A lot of those were collected on my travels. I don't know where I'd find the like of them again, even if I did have the opportunity to go adventuring. And I'm not sure that lifestyle suits me anymore, truth be told. There was one odd thing, though." The Shopkeeper crossed the room and pulled a fez off the coat rack, identical to the one he had on, but well worn and sun bleached.

"Your old one?" said Panda. "Don't you take care of them?"

"I do own more than one," the Shopkeeper admitted. "But this one is ancient. It looks like one of mine, but I don't remember owning it. I certainly didn't put it there."

Iris sat bolt upright. "I've got it! What's the nicest hotel in town?"

"Um … Well, that'd be Mrs. Tlohtoxcatl's Inn. It's a nice little place, tucked over on Crouch street. Just a block or two over."

"In the novels, Lupin always travels in style, doesn't he? Where else would you find him? I doubt he could make it all the way to one of the local Lord's homes with all those costumes, but a quick jaunt over a couple streets? Child's play for a master thief. And I'm sure he has them in a cache somewhere along the way. The boot of a motor car, perhaps, or in a parked carriage."

"Iris, that's brilliant! I'll go get Constable Wallace. If nothing else, it's a lead." He dashed out the door.

As soon as he was gone, Iris leapt up and began rummaging through costumes, desperately searching for … something.

"Iris, what are you doing? I thought you'd solved the mystery?" Panda asked.

"I have! A fez, a vest. Quick! Before he gets back! I think I've really solved this, but he'd never believe me."

Together, they pieced together a better quality fez from an Otto of Greece, a vest and shirt from a James Bond, striped slacks from a Jeeves, glasses off a Ben Franklin, and a bow tie from a Karl Marx. She looked pretty much like the Shopkeeper, as she studied herself in the stand alone mirror next to the bolts of fabric.

"Are you going to tell me the solution yet?" said Panda.

"Just think about it, darling. Who's the only likely person we've met? Who else could it be?" Iris said with a smile, whipping open the changing room door and leaping through the shimmering surface, dragging Panda along with her.

"Hello Iris," said the handsome young man in the tuxedo, top hat and monocle, seated in the wooden chair on the other side of the mirror. A fez sat on the end table to his left. "How did you find me?"

"It was easy, once I put on the costume," said Iris. "There was no way a single person could move or hide all those costumes, and no way for the current level of technology to allow for someone to bring transport and escape silently.

"The house was locked, and remained locked. What other manner of entrance was there? Through the mirror, you could take as many trips back and forth as you'd like. Child's play for a master thief, or someone pretending to be one. But it's about time to come out, don't you think?"

"I'm astounded! How'd you put it together?" the man said.

"First there was your comment about who you rent costumes to. Shopkeepers, eh? Then, your choice of calling card. Garamond is a font that became popular in the 16th century when it became the official font of Cardinal Richelieu's Royal Printing Office, so I knew it had to be someone from the past. But it was the fez that really clinched it for me. Who else but the Shopkeeper himself would be able to slip through his own mirrors and pilfer his own costumes? But you forgot yourself, and hung your fez on the hat rack like you always do when you changed into the Lupin costume. The Longstreet effect must have hit the fez when you opened the portal without having it on, leaving it to age two hundred and fifty years' time overnight. It happens sometimes, with time traveller's clothes."

The man smiled, removed his monocle and top hat, and put his fez back on. "I guess I got a little carried away, didn't I? I hope didn't do anything too bad," said the Shopkeeper.

"Well, you only –"

"Just how many of those things do you own anyways? Do you have a milliner hidden somewhere?" Panda exclaimed. "Well! I suppose stealing from yourself hardly qualifies as a crime, does it?"

He inspected the room further: it was a bare, wooden floored place, with a solid thatched roof, a small iron stove by the bed, and some small chests of clothing stacked side by side against the wall.

Some lumber was stacked by the wall, with rough cut nails, a hammer, a saw, hinges, and a centre bit laid nearby. Bolts of fabric and a table covered with thread, shears, and needles sat opposite. And carefully set far away from everything else were three beautiful mirrors, out of which Iris and Panda had just leapt. They were simply constructed, rectangular in shape, but the surface glistened with a liquidy quality that was cleaner and clearer than any mirror he'd ever seen before.

"I suppose some explanation is in order," said the Shopkeeper. He removed his cape and coat, and put his glasses back on; stripped down to his vest, with his fez and glasses restored, he looked a lot more like himself. "The year is 1643. Soon, Samhain will be a small collection of folks fleeing the civil war. Farmers, priests, parliamentarians, aliens, the time displaced ... People who need a way to escape and relax, to pretend to be someone else for a while, to go help someone else and forget about themselves. Just like I did when I left with you."

"I say!" said Panda.

"I'm sorry, but I don't remember ..." Iris started.

"Because it hasn't happened yet," said the Shopkeeper, smiling. "Not for you, anyways. But we went everywhere and the adventures we had ... the cave of Orc, the Toynbee convention, meeting the sons of Uriel ... even that incident with the Faction Par–"

"No, no, don't tell me too much," interrupted Iris, smiling. "Don't want to ruin the surprise, do you?"

"I expect you'll want me to give everything back, won't you?"

"On the contrary. I expect if you don't get a good collection right off the bat, this place will never get off the ground. Mind if I take a look?"

"Be my guest," he said, gesturing with a hand towards the chests.

"So, these mirrors," said Panda. "How did you make them?"

"Oh no, I didn't," said the Shopkeeper. "They were a gift from Miss Iris. A going away present, if you will. She wouldn't tell me where she got them from. I'm frankly surprised they didn't get broken with the way she drives."

"Now I sure you're not lying," said Panda, retrieving the flask from the pocket of his jacket and taking a pull. He offered it to the Shopkeeper.

"No thanks, I don't anymore."

"Suit yourself."

"A ha!" cried Iris, springing up from the pyramid of costumes she had erected around herself. "Did you know Arsene Lupin had a grandson who was every bit the master thief?" She tugged on a bright red jacket, and switched her bow tie for a yellow one with a silver clip. "A grandson with two trusty sidekicks, and an equally untrustworthy girlfriend, who pulled off crimes even more extravagant than his ancestor?"

Before he could say anything, the Shopkeeper found his fez replaced with a slouched fedora that completely covered his eyes, and Panda a grey kimono tossed over his shoulders.

"What are we going to do?" said the Shopkeeper.

"Go even further into the future, and really get you set up right. Just make sure to stash them in a trunk in the basement or something and leave them there when you're done, so your older self won't feel robbed."

Iris pulled on a pair of white cotton gloves from her pocket, and gestured that the Shopkeeper ought to do likewise. He retrieved the pair from his old costume.

Iris fiddled with one of the mirrors, running a finger across the surface, sniffing it, listening to it, looking really close with one wide eye.

"Are you going to explain this scheme of yours?" said Panda.

Iris nodded. "You're going to stand in the middle of the mirror to keep it open, once I get it set to where we want to go. We're going to take the other two mirrors, and, if I've got this right, we should be able to reflect the contents back through this mirror right quick."

The Shopkeeper's hat moved, as if he were raising an eyebrow, but before he could say anything, the surface of the mirror began to glow.

"Come on now, chuck, don't wanna miss the window." She hefted up the mirror, and stepped through the surface, around Panda, her potato shaped shoes silent on the plush carpet on the other side.

It was dark in 1977. Even after she slid the curtain to the changing room aside, the room was lit only by the soft blue/yellow glow of the lava lamp. She motioned to the Shopkeeper, who slid through the glowing surface — somehow the mirror's glow didn't seem to project into the rest of the room, as if the light were trapped all on the other side, back in 1643. Panda kept his little arms outstretched between both times.

Iris angled her mirror so it caught both the far wall of clothing and the Shopkeeper's mirror. The Shopkeeper nodded, and angled his mirror to catch Iris' and the changing room's. With a flash, the clothing, racks and all, disappeared into Iris' mirror, then into the Shopkeeper's, then into the past.

Iris nodded, and the pair quietly padded back through the glowing mirror, Iris making sure to draw the curtain shut behind them.

The next morning, Iris and Panda walked through the shop door, and the Shopkeeper appeared, frantically waving his hands. "Where've you two been? My goodness! I was starting to worry."

"No, no, we're just fine. Had a few hiccups, but otherwise a delightful little journey," said Iris.

"Your clothes are different."

"Yes …" Iris paused. "A few hiccups, as I said."

"You didn't … lose … the costumes did you? Because there's been …"

"Not lost, per se, old man," said Panda. "There's a situation you should probably be made aware of …"

The backroom was only half empty.

"Huh," said the Shopkeeper, taking it in. He picked his fez off his head, twirled it in his hands, then placed it back on his head. He removed his glasses, wiped them with a clean handkerchief, and put them back on. He resettled his suspenders on his shoulders, under his vest. "Well …"

"It's hardly stealing," said Iris. "Seeing as how it was you, and all."

"Yes, I'm taking that in. I don't remember any of it."

"And it's all done, anyways," said Panda. "No sense in crying over spilt milk."

"And you say they should all be in the basement?"

Iris nodded. "Sure. It's one of those time things. You use them in the past, then box them up, and they sit safely there until you open them up again in the present." She grinned.

"But this building doesn't have a basement. Never has."

"Oh." Iris' face fell.

"Then where are they?" asked Panda.

"I'm sure they'll turn up … eventually," said Iris.

"That's one of mine, isn't it? The costume," said the Shopkeeper. Iris nodded.

"Lupin's schemes rarely go quite as planned, do they? Still, I suppose I can hardly be mad. After all, you got me my start. Twice." He smiled a helpless smile.

"That's the attitude, chuck. Say, you wouldn't happen to have anything laying around I could change into before we go, would you?"

"I've got just the thing," said the Shopkeeper pulling out a black and blue (or was it yellow and gold?) striped dress, zebra print jacket, gigantic red hat with flowers, and red boots to match.

"That's ridiculous. Who'd wear an outfit like that?" Iris asked.

"Don't forget the scarf," said the Shopkeeper. It was red, matching the hat and boots.

"So, does that settle our little argument?" Iris asked. The bus was warming up, as it did from time to time.

"It most certainly does not," Panda said. "If the Shopkeeper knew that we were going to break in in the past, to steal from the future, why would he set up security in the first place? And wouldn't that create an infinite loop? And what happens to the costumes? Now that they're back in the past, what if they don't make it here to the future to be stolen again? And where did he get that Lupin costume from in the first place, anyways?"

Iris shrugged. "Probably from the pile we just stole. Anyways, we solved the mystery, darling. That's what's important." She tossed the red hat back into the pile behind her and shook out her hair. "An improbable solution, sure, but ..."

"Yes, yes. But not impossible." Panda crossed his arms as if still annoyed, but his face and posture relaxed and finally he grinned, as much as his stuffed face would allow. "You win this time, Wildthyme. Not quite a fair mystery. Certainly no way for the police to ever solve that one."

"Cops never do in stories like these. That's why we were the private detectives. And anyways, in that outfit, whatever I came up with was bound to be correct."

"Where to next, then?" He hopped up on the console by the steering wheel.

"Fancy seeing if Stropworth-on-Hamble Brook actually exists?" said Iris, pushing the Abba 8-track into the dash and shifting the bus into gear.

"Only if they have a pub as good as the Fox and Owl."

"You want a drink with the Vicar, darling?"

"No, I want to ask Verger Chambers how she manages every week. Being a sidekick can be exhausting."

DOLORES SMITH AND THE BIRTHDAY BEAR
KARA DENNISON

On the 11th of July 1999, Dolores Smith made a wish and blew out the ten little candles on her birthday cake.

When her father asked after dinner and presents if she'd gotten her wish, she said yes, it had been her new ballet slippers. It hadn't been, as nice as the new slippers were, but she knew saying so would make her parents happy. In truth, she hadn't gotten her wish – but it was only 6:07. She still had just under five hours.

By the time she was in her pyjamas and sent off to bed at 9:00, nothing had happened. But there was still time. She kissed her parents goodnight, switched off her Peter Rabbit lamp, and waited.

Her parents went to bed promptly at 10:00 so they could be up in time for work. Dolores waited until the light from their doorway clicked out, then slipped out of bed as quietly as she could. She put on her favourite pink fluffy jumper, her jeans with the patch on the left knee, her digital watch with the butterflies on the strap, and her warmest house slippers so as not to make any noise on the wooden floors.

At 10:26 PM, with 34 minutes to spare, Dolores Smith set off for the park. Two and a half minutes later, she found her wish half-buried in the summer snow.

It was a bear. Not a real bear (though she wouldn't have said no to one under the circumstances), but a cuddly one, less than a foot high and flopped over on its side unceremoniously. She picked it up, brushed the snow off its nose, and tucked it under her arm.

"You aren't really what I had in mind," said Dolores to the bear as she continued to walk, "but you'll do."

"Do for what?"

Dolores paused and looked around. No one seemed to be following her. "What was that?" she asked cautiously.

She felt something brush against the sleeve of her jumper. With a start, she lifted up the cuddly bear and held it in front of her.

"I said," repeated the bear, "do for what?"

"I didn't know teddy bears could talk."

The bear tilted his head. "I'm not a teddy bear," he said, slurring a bit, "I'm a Panda."

"I didn't know pandas could talk, either."

"I told you," the Panda said, "I'm a Panda. Not a panda. Er. Oh." He looked down.

"Why have you gone and put the ground all the way down there?"

"Are you my birthday wish?" asked Dolores. She was almost beginning to hope he wasn't. His beady eyes seemed unfocused, his words ran together, and his fur smelled a bit of grown-up drinks. In all fairness, though, she hadn't been terribly specific.

The Panda struggled weakly in her hands. "Do you think you could put me down?" he asked. "Not sure I fancy being carried around like a helpless toy."

Reluctantly, Dolores put the Panda down next to her. "Are you all right?"

"I'm half knackered," said the Panda, wobbling on his stumpy feet. "Well, really more like thirty percent knackered. And falling. In about half an hour I'm going to be very miserable indeed."

"Is there anything I can do?" asked Dolores.

"A drink would be fantastic."

"There's water or ginger beer back at the house."

The Panda swayed a bit. "I'm starting to think I might like to be somewhere else," he said thoughtfully, and plopped down on on the sidewalk with a soft thud. "Say, can we revisit the 'carrying me like a helpless toy' idea from earlier?"

Dolores picked him up again, hugging him against her chest with both arms so he was facing forward. "Better?"

Rather than answering her question, the Panda asked, "Where am I?"

"Samhain," Dolores answered, deciding she'd better get back to walking if she was going to be at the park in time.

"I mean when. Right. Yes. That's the word. When."

"My birthday."

The Panda fidgeted, then moaned as though the fidget had caused him some pain. "I don't know when your birthday is. I don't even know who you are."

"But you're my birthday wish, aren't you? Shouldn't you know?"

Dolores felt a rumble from the Panda, as though he'd growled or groaned very quietly. "If you wished for a knackered, progressively more and more annoyed Panda, then yes, I suppose so."

"I wished for a friend."

"Did you."

"Mm. A friend to come with me to fight the monster in the park."

The Panda tensed, turning his head slowly to look up at Dolores. "... what monster?"

Dolores was beginning to wonder if the Panda was the answer to her wish after all, but it was getting late, and it seemed he was all she was going to get. "Every year on my birthday at 11 o'clock at night, a monster appears in the park behind my house. I can see it from my bedroom window every year."

"That's ... specific."

"I don't know what it wants," Dolores mused as she turned a corner. "It's never actually come after me, you see. But I can hear it calling to me. And when I've been by the park in the past – to try to get a closer look, you know – I can feel it watching me."

The Panda pawed at his eyes a bit. "What does this ... monster ... what sort of monster is it?"

Dolores summoned up the image in her mind. "Tall –"

"I imagine everything's tall to you. Skip that."

"... it breathes smoke from its nostrils," she resumed. "And has one glowing eye."

"Crikey."

"And it's big and ... and furry."

"That's all you've got, then?"

"Yes," Dolores admitted. "I've only ever seen its silhouette, you see. But when it speaks to me, it's in a strange, croaky voice. It always says the same thing. 'Come to me, little one,' it says. Over and over. 'Come to me, little one.'" She did her best approximation of the voice, but it hurt her throat to try.

"Maybe it just wants to say hello," mused the Panda.

Dolores shook her head. "Mmm. It always sounds ... threatening. Like it's looking for me. Like it has plans for when it catches me."

"And ... so you're ... going to make its job easier?"

"Here we are!" Dolores said quickly, trying not to dwell on the Panda's words.

The park was in clear view of Dolores's bedroom window, as she had said, but walking to the front gate meant going the long way around some neighbours' houses. Though the gate was locked for the night, Dolores was small enough that she could slip between the bars. She helped the Panda through first, then squeezed through after. The Panda trotted ahead of her as she brushed the snow off herself, but he moved in a precarious zigzag. A few feet ahead of her, he lost his bearings, windmilled his arms while wobbling on one foot, and fell over into the patchy snow, muttering a few of those words her Aunt Rebecca said a lot (but that she herself wasn't ever to say).

"Are you all right?" Dolores dashed ahead to help the Panda to his feet again, though she was beginning to wonder if there was a point.

"You didn't tell me it was a moving floor!" the Panda snapped. "That's not sporting at all. If you're going to play like that, I'm leaving."

"But what about my monster?"

The Panda froze with one foot in the air. "Ah." He started to sit down again, but Dolores grabbed him by one forepaw and walked them both over to the swingset instead, sitting him down in her lap.

"I first saw it when I was two," Dolores started, but the Panda interrupted her.

"You said every birthday."

"Well, I can't remember the day I was born, can I? And I can't really remember being a year old." Dolores swung gently, digging two lines in the snow beneath the swing with the toes of her slippers. "I asked Mum and Dad if it had been here on those birthdays. They said 'No,' but it wasn't a proper 'No'. I could tell they'd not actually thought about it. It was more like –"

The Panda tapped her hand urgently with one paw. "Could you stop swinging? My head's doing loops."

Dolores dug her feet in to stop herself. "Sorry."

The Panda prodded his head carefully. 'Urf. You have stopped, yes?"

"Yes."

"Urf."

"So I'd had a bad dream," she continued, "about something outside my window. I remember waking up to check there was nothing there ... but then I looked out toward the park and there was."

She did her best to summon up her first look at the monster in her mind, faded though the image was by the passing of eight whole years. There had been a sprinkling of snow glinting as it passed by the streetlamps, flakes tapping lightly against her windowpane. She remembered the eye most, glowing bright and orange through the freezing night. Of that night in particular she remembered little else, for she'd pulled her curtains closed and run to her parents' room, crawling into bed between them and burying her face against her mother's plaid nightshirt until the mental image of the glowing eye faded.

And fade it had, into the same dark corners as her nightmares about the snapping turtle who chased her up her bedroom wall and the chalk figure challenging her to dance. But then her third birthday had come, and she'd snuck out of bed when her parents were asleep to play more with the new doll she'd gotten from her grandmother. She couldn't tell time yet, but at what ended up being the right time, she happened to look out her window … and there it was. But there were no flakes to obscure her view, and she could see that the glowing eye, besides being very real, was set in a very real, very large figure. She'd dropped her doll and opened the window.

"Hello?" she'd cried out, though to this day she couldn't think why.

And then she heard it for the first time. "Come to me, little one." The odd voice distorted as it echoed across the street, but the words were clear. "Come to me, little one." And that had been enough to make her slam the window shut and crawl … well, this time, she'd crawled into her own bed, clutching her new doll tightly for comfort.

On her fourth birthday –

"I say, could you throw me in the snow?"

Dolores stopped talking and looked down at the Panda in her lap. "What? Why?"

The Panda rubbed a paw against his forehead. "It's all catching up to me," he muttered. "My head feels like it's full of cotton wool."

"Isn't it, though?"

"Throw me. Honestly."

With a shrug, Dolores chucked the Panda lightly into the snow drift a few feet ahead of her. He let out a sigh somewhere between agony and relief, wiggling his paws contentedly.

"Are you all right?" Dolores asked.

"I'll do for now," the Panda replied in a strained tone, "but once we've killed your monster I hope I can trouble you for a splash of something medicinal."

Dolores stared at the damp toes of her slippers. "I'm not going to kill it. I don't think, anyway."

The Panda turned his head sideways, still pressing as much of himself against the cold whiteness as he could. "No? What was the plan, then?"

"I'm ... not sure." Dolores blinked. "I'd thought at first I should get rid of it somehow, but I don't know if that's the case now."

Certainly, as she went on to tell the Panda, on her fourth birthday she'd had nothing but that on her mind. Her older cousins, both boys, would play-fight with wooden swords and shields like the dragon-slaying knights in her storybooks. She'd asked them to come fight the monster with her, as they were much older and tougher (seven and nine, respectively). They lived two streets down, and the three had snuck out at what Dolores believed to be the right time and waited by the gate of the park. But time passed with no sign of a monster, and the boys eventually packed up their weapons and shuffled home – making sure to throw a few choice words over their shoulders at her.

Dolores hadn't been sure what to feel. She knew she should be relieved that a birthday had apparently gone by monster-free, but her cousins' taunts – and, most of all, being hugely and embarrassingly wrong in front of older boys – left her embarrassed and ashamed. "Stupid monster," she'd spat toward the park gates as she got up to leave. But just as she walked past the gates in the direction of home, she heard it.

"Come to me, little one."

It was a far stranger voice up close: cracked and weathered, the sort of voice a desert would have if deserts could talk. She looked up and behind her, and there it was: still shadowy, still unclear, but certainly there, with the one glowing eye turned straight toward her. Her previous bravery evaporated and she bolted home, skidding on icy patches of sidewalk as she went.

"I checked the clock on the stove when I got home," Dolores explained to the Panda, who may or may not have been listening at this point, "and it was just after eleven."

"Mrrglph."

Dolores nodded thoughtfully. "I had a bit of a scare, seeing it that close, so for the next year or two I tried to ignore it." Tried, certainly. For two birthdays in a row she'd intended to go to bed and sleep straight through the night. But it seemed as though a tiny alarm clock in her brain had been set for 11 o'clock from there on out, and she found herself wide awake. Both times she lay in bed and willed herself to sleep. Both times it failed. Both times she slid out of bed, crept toward the window, and tentatively opened the curtains. And both times … it was there.

She knew opening the window meant she would hear it speak. But she'd done just that, both times. And she'd been right. And she'd slammed the window and crawled back into bed and swore never to go looking again.

Then she'd turned seven. And finally, she'd told her parents.

She wasn't sure what she'd been expecting. Part of her knew she wouldn't be believed. But she'd told them – that was when she asked about her first two birthdays – and received a pat on the head and a comforting hug. Of course there'd been no monsters looking for her when she was a baby, they said reassuringly. She'd tried to explain that she wasn't asking for comfort, that it was a genuine question, but they didn't seem to understand.

"Nightmares can't hurt you," her dad had said.

"But it's not a nightmare," Dolores had shot back tersely, "it's real!"

"You've only ever seen the monster from your bedroom window, though," her mother had replied gently. And Dolores had nearly protested, but stopped herself; protesting would mean admitting she'd snuck out of the house after hours when she was much younger. So she'd shrugged and nodded, realising there were no answers to be had from her family.

That night, she'd gone out again. Not all the way to the park, but into the garden outside her bedroom window. Close enough to home to be safe, but far enough from her bed to know that what she was seeing was real. And again …

And again …

Dolores looked down at the snow in front of the swing set. The Panda was gone.

"Panda?" She hopped off the swing, looking around in all directions. He couldn't have gotten far, considering how much trouble he'd been having with standing not long ago. "Panda, are you still here?"

She heard a scuffle and a thud a few feet away, and ran in the direction of the noise. The Panda had made his way to a nearby tree, where he was pawing through the snow.

"There you are! What are you doing?"

"I've remembered something extremely important," he muttered, continuing to dig. "Something very important indeed."

Dolores sat down next to him. "Is it about the monster?"

"What?" The Panda lifted his head, pausing in his work, and regarded Dolores blankly. "What monster?"

"The one I've been telling you about."

"I don't know the first thing about your monster."

"But –"

The Panda dug until he reached dirt, then snuffled at it.

"Hmf. I could have sworn …"

Dolores hugged her knees impatiently. "What have you remembered?"

"Bubbles."

"Bubbles?"

The Panda nodded.

"Yes. Bubbles. Obviously." He sniffed around a bit more.

"What can you smell?"

"Bugger-all." The Panda flopped back down in the snow. "I don't know what I was thinking."

Slowly, Dolores scooted over to sit next to the Panda. "Were you smelling for clues about the monster? Because I can tell you it smells a bit of –"

"Oh, for God's sake!" the Panda snapped. "I told you, I don't give a damn about your monster! Do stop going on about it!"

Dolores swallowed. "But. But. My birthday wish."

The Panda hopped to his feet, wincing a bit and rubbing one eye with a paw, but recovering quickly. "I am not your birthday wish! I am not your new best friend! I don't even know your name! Do you know what I am? I am a very irate, very confused, very lost Panda who's come a very long way and just wants to get his wits about him and find his friend."

"Well that's –"

"Not. You."

Dolores felt as though the floor had dropped out from under her heart. "You're ... not my friend?"

"I'm not whatever you're looking for, that's for sure."

The air fell silent as the two stared at each other.

"Oh. Oh, no. Oh, look, don't ... no, don't cry."

Dolores felt tears brimming up in her eyes. She bit her lip to avoid sobbing aloud. The Panda waved his paws in front of him nervously. "No, no, not tears, I don't know what to do when humans do tears. Um ..."

"I just ..." Dolores wiped the sleeve of her jumper across her eyes, doing her best to keep her voice from shaking. "I just didn't want to come out here alone. I was scared. I said if the monster didn't stop watching me I'd come see it on my tenth birthday. I've been trying to get brave enough to do it. I thought I was. But I'm not. I thought about it this morning and I got scared. So I ... I made a wish. I wished for a friend because maybe it wouldn't be so scary then."

The Panda fidgeted where he stood, looking everywhere but at Dolores.

"Well. That's. Well."

"I'm sorry I wasted your time," she sniffled. "And stopped you from finding your real friend."

"When you say it like that —"

"And ..." She took a deep breath. "And my name is Dolores Smith."

A dog barked somewhere. Panda cleared his throat.

"... eight."

Dolores looked up. "What?"

"You ... only got up to your seventh birthday. What about your eighth?"

The last thing Dolores wanted to do was smile, but she did. She gave her face one last good dry-off with her sleeve, took another deep breath, and picked up where she'd left off.

By her eighth birthday, she knew she was in this alone. She couldn't talk to her cousins about it after her last embarrassment, and her parents took no interest. The only thing she didn't understand was why. Why her? Why the park? Why her birthday? And why the same thing every year, with that glowing eye pointed straight at her? Had she done something bad? Was it because she never ate her vegetables? Or, worst of all, was there simply no reason for it? Was she just an unlucky victim?

And why did it never leave the park? It was looking for her – it looked through her bedroom window late at night on her birthday. And it called to her. Was there something special about the park? ("Not really," the Panda interrupted, "unless you count the swings' special propensity for possibly giving everyone tetanus.") Did it lock the monster in? And where did it go overnight?

After watching the monster quietly from her bedroom on the night of her eighth birthday, she resolved to take action. What sort of action, she wasn't even remotely sure. She spent her lunch breaks at school in the library, reading every book that had anything even remotely beast-y in it. She looked for anything that fit what little description she had of her monster. Nothing. Perhaps if it had the decency to show up in daylight ... but she had very little to go on.

The year flew by fast, and on her ninth birthday she had nothing to show for all her work. She stood in the garden again, watching and listening from a safe distance, and wondering.

"It hasn't actually tried to hurt me," Dolores said thoughtfully. "But it's watched and waited and stared. It never says what it wants. It just wants me to come to it."

"I," the Panda said thoughtfully, "would suggest not being here, then."

"But –"

"Dolores Smith, listen to me." The Panda stood up straight, puffing out his chest. "Do you fancy being eaten by a monster?"

Dolores shook her head.

"Good. Neither do I. I suggest we both –"

"But I want to meet it."

The Panda peered at her with its shiny eyes. "For God's sake why."

Dolores fumbled with her fingers, staring at the ground. "I ... I don't know. I guess ... I guess I want to see what I've been scared of for all these years. And ten years old is practically grown-up, isn't it?"

"Not really, no."

"I'm terrified. I mean, it might want to hurt me. It might want to eat me. But ..." She stared at the Panda earnestly, feeling herself close to (of all things) smiling. "I want to see the monster. I want to meet what's been scaring me."

"And then get devoured."

Dolores flinched. "Maybe."

The Panda cocked an ear. "What's that beeping?"

"Huh?" Dolores looked down at her left wrist. "Oh, my watch. I set it for eleven. It's ..." She swallowed, pressing the tiny button on the side to silence it. "It's time."

The world went still. The back of Dolores's neck tingled cold. Her hands tingled hot. The Panda, in spite of himself, jumped into Dolores's arms and clung to her jumper.

"This is not how I imagined it all ending," he muttered quietly.

"Shh."

"I always thought there'd be a flaming spaceship, you know. Or a laser gun shoot-out. Or something. But here I am in the middle of July in a snowbank, about to be eaten alive by a little girl's birthday stalk ... mmph!"

Dolores slapped a hand over the Panda's mouth, shuddering. She'd never been inside the park with the monster before. She didn't know what would happen.

There was a sound like a lorry racing through at top speed, minus the lorry. Then a bursting sound, then for a moment the world seemed to bounce a bit as though everything had been hit with a rubber hammer.

And there it was, just a few feet away, still in silhouette. Half again as tall as Dolores, covered in some sort of fur, with a broad, feathered head. And the eye. The glowing eye.

Turned straight toward her.

"Come to me, little one," came the familiar voice.

The Panda's ears went flat, then pricked up again. He lifted his head. Dolores took a deep breath, clutched him tighter, and stepped forward.

"Hello," Dolores said in a voice that was much weaker than she'd intended. "I ... I'm here."

The monster tilted its head, the eye still squared on her. "I know you've been looking for me," she went on. "And I ... I don't know what you want, but here I am. So ... so ... do your worst." She bit her lip, squinting her eyes shut, and waited.

"What?" The monster made what Dolores initially thought was a rattling, growling sound. But it resolved into a laugh. "Oh, not you, dear. The little blighter hiding his face in your shirt."

"Huh?"

The Panda began to struggle wildly. "You!" he shouted, flailing against Dolores's arms until she released him. He pounced on the monster, which stepped forward to catch him awkwardly. And now, slightly out of the shadows, she could see the glowing eye was no eye at all, but the lit end of some sort of fancy pink cigarette.

"I've been calling for ten minutes, chuck. My voice isn't half frayed. Where've you been?"

"More like ten years, if you listen to her." The Panda waved a paw at the baffled Dolores, who was still trying to resolve the image of the woman in the fur coat and feathered hat to her shadowy monster of ten years. "You've gone and given her a complex, you daft woman."

"A complex what, love?" The woman laughed again, but it lapsed into a cough. "Augh, I'm parched. We're travelling the old-fashioned way from now on, and stop me if I say otherwise!"

Dolores cleared her throat nervously, and the woman looked down at her. "Yes? Oh, you're still here?"

"Are you the one who's been coming to the park on my birthday all these years?" Dolores asked hesitantly.

"Years? Heavens, no, can't have been more than a few minutes, surely." The woman grabbed for her handbag and began shuffling through it. "It's ... oh, what year is it, pet?"

"1999."

"Nineteen-ninety-something! Yes!" She came up with a watch, which she checked only briefly. "Knew if I stood still it'd sort itself out eventually."

Dolores wanted to ask a dozen questions, but her mind wouldn't latch on to a place to start. The Panda, meanwhile, had draped himself over the woman's shoulder and turned his attention back to Dolores. "This is my friend I told you about. Iris Wildthyme. Not a monster, just a confused old woman."

Iris Wildthyme gasped and swatted the Panda on the nose. "Why, that's the sweetest thing you've ever said to me."

"Iris, this is Dolores Smith."

"Hi," Dolores said quietly.

"It's Dolores's birthday," the Panda added.

Iris smiled widely. "Is it just? Why, mine, too!"

"Really?" Dolores asked with a smile.

"Oh, no, dear. But I'm willing to drink like it is. Speaking of which, Panda chuck." She tapped the Panda on the nose. "We should get another splash in us before we sober up."

The Panda groaned quietly. "Too late."

Iris turned to leave, then paused. "Dolores Smith, did you say? Tell me, what did you get for your birthday?"

Dolores looked at the Panda, hesitating. "Ballet slippers," she said after a moment.

"Ohhh! Going to be a ballerina, are you?"

"Yes, ma'am."

Iris smiled. "I should say. I thought the name sounded familiar. Dolores Smith, prima ballerina! You'll be known the world over!"

"Really?" Dolores beamed.

"Yes, indeed, but only if you keep practicing and look after yourself. So you'd best get home and get your beauty rest."

Dolores felt herself blushing. "Yes, ma'am!" She started for the park gate at a run, then paused and turned.

"Miss Wildthyme? You're the nicest monster ever."

Iris gave a blustering laugh. "Oh, well did you ever!"

The little girl's footsteps scuffled off in the distance as Panda settled himself on Iris's shoulder. "Well," she muttered, stubbing out her Sobranie against the tree Panda had been sniffing at moments prior, "that was a bleeding misery. My head feels like I've been stood spinning in circles for hours."

"You've been blipping on and off this spot for a decade at least, if she's to be believed. How did you manage that?"

Iris hiccuped lightly, staggering a bit as she did. "Not the faintest. What about you, chuck? Bounced about at all?"

"Dropped right here," Panda huffed. "You made me wait almost whole hour."

"What sort of time traveller do you call yourself? An hour's nothing!"

Panda snorted. "Well, I'm glad you think so, because there's no knowing how long we're going to be stuck here in East Snowdrift thanks to your little oversight."

"Pah!" Iris gave Panda another tap on the nose. "I think the bus can handle being a tiny bit –"

"Destroyed?"

"A tiny bit destroyed, yes," Iris said with a shrug. "I can call in a few favours and get it fixed up good as new. We'll be on our way in no time, you'll see."

Panda glowered, growling something about a handbrake, but was otherwise unresponsive.

"Good? Good. Come along, then. Still a bit before midnight. Something must be open."

"Good-o," Panda muttered darkly. "Might as well go about choosing a local."

The two clambered awkwardly over the park wall, Iris shooting a hand back quickly to rescue her hat.

"Say ... is she really going to become a famous ballerina?"

"Not an earthly," Iris chuckled, fishing out another Sobranie and lighting it up. "But she'll certainly be trying a lot harder for it now, won't she?"

That night, for the first time in her life, Dolores Smith slept soundly on her birthday.

THE GIRL WHO WENT UP IN SMOKE
GREG MAUGHAN

Iris Wildthyme stepped back into the changing room of the costume shop and made an attempt to put on the jumper that the funny little man who ran the shop had handed her. It was itchy and oddly shaped; fumbling round inside it, her head found an arm instead of a neck and Iris wondered whether that shopkeeper deliberately gave her ill-fitting costumes for his own amusement.

As she stumbled around blindly, what she expected to be the back wall of the changing room opened out and Iris tripped up some steps, gaining pace as she attempted to keep her balance in the dark. Having extracted her head from the jumpers arm, Iris was busy trying to squeeze her bouffant doo through the neck-hole when she suddenly stopped stark still. The sting of salt air hit her face even through a thick, itchy layer of wool; the ground beneath her feet lilted in a way that it shouldn't before her mid-morning G&T; while above her, the sky was filled with the soothing melody of gulls doing loud impressions of other gulls being violently killed. She had been transported. Again.

Jumper on, a sea vista from the boat she was somehow now on was revealed to Iris. The sea was blue-grey and choppy, with spray reaching over the sides of the boat and onto the deck. Iris looked around her and then down across her body to try and give some context to where she now found herself. The itchy garment that she had wrestled with on her way into this story was now revealed as a rather unflattering Fairisle jumper, clinging in all the wrong places and showing off all her lumpy-bumpy bits.

"This doesn't look promising ..." she murmured to herself.

"Iris!" called Panda, drawing her attention to him for the first time in this new world.

He was stood at the bow of the boat and looked decidedly more pre-occupied and brooding than Iris had come to expect of him. Well, as brooding as a sentient stuffed Panda could get away with. Which is not that brooding, really. It occurred to Iris that he looked more sort of pensive and slightly chilly. It's his own fault, really, she contemplated. Panda too was squeezed into a Fairisle jumper (of inverse colour scheme to Iris', natch) and wore a woolly yellow fisherman's hat, but was pointedly lacking any trousers, underwear, socks or shoes on his stuffed lower-half.

"Iris, it's bloody freezing," he complained.

"I'm not surprised! You'll catch your death with your rear-end hanging out like that, chuck" she chided him as the little boat drifted in to dock. "Now, should we get out and see what this is all about, then?"

The dock that their boat/changing room portal had moored itself up to was small and almost empty; the dock of an actual, working fishing village on a grim mid-morning. A thin, serious looking young man with harsh cheekbones and steel-rimmed glasses called out to them, enunciating to be heard over the rising wind; "Hello there! You must be DCI Panda and Inspector Wildthyme, from the mainland."

"Erm, yes. I suppose we must be. But you can call me Iris, love."

"If you insist, sir, ahem, Iris," the young man replied. "I'm Sgt Blomkvert. I've been instructed to bring you up to speed and take you directly to the scene of the incident."

"All in good time, dearie," said Iris as she strutted past and ahead of the young man, towards a dark car waiting at the edge of the dock. As the only vehicle in sight, she thought it was a safe bet that this was how they were going to get to 'the incident'. Panda brought up the rear of the group, while Blomkvert darted his look agitatedly between the two. "First, I want a few questions answering. Where I am and what language am I supposed to be speaking."

"Ah, well; I believe you're speaking Danish, same as me. I'm a native Faroe speaker, but with you being from the mainland and all, I thought Danish would be better."

"Speak what you like, dearie. As long as I write it in English in my diary, we'll be able to follow fine. Now, Faroe you say? Like our jumpers?"

Blomkvert ushered Iris and Panda into the car for what he felt was going to be a decidedly long high-speed charge to the scene of the crime; "Well, no. You see, that's a Fairisle jumper and we're in the Faroe Isles. It's, well, different. Less Scottish…"

The room was small and shabby. Square windows were covered by too thin curtains, a dulled twilight version of the bright winter sun outside seeping through and giving everything a coating of murk. A tap dripped just out of time into a sink containing unwashed dishes; next to the sink more dishes waited, piled on the bench, flecks of food hardened on them now. Thick, old-fashioned wallpaper clung precariously to the walls; the kind that once adorned school exercise books. Round the sink, moisture ate away at its edges, while towards the hob a layer of grease was visible.

In the centre of the room was a battered, old table and two chairs. One of the chairs looked as though its leg had come off and a crude attempt had been made to reattach it, so the offending leg now hovered a quarter inch above ground-level. Amongst the detritus on the table was a half-empty cafetière, an ashtray that butts had overflowed and escaped from and an open tub of margarine with knife embedded. A grubby white coffee cup had fallen to the floor and broken, the coffee stain now dried in. To the right of the coffee stain and towards the door, face up, lay a dead body. Pallid grey and naked, the corpse had been a young woman. Around her, a pool of blood had dried solid just short of mingling with the coffee stain.

"Oi! Perv! Stop staring, she's young enough to have a stuffed panda of her own," chided Iris, snapping Panda from the photograph. The room they were in was identical, only where the young woman's body had lain was now marked out in chalk.

Blomkvert ducked in front of them, adding a tall, nervous man to the tableaux; "We found her yesterday morning after neighbours complained of noise in the early hours. So far we've kept it out of the papers. She wasn't just any sort of girl. It's, erm, sensitive. That's why we sent for detectives from the mainland with, well, experience of this sort of thing."

"Who's just any sort of girl, you lanky pillock!" erupted Iris as she raked around for her ciggies.

More calmly, Panda interjected; "Who was she?"

"Mim Artesië. She was the granddaughter of Genfødt Artesië, the millionaire. That's why it's not in the papers yet. Genfødt owns half the restaurants in Faroe and, well, he's asked that we keep things quite. The families taken it pretty badly."

A grim determination set into Panda's plastic, sown-on eye; "We need to talk to the family. Now."

The Artesië family home was set alone in a woodland clearing, at the end of a road little more than a dirt track that twisted through towering firs. It was a modern-looking building of concrete and harsh angles, with porthole windows dotted around the upper floors and a panoramic window taking up an entire wall of the ground floor. Through that window, Iris and Panda could see an old man hunched on the edge of a chair, staring out, oblivious to them.

Blomkvert darted ahead of them and knocked on the glass. The old man did not react. Instead, another man, this one in his mid-forties, wearing a polo neck and thick spectacles, emerged from the shadows at the back of the room, approached the glass and opened a sliding door for them. "Come in, come in. Please. Do not mind my father."

Panda fixed the man with a hard look: "You are …"

"Aksel. Aksel Artesië."

"Mim was your daughter?" Iris noticed that despite the synthetic fur covering his whole body, Panda was now also sporting a thick five o'clock shadow. None of this bode well.

"Yes. Yes, she … was. A wonderful girl, but troubled. No one in the family had heard from her for three months."

"Oh?" Panda took in the scene. There was a slight stoop to this man, fawning. He had positioned himself directly between the new arrivals and his father, blocking Panda's line of sight to the old man. As Panda craned his neck slightly, so too did he shuffle this way and that. Not so much that it was obvious, or even intentional, but Panda felt the old man was guarded. "Genfødt, is this true?"

After a pause, "Aye." The old man delivered the word at a pace that added syllables, without adjusting his gaze.

Panda's gaze was now firmly back on Aksel; "Was there an argument? Did anyone try to get in touch with her? You don't just suddenly forget to stay in touch with your own daughter."

"Well, you know how it is. The daughter of a rich family, we gave her everything she could want and she resented it. I think she was living in that flea-pit to try and make some sort of point …"

Iris was getting agitated; "Well, thanks very much, dear. We'd best be on our way now."

"Before that," cut in Panda, "where did all this money she resented come from?"

Aksel frowned slightly and adjusted his spectacles; "Surely, you must have heard the story of the Artesië restaurant empire? My father had humble beginnings as a simple café owner, but when Artesië's became a favourite of Sir Frederick Mason during the war his fame spread throughout the islands. Following the outbreak of peace, my father opened up a second and a third and soon we are here now."

"Wasn't it a bit difficult to keep a chain of restaurants going while food was still rationed?" chipped in Iris.

"Ah, but here we are blessed with all the herring a man could wish for," said Aksel wistfully.

"Aye," chimed Genfødt as glaciers flowed.

Panda was agitated as they left the Artesië family home. The evening was setting in, but he insisted on returning to the scene of the crime immediately. No, not the scene of the crime. That was too clinical. Bleached. The place of death. The place where a young girl's life was cut short, for reasons unknown. Reasons Panda now pledged himself to set out on the path to uncover. For it was these reasons that would lead him to the killer.

Iris flitted about behind her chum. "Why are you so set on going back tonight, dearie? It was grim enough before it got dark." She tried to hide the look of worry on her face. "Would you not rather a quick drinkie-poos and then settle in at the Five Star Accommodation that's been promised to Denmark's Finest?"

"Just give me a few minutes, Iris. I need to look back over the room. There must be something we missed, and it could be the key to finding Mim's killer."

Panda creaked open the door and flicked a dusty light switch, which produced a dull glow from the low ceiling. He squinted.

"Somethings been moved. No, something's gone." A rectangle of clean marked out on the grimy kitchen table revealed where something had been and now was not. "The killer returned for something ..."

"Or, someone in the family called to collect a memento. Or her friend. Or some strange but essentially harmless crime groupie. Stop jumping to the darkest conclusions, love. It'll do you no good."

A creak in the next room. "He's still here!"

Panda darted through the door in time to see a leg climbing out of the window, then – clang, clang, clang – down the fire escape. Panda gave chase. But his wide, downy behind wasn't designed for hot pursuits. He shuffled down the ladder of the fire escape as fast as his paws would allow and doggedly broke into what, for him, passed as a sprint. As he panted along, heavy footfalls disappeared into the dark distance before him.

Sweating and heaving breath, he let out a mournful cry and dropped to all fours in exhaustion.

Blomkvert had found Iris and Panda rooms at a local hostelry and Iris had spent a fitful night tossing and turning in functional, starched sheets. Things didn't feel right. She didn't mind a mystery; solved them all the time. But she was used to waltzing in, mucking about, home in time for G&T. She knew how to stay above it all. This time it was all decidedly grim, and she didn't like how Panda was acting. Old Iris liked a mystery as much as the rest of them. But whatever happened to a little lightness of touch? A little fun. A little pizazz? A little, dare I say it, camp!? Who says murder can't be a little bit camp, she thought. Can't be a romp? Or a game to distract from the dying of the light? Not like this.

Morning came too soon and, after Iris had put on her face, the hostelry was filled with a strange sort of wheezing groaning sound that always accompanied her first fag of the day. Then, she materialised in the breakfast bar. Panda was already there, staring into the middle distance. In front of him was a traditional breakfast of Ryvita, hardboiled egg and whisky. His five o'clock shadow from the day before had been added to and his patches of black fur failed to disguise the bags beneath his eyes. Now he looked brooding.

"There's something he's not telling us," Panda murmured to no one in particular.

Iris sat down with a coffee and a Danish. "What?"

"Aksel. There's something he's not telling us. About Mim. Or the restaurants. Or his father. Or all of them. We need to talk to them again. Bring them in and see how they talk sweating under a lamp at the station."

"Oh, ok dear," Iris gulped down her coffee. "But I need to pick up another pack of ciggies on the way. Shall I meet you over there, chuck?"

Before Panda had a chance to reply, Iris was up from the table and off.

But she never came back. Off for a pack of fags, and then up in smoke!

So that was it. Panda was alone. Alone in a bad world, setting off down a dark road. There was nothing to be done except suck it up and get on with things, he told himself.

As he left the lodgings, the cold hit his chest; he coughed, spluttered and swore to himself. Leaning into the wind, he made his way back towards Artesië's. And Mim's face called out to him, the thought of it pulsating at the heart of the shapes and colours and smells that drifted in and out of his mind. As purple faded to black faded to grey, with each beat the image of that photograph flashed up. With each beat, burnt into his mind's eye, the tableaux of the murder flashed before him again. And each flash was a step closer. Each flash focused and zoomed in on the one thing he was drawn back to over and over again. With each flash, the death mask of young Mim Artesië. Pale as eggshell; a snap-shot frozen in time of a life lost. Every thought around it drowned out by that one perfect image of death. Who could have done such a thing? Why would they? Panda had to find out, had to understand to be free of that scene.

The interviews with her family turned up nothing. The site of the murder turned up nothing. An old passport photo where, if anything, Mim looked paler than in the shot that Panda could now not escape. An old passport photograph, framed on a hurriedly laid out poster appealing for information. It punctuated the street corners and telegraph poles across the island like a processional route. But still nothing. This was a long haul. No short, sharp glamour here. No suspects to pursue, to chase at high-speed and beat mercilessly until that image was gone and that taste was gone. No photo opportunities. No short-cuts. Panda had to go deeper.

He was still living out of the lodgings he and Iris had been hurriedly booked into on that first night, which seemed so long ago now. His tiny room, a clutter of paperwork. The case consuming every waking hour. Maps. Photographs. Hurriedly scribbled notes. Every inch of wall space covered. Interview transcripts. Diaries. School reports. Piled across table and dresser and draw, and over onto floor space so a path was drawn out from door to bathroom to bed with skyscrapers of paper lining the route.

He felt closer now than ever to Mim. Her school reports; happy-go-lucky gave way to teenage angst. Overachievement gave way to disengagement, boredom. Panda lit a cigarette, poured three fingers of whisky and picked up her diary again. Same story. Mim starts off happy, gossipy in what she writes about only to be pulled towards awkwardness, resentment, embarrassment. She sees her families money, sees others without. She notices how they look at her and becomes stilted. But there's more to it than that. The later entries hint at something. Something Mim found out. It's more than just an embarrassed little rich girl. There's something she won't even say in the pages of her own diary. Something rotten at the heart of that family. And Panda knows that's where he must go.

Poor Mim. That death mask flash, again. Closer now than ever, the gap between what he knows and what he can never know tightens an inch. But she's gone, and there will always be a gap no matter how small he manages to make it, and it stings.

It had been six months now since Panda had last seen Iris. As he headed down a dark lane, walking back from another evening brooding at a dirty bar, Panda cursed her again.

"'Just nipping out for a pack of ciggies,' she said. That's the last I'll bloody see of her! Just because she can't ever take anything seriously. This is important!"

But six months and no closer, he thought to himself. He'd visited the crime scene over and over again, interviewed everyone who knew Mim repeatedly, scoured the evidence from every angle. What was he missing? A clammy sweat crept around his shoulders and Panda realised that after days of fighting it, he had to rest. So when he reached his room, he staggered through the door, past the towers of files, crumpled in to bed and slept. He slept and dreamed.

In his dream, he heard music. It seemed to be coming from the next room; persistent strings and persuasive rhythms. His mind's eye floated from the room that had been his home for months now. It floated out of the window and took in a side-view of the flea-ridden lodgings.

The window to the right of Panda's framed a silhouette. The mysterious silhouette swayed from side to side, almost but not quite in time with the music. As Panda's view drew nearer, the shadow was lifted to reveal the perennial Ms Wildthyme. But not as she was when Panda had last seen her. This was a younger Iris, back when she was older and would usually wear even more cardigans than in her current incarnation. But this time, she'd left the cardigans at home. And everything else, by the looks of it. In her left hand she gripped a very large G&T, while on her right side a nipple bobbed in and out of sight. It danced above and below the frame of the sill as Iris swayed in a style that displayed an increasingly vague connection to the coquettish rhythm that filled the night air.

Iris cleared her throat of what sounded like half a lung-full of Silk Cuts, and began to sing; "Heigh ho, who is there?"

What should have been soft and sensual in tone had a decidedly dwarfish ring to it. She continued; "No one but me, my dear."

In her most boastful moments, Iris claimed her voice could pass for a young Dame Shirley Bassey, but in truth this was more like a two-star Cardiff karaoke.

Suddenly, Iris necked her G&T, threw down the glass and started slapping her arms, belly and thighs in a drunken, naked hakka. Panda's viewpoint flipped and cut to inside the room from behind, where Iris continued to sway, stagger and spank out a rhythm on a behind that was almost but not-quite recognisably somebody else's.

"It's been a while since the Old Girl's had a night like this," Panda said to himself. "She'll sleep well once she's tired herself out."

The next morning, Panda awoke feeling more confused than refreshed. On his windowsill, two snails were entwined making love, on the near-by shoreline, herring spawned and as the sun rose, a new story had begun.

But Panda was still trying to piece together the old story. You could see the stubble poking through his polyester fur and he was coated in a sheen of pallid sweat that a cuddly toy really shouldn't get. He felt the story goes much further back; Mim found something out from long ago and it got her killed. The islands house of records is a post-war building, angular and concrete. Brutalism represents mastery of the future, but no one gave the town maintenance department that memo and the buildings bold, white concrete has fifty years of soot and muck coating it now. The future might have looked bright back then. Bright enough to blind people to what it was built on. Of misdeeds long buried, hoped forgot. But traces remain. So Panda dug through files. The records slowly built a picture. Of Genfødt's rise after the war. Bold.

Rapid. Surprising.

And he sees what he's looking for, and he takes it, and he paces out of the records hall, back into the bracing cold. It hits his chest, and that blessed cough once again. And the sweat. And the grime of days without end and too many nights without sleep. And he leans into the wind and paces out, heading to Genfodts modernist family seat, all glass and angles. And he turns the corner to head once again down that dark road. When out of nowhere pulls up a bright red Routemaster bus, the kind you used to get down in London. The Number 22 to Putney Common, in point of fact. Out of the bus, bold as brass, steps Iris Wildthyme, Transtemporal Adventuress:

"Miss me?" she says, with a grin.

It was raining heavier than it had at any point since they arrived on the island. Mud gathered around Panda's hind paws and thick dollops of rain impacted like shells as he stood, slack-jawed, staring at Iris, unsure what to say.

"Well, *did* you miss me?" Iris chimed in to end the hanging silence.

"Miss you? You nipped out for some fags and disappeared for six months. Miss doesn't come into it, I'm livid with you!"

"Look, luvvie. I thought you were gone, changing so I'd never see my friend again. I've seen it happen before. Remember Karl? When we had that Adventure with The Girl with The Lizard Transfer? He became absolutely insufferable! The old letch was convinced that every female protagonist we came across was inexplicably drawn to him. And this despite a series of increasingly poor life style choices leading to chronic obesity and early-onset heart disease! But it's ok. I'm not going to lose you. I've figured it out."

"I have got no idea what you are talking about," Panda yelled. "This is real. Too bloody real. A girl has died. Been killed. By someone evil, someone who thinks protecting themselves is worth more than that girl's life. And it took six months on this dark, cold island to get there. Six months with the fug of a hangover at all times and stale smoke clinging to the back of my throat and a bloody cold that I can't shake off, but I've figured it out. I'm going to get her killer. I will bring them down and Mim will be avenged!"

"But I've found a better way."

As Iris and Panda stared at each other, the rain got heavier still, until Panda tore himself away, paws squelching out of the mud, and stormed past her towards Genfødt's place.

"Genfødt," shouted Panda as he barged into the fish tank of a home. "I know where the money came from. I've seen the records and I know what you did; what you sold and how you got it."

As Panda faced down the old man Iris slunk in behind him, "I've figured it out too, you know."

"Ignore her! I know about the German Airmen!"

Genfødt held himself as impassively as he could, but slowly that stillness gave way to a shake and then a sob and then a wail. "It's true! The war was a different time, but we were stuck between a rock and a hard place. The British were good customers. But those Airmen, if we hadn't agreed to hide them when they were first shot down, they'd have killed us. So I made the best of it. What else could I do?"

"And the painting you took as payment for harbouring fascists put you on the road to riches after the war. The records of the sale are here in black and white." Panda held up a typed auction record which Genfødt cowered from. "Mim found out too. So you killed her to save your fortune, didn't you?"

Genfødt features darkened and his voice started as a slow rumble, deep in his diaphragm. "You stupid Panda! How could I kill her? I am an old man and barely leave the house now."

"Can I just say," Iris cut in, "All the money in the world wouldn't have help you set up a restaurant in the middle of the post-war herring drought."

Genfødt straightened up and tried to regain some of his poise, "Well, erm, the drought only lasted two seasons. Everyone knows that after that, we were blessed with an abundance of oily fish that has continued to this day."

"But not this year, ey?" Iris had a mischievous glint in her eye. "When we arrived, the harbour was dead. Where were all the boats overflowing with the days catch? Where were the fishwives squabbling and gutting by the harbour steps? There's another drought, isn't there?"

"So what if there is?" snapped Genfødt.

"How did you fix things last time? With an offering to the Great Old Herring God! And this time, you'd give your own granddaughter. How could you?"

Genfødt darkened further still, "You'll never understand the true

nature of sacrifice, Iris."
"This is ridiculous," Panda gritted out. "We've got to go. Now."
And he dragged her by the arm back into the rain.

"What were you doing in there?" Panda yelled.
"Changing the story."
Panda starred, disbelieving, at the woman who had been his best friend. "I've no time for this rubbish. If Genfødt couldn't have done it, then it had to be his son. He had just as much to lose, so he killed his own daughter."
Iris laughed. "No, dearie. It wasn't her dad, because Mim's not even dead!"
"What utter rubbish! I've stared at the photograph of that poor, dead girl every night for the last six months!"
"It's a fake! She's still alive, and we can save her." Iris chivvied Panda along the road back towards the docks.
"What are you doing?" demanded Panda.
"Isn't it obvious? Mim's being held captive to be sacrificed to this weird island's herring god. Frankly, I can't believe you didn't figure it out yourself, dearie. But don't worry, well find her. And we'll save her."
As the rain started to ease and lift, they got closer to the dock when suddenly something caught the edge of Panda ear. "Iris, what's that ..?"
"No one needs vengeance when you can just bring them back, dearie," Iris said with a smile.
The air seemed to warm, and carried on its gentle breeze a drum beat flitted in the background.
"Are you sure you know what your conjuring up here?" Panda conceded. Iris shushed him and stood still, trying to take in what she heard. A simple drum pounded out a simple rhythm, echoed by countless blocks and bells. Iris waved to Panda to creep forward. As they reached a ridge in the path, the rhythm got ominously louder, until just round the corner they saw a terrible sight emerging.

Old Genfødt was wearing the ragged layers and dirty work-pinny of a fishwife. Atop his head was a slimy wig of seaweed. He was out of his chair and unsteadily but with growing confidence skipped to the ritual beat. Behind him, young and old spread out in procession. They wore costumes of the sea, of mixed quality. One young girl was dressed as a radiant squid, with an intricate pulley-system hidden under her skirt to operate bejewelled tentacles. Behind her, an old man stared and ogled. He had tied some string to a bucolic stingray and wore it as a flaccid cape. Many of the people of the island had opted for papier-mâché herring masks, with gapping maw and egg-like staring eyes. One of these herring masks was being pushed, pulled and cajoled to the front of the procession.

Panda's heart jumped; even masked and clothed, he could recognise that frame.

"Iris, you did it! It's Mim!" Iris and Panda rushed down to the front of the march, Panda grabbed Mim by the arm.

"Run!" he yelled.

The returned Mim took the hint and led the way. Panda and Iris struggled to keep up, as she darted into the brush and over the horizon. Mim raced up and down over the undulating ground, taking sharp seemingly random turns like a mad march hare. In the direction she now ran, something large and dark punctuated the skyline, and before it, Genfødt. "Mim, not that way," called out Iris. But ignoring her, Mim ran straight into the arms of her grandfather.

"Thank you Iris," Genfødt boomed, as seaweed-juice dripped down his forehead. "You'll never know how much you've done for me. Cross-dressing Paganism is so much more fun than collaborating with Nazis! It's such a same you have to go. But the Herring God must be appeased!"

As Iris and Panda moved tentatively closer, the structure behind Genfødt came into focus and the penny dropped.

"Oh god …" Iris murmured to herself, as it slowly dawned on her just exactly what her ritual had produced. "Jesus Christ …" she sighed resignedly as in all its glory a 100ft tall wicker representation of a Fairisle jumper stood in front of them. Be-robed locals wielded flaming torches at its base. And with a crack to the back of her head from one of the robed figures, Iris's view faded to black.

"Iris! Iris, wake up!" yelled Panda, with real panic in his voice.

Iris slowly came round and shook her head to try and clear the cobwebs. She breathed in a lung-full of air and coughed hackily. "What is that stink? It smells like bad barbecue and goats piss!"

"We're in the Wicker Jumper," quivered Panda. "And those mad fishy bastards are burning it!"

Hot flames danced below. They had swallowed up the midriff of the jumper, caught on the cuffs and were rapidly making their way to the neck-hole that Iris and Panda were perched on. Panda was sweating through heat and fear; this wasn't the same pallid sweat that had clung to him for the last six months as murder had consumed them. This was the sweat of primal terror.

"My fur's a polyester blend, for god's sake! I'll go up like kindling!" He paced and turned in their tiny collar-cell, starting to hyperventilate.

Iris began to laugh.

"What on earth can be funny at a time like this, you mad old bint!" Panda yelled, with real conviction.

"It's just, it worked, dearie. It might not quite have been the story I was after, but at least this has shook you out of your funk."

"Alright! It did the trick," Panda conceded. "Now can you get us out of here?"

"Erm …"

ONESIES
STEVE PALACE

The plan was to get some ice cream.

Iris and Panda had "rocked up" in Samhain, worse for wear after a succession of cheap ciders, urgently requiring a knickerbocker glory and a village green. The green so Panda could explain to Iris how cricket didn't work when you were drunk – Iris arguing it improved the game no end – and the dessert because they fancied one. Whether the two went together remained to be seen.

They failed to find an ice cream parlour and the bearded Yorkshireman at the sporting goods concern refused to serve them, so they wound up dejected, plonked on a bench overlooking a sea of grass and dog dirt. It was then that the trouble started.

"Hey I like your onesie."

They were being addressed by a trio of youths, more specifically the ringleader, who was clad as a leopard. Their chunky accents descended on Iris and Panda, borne on streams of fogged breath:

"How'd you fit your baby in there?"

"He looks like a toy panda."

"Can he not breathe?"

Panda's unexpected and abrupt retort had led to a pitch battle of sorts, which left Iris flat on her face and her little friend the wrong way up in a bag of soggy chips on top of a bin. Worst of all they took her parasol. Iris was rather partial to her parasol, and if you needed a replacement in Samhain fast there was only one place you could go.

Inside, the shop was warm as toast. They found the Shopkeeper on his knees amongst the colourful ensembles resting on wooden dummies.

"I didn't know you were a screwdriver with a dab hand," Iris remarked, battling to stay upright as the heat stewed her inebriated brain.

Laid out on the varnished floor were various heads, torsos and limbs. Such a sight would sway a less hardy soul, but she'd seen worse. When she got a look at one of the faces however her system froze all over again.

"What the hell is Tom Jones doing here?"

"Getting reprogrammed," The Shopkeeper replied, fez askew. "I know you two had your differences, but I reckon with a bit of recalibration he could help me around the establishment. Plus he's got a lovely wardrobe."

"Differences?" Panda spluttered, becoming aware of the stench of vinegar on his cheeks. "He did try and assassinate us you know!"

"Yes, but his heart's in the right place." The proprietor spotted a small valved attachment by the fire exit. "Hang on, no it isn't." He scooped it up and plugged it back into Tom's chest cavity. "This is turning into a pickle of an afternoon. Cup of tea perhaps Iris?"

"You'll find it happens all the ti-ii-ii-iime …" The lyric drifted from a discombobulated voice box. The Shopkeeper gave it a whack and it stopped.

Over steaming mugs Iris and Panda relayed their tale of woe. How they'd been set upon by wayward teens and how one of them resembled an extra from The Banana Splits.

"A lot of them do Mr Panda. It's the onesies you see."

"Onesie." Iris was starting to think more clearly. "That was what he called you, wasn't it Panda? The ringleader."

The Shopkeeper's face darkened. "A few years back I noticed people were wearing those things. In the city, when I had to venture out for novelty supplies. I thought they'd never reach Samhain, but the local tearaways have taken them on with a vengeance." Starting to sober up, Iris asked what he did by way of parasols, but discovered to her chagrin he'd hired his last one out to a spinster named Mrs Flowerday. However, never one to let down a customer, he suggested there might be one in the back room, where he kept spoiled fabric for collection and general loose ends.

The Shopkeeper led them through to the rear of the building. As with any shop it was utilitarian and stained. He pushed on the door to the back room, which immediately swung open and banged on the wall. A stiff breeze blew across them, iciness cleaving the heat.

They squinted into the room.

"You'll find it happens all the ti-ii-ii-iime …"

Through the doorframe was a wall. At least it seemed like a wall. A concentrated aroma filled everyone's nostrils. The heavy scent of an old room laced with the smell of a zoo. Their adjusting eyes made out a blanket of fog where the ceiling should be.

Panda tugged at Iris's coat tails. "It's another dimension isn't it?"

Iris nodded and wrinkled her wrinkly nose. "That smell. Something organic."

"Well it is full of old clothes," said The Shopkeeper. "Alan The Widower was supposed to collect a lot of this stuff ages ago."

She turned her head so sharply the feathers lurched. "How long has this room stayed unattended?"

"I don't know." The Shopkeeper shrugged. "Couple of weeks?" He furrowed his rather fetching brow. "Wait a minute ..."

He was checking out something wedged into the base of the wall. "There are those sack coats I've been looking for ... and the whalebones!" Iris and Panda jumped as he emitted an almost girlish squeal of delight. "And the Homburgs! I thought this stuff had been lost forever ...!"

"You mean to say this is the missing stock?" Steam nearly shot out of Iris' lugholes. "These costumes have been left to their own devices since the seventeenth century!"

"What do you mean left to their own devices ...?"

"And you running a costume shop and everything! I'm surprised at you!"

"Hang on ..." The bewildered proprietor took another squint at the dim mass ahead of them. "Is that entire wall made out of ...?"

"Put it this way chuck, the brick fairy didn't come in the night! If used fabric is ignored for too long bad things happen, especially if it used to be on someone's back."

"Iris I know you specialize in the ridiculous but even by your standards ... that's ridiculous."

"Why do you think charity shops drench their fabrics in synthetic scent? It's a weapons grade disinfectant!"

Panda chipped in from knee level. "Think of a city trader." They all did and shuddered. "He ..." Iris nudged him. "Or she ... spends their days mired in stress. They scream and shout but those strong emotions also escape through their pores. Soaking into their collars and lying preserved, like flies in amber."

"The emotions are dormant but can be triggered, especially if left in the vicinity of other neglected fabrics. They feed off each others' stains, creating a swarm of abandoned feelings." Iris marvelled grimly at the weird wall. "I've never seen anything on this scale though. The amount of clothing all meshed together, stemming from that little clutch of headgear and corsetry. Do you know how much fury is embedded in the average corset? It must have generated a sizeable quantity of psychic energy."

Suddenly a scream was heard, its echo absorbed into the fabric pile before gunfire accompanied it, rattling from the distance. Both sounds emanated from the room, but seemed half a mile away.

"Well that tears it." Iris gave her companion a sympathetic smile. "Sorry Panda, looks like we'll be staying here a while."

Panda gazed upwards with a hopeful yet shifty little face. "Iris, couldn't the British Heart Foundation sort this one out? I'm sure if you called them they could bring a truckload of disinfectant and …"

She knelt down and squeezed his paw. "If someone's in mortal danger we've got to go and help. It's a bugger chuck, but that's the way it is."

Iris stepped inside the room, joined by Panda, who was frightened but didn't want to abandon his best drinking buddy.

Now they were closer they could see the detail of the wall. Thick, tight ribbons of fabric, twisted together in various hues, bonded into what was almost an imitation of muscle. To the left it met the plasterwork, stopping dead in a clean line. To the right there was a corridor effect as the cloth structure branched left to run parallel with the shop's opposing wall, itself coated in a layer of assorted glad-rags.

"Ready to do something potentially stupid?" Panda nodded.

Slowly and carefully, they made their way along the corridor. A fresh breeze carried a musk that nearly floored the pair with its pungency.

The passage opened out on the left into a strange parody of the World War One trenches. The sides were compacted trilbys, torn t-shirts, embarrassing Bermuda shorts, all plaited into solidity and forming a network of hemmed-in pathways. Iris noticed her heels clacking, the ground beneath still linoleum. The realm was well-lit, the fog above bright like a cold torch.

Behind them, the branching wall swung back in a slow but inexorable motion to bond against the opposite side. Iris and Panda turned round in time to see shirt sleeves and shoelaces and apron strings whip out from the mass to knot it together, forming a join. They were sealed in.

"Yep," Panda said. "Pretty stupid."

Iris shivered and pulled the wide brim of her hat down against the light. "What does all this make you think of love?"

"The world's angriest wardrobe? I know what you mean though. I keep expecting to see a Tommy whistling Pack Up Your Troubles In Your Old Kit Bag."

She pondered. "There's a snifter of the Great War. But I reckon it's more like a maze." She indicated the layout of the network, which twisted and turned. "Trenches are straight lines. This place is definitely a puzzle."

"Hey baby. I was startin' to think you were lost for good." The voice was deep and rich and American.

A large black man had appeared at the entrance to one of the pathways, sporting a tidy afro and a moustache just the right side of a porn film. He was clad in a knee length, wide-collared leather coat over the top of a turtleneck, flares and boots. Effortlessly clutched in his hand was a sub-machine gun. He wore a confident expression which shifted on seeing their faces. He recognized them, but something bothered him. However he was feeling, Iris ruefully concluded all hope of flirtation had evaporated into the fog.

"You've found us, whoever you are," she replied, a little crestfallen.

The stranger took strides toward them with a wary gait, eyes darting about.

"Everybody goin' their separate ways was one bad idea. We never should have listened to that uptight honky."

"And who might this honky be?" Iris enquired.

That irritated him. He clearly expected her to know who he meant. "That talkin' peanut who thinks he's cleverer than everyone else! Let's pray the phantoms got to him first or I might just kill him myself."

"Phantoms?" Panda threw his paws up. This was the end to a perfect afternoon.

"Now then chucks, don't get exasperated. My name's Iris and this is my friend Panda." She held out her hand.

The man sighed, as if being made to play a little game. "The name's Shunt … Joe Shunt."

"Cool as a cucumber aren't we Mr Shunt? Don't even bat an eyelid when an old lady appears out of nowhere with her endangered companion. A talking one to boot."

He snorted. "Listen lady, we'd better get movin', or we're gonna be up to our necks in some bad business."

They made their way along the path he'd emerged from, walls of stinky, compressed fabric looming up either side. Panda's soft feet didn't agree with the lino and he frequently slipped, at one point landing with his head an inch from a bundle of clown pants. It bristled as Iris helped him up.

After a few minutes they came upon a pocket of free space, a circle of sorts from where you could select several pathways deeper into the maze. Occupying it was a reedy-looking bald man in glasses, a check shirt, corduroys and shiny shoes (who Iris presumed was the talking peanut). Aiming a gun between his eyes was a bulky Italian American, in the process of losing his hair, wearing a short-sleeved vacation shirt, shorts (regrettably) and moccasins.

"Mr Soprendo, I urge you to see sense!" The man – another Yank – was imploring his generously proportioned aggressor in pedantic tones. "We are in a mutually inconvenient situation …"

"I'm gettin' sick of all your fancy words cueball!" Soprendo readied his chunky trigger finger. "Just shut your yap and think of a way to get us out of this!"

"What is it with you boys? You're left alone five minutes and already you're trying to propel hot metal into each others' faces …" Iris adopted a grandmotherly tone as she stood between them. Her tactic certainly shut them up, but they stared at her the same way Shunt had, displaying an odd familiarity. Shunt himself watched from the sidelines, chuckling at her bravado.

"What happened to you?" snarled Soprendo at Iris.

"That's what I'm wondering," she replied. He stomped away, muttering elaborate epithets.

Peanut Head approached Shunt with an oily posture, wringing his hands. "John. Good to see you've avoided all the unpleasantness so far."

"No thanks to you four eyes. Kel Boy bought the farm out there."

"Well thank god for that. I couldn't have abided another spiel about discount Latvian trouser presses."

Iris reasoned Kel Boy must have emitted the scream they heard back in the shop.

"You callous sonofabitch. I told you we shoulda stuck together." Shunt checked the mechanism on his weapon.

Peanut Head took a step back before sidling up to Iris. "We're having enough trouble being whittled down by those ... things ...without turning on each other."

"How many of you are there? Or rather were." He gave her a quizzical look. "Humour me. Pretend you've never met us before, even though it seems you have."

"What happened to your face?"

"What happened to yours chuck? You look exhausted."

"I have some ... health issues I'd rather not discuss." He coughed markedly against his hand before continuing. "You know what happened. Dozens of us were summoned."

"You're saying someone or something has brought you here ...?"

"It's like we're running round this rat-trap for a purpose, but I can't think what. I'm a chemistry teacher, not a philosopher."

"Oh, you sure ain't that." Shunt was getting itchy feet. "Listen up people, we gotta stay one step ahead of these monsters. If we don't ..." He paused for breath. "Man, we are toast."

"Stop it, you're making me hungry." Iris gave Shunt a wink, but there was something wrong. The oak of a man appeared to be having difficulty standing upright. He gasped for air as his long coat tightened, constricting across his back. Everyone noticed when it split and fell away, sections twirling in the air. Shunt swore as the leather wound itself into the wall.

"I paid a hundred bucks for that coat!" he panted.

"Gives a whole new meaning to the expression 'the cows are coming home'," whispered Panda.

Iris failed to quip back, her face focused in concentration. "It's getting smellier in here. Why do I get the feeling the pack are readying for a kill?"

Around a corner came two shapes. Iris and Panda were surprised as they thought their assailants from the park had found their way into the maze. Two onesies – a badger and reindeer, foam antlers cock-eyed over a dark hood – faced the gathering.

"Get back!" yelled Shunt, lifting his firearm as they backed against the wall. It practically snarled at them, making them jump and inch back toward the eerie visitors.

The onesies took spongy steps, like astronauts. Their limbs were stuffed and tubular, scraps of fabric dangling from the sleeves and material clenched into balls where the feet should be.

Shunt let out a spray of lead across the animated suits. They jerked under the impact as the bullets went straight through and buried themselves in the wall. The gun clicked and he hissed. "Out of ammo."

"Step aside boy," sneered Soprendo. "Time to take out the laundry." He squeezed the trigger, tearing holes in the onesies. The reindeer toppled and the bloated gangster sensed victory. But he was wrong.

The lolling antlers pulled the hood back slightly and Iris studied the "head", a fisted wad of various fabrics. Suddenly a stream of cloth burst from the centre, wrapping itself round Soprendo's neck. He yelped and dropped the gun, trying to make a break for it, but the tether tugged him down onto his knees with surprising ferocity.

The badger towered over him, the flattened cartoon of a face staring down atop the hood. Without warning, all the fabric erupted from the badger in a torrent, whirling into a thick tentacle, the pointed end hovering to accuse before it hurtled at his gaping mouth. Soprendo's arms and legs rocked mightily over the edges of the cradle of his form, the onesie unloading itself down his gullet while his eyes juddered into the back of his skull. The badger's polyester and cotton skin collapsed in a heap as blood started to seep from the hairline gaps in Soprendo's stretched lips. By the time it had finished, it left a rose-shaped stopper against his mouth and the man was dead.

The horrified group barely had time to react before the reindeer was back on its makeshift hooves, bloodied tether retreating into its face. They tried to reach an escape route but it was alarmingly agile, dancing with a new-found vigour as it blocked off whichever avenue they chose.

"Split up!" shouted Peanut Head.

"I hate to agree with this asshole, but he's right!" added Shunt. "It's our only chance!"

To Iris's amazement Peanut Head grabbed Panda, darting for a trench with the onesie in hot pursuit. As it closed ground he pitched the little bear at the reindeer's head. Panda cried out as the animal sucked him into the dark hood right up to his waist.

She thought fast, rifling through her unfeasibly deep pockets. A lighter. The tragic remnant of a smoke-free existence. The flame wasn't enough to ward off a mosquito let alone this obscenity. But there was something else that would do the trick.

Reluctantly, Iris took out her hip flask, triggered the lighter, took a mouthful of gin and spat fire across the reindeer. A relinquished Panda bounced on the lino as the floppy predator retreated, leaving silence and fog in its wake.

"Lady ... I like your style!"

Panda barely contained his outrage. "So you did have booze!"

After gathering their wits the three of them were on the move. It wasn't long before they encountered Peanut Head. He was lost and shattered. Iris's clout over the head didn't help him.

"I apologize if my actions were extreme," he explained. "But when you're in a survival situation the primary instinct is self-preservation."

"I'd say your primary instinct is being a shitbox," replied Panda.

"Panda please... language," Iris went to lean against the wall, but Shunt caught her just in time. She gratefully leaned on him, taking the weight off her ankles, shot through from running in heels.

"You ever thought about removing those things baby?"

"Oh you wouldn't appreciate that chuck. I haven't trimmed my toenails in millennia. I'm liable to have your eye out." He laughed, his chest cavernous.

"Could we keep the noise to a minimum?"

"Hey no-one's talkin' to you, you backstabbin' cracker!"

Peanut Head sank onto the lino, drained and muffling his coughs with a hanky. He obviously was not a well man and the flight had half-crippled him. The hanky broke loose from his hand and joined the wall, like the abandoning of a sinking ship. "You may not trust me, but we're all going to have to work together if we want to get out of this place. Now admittedly I'm no expert ..."

"Won't stop him having his ten pence though," mumbled Panda.

"I'm no expert ... but I've been studying the layout of this maze and the way the paths curve and join up ... they seem to mirror the surface of the human brain."

"Ah heck, we ain't got time for these crazy-ass theories!"

"No wait." Iris stooped to be at eye level with Peanut Head. "I think the uptight honky's onto something."

He was rapidly weakening, drawing strength from the light in Iris's eyes. "I wonder … if this whole place is an organism … then maybe … it has a heart …"

She felt inspired enough to forget her raw heels. The onesies had to be feeding off an incredible power to do what they did to Soprendo. She'd wager a bet the source of that power lay in the centre of the maze.

The pedant's head wilted, touching the floor. With that, he was gone.

"Mr Shunt," she said abruptly. "D'you mind if I sit on your shoulders …?"

Panda squinted into the fog, the freezing atmosphere paralysing his skills of observation.

"Mercy me, it's cold up here!"

"Try to focus chuck, it's important!"

The little bear balanced on Iris's hat. Iris had her thighs round Shunt's head. Shunt didn't appear to dislike the experience.

At an altitude of twelve feet ten inches Panda had a reasonably clear view across the fabric trenches. "I can see a … this is going to sound odd …"

"Impossible in this situation friend," said Shunt from below.

"It looks like a … castle …" He screwed his resin eyes tight to block out the sinus-numbing chill.

When he opened them again he was face to face with a onesie.

Standing on the wall, this one took the form of a lurid green frog. A tongue of scarlet fabric unspooled from the bunched interior and sealed his mouth before he could protest. He could hear Iris and Shunt flirting under him. Typical of her when a crisis was happening right under her nose, or in this case over it! Oh well, if he was going to die it may as well be at the hands of something funny …

All hope jettisoned, he received a big surprise when something javelin-esque streaked through the air and impaled his garish attacker. Iris and Shunt stopped dead as the frog landed on the lino with a plush thud, a parasol stuck through its innards.

It skittered on its side, unable to extract itself. She saw the handle was inscribed. Embossed initials. "I.W."

"I think you'll find that belongs to me chuck."

Iris turned, the hairs on the back of her neck elevating.

Walking into view was herself. Yet not. Her attire matched Iris's perfectly but it was coordinated and most of it was PVC. She was younger. Worryingly so. At most forty. Accompanying her was a stumpy individual encased in a panda suit.

The newcomer came to a stop with poise and elegance. "Ida Windchime. And this is my associate Panda."

"There you are baby, where you been hidin'?" Shunt dropped Iris's hot brick-shaped presence and headed straight for her.

"Can I get some help down here please?" The real Panda lay a few yards away, half-tangled in the limp tongue. A simmering Iris broke off from glowering to assist him. The stitched amphibian appeared dead on her approach. Suddenly it reeled in its protuberance, threatening to swallow Panda whole.

Ida put a stop to that – she stamped on the tongue with her spiked heel and administered a few squirts of disinfectant via a bottle in her designer handbag. Shunt looked on adoringly as she extinguished the beast.

"If any chaps or chapesses are experiencing any extreme emotions, best start suppressing them now. Especially paranoia." Ida paused, apparently for effect. "They seem to like paranoia."

"Oh man …" Shunt was staring at the far wall. Jutting out was Peanut Head's lifeless hand, vanishing amongst pantomime horse tails and mad scientist coats.

"The mind is getting more aggressive," said Ida. "Evolving. First they mimic us. Then they try and inhabit us. Once they establish they can't be us … they wipe us out."

"Of course you're referring to the fact this place is a mental landscape," Iris interjected confidently, recalling Peanut Head's dying words. "You are doing that, aren't you?"

Ida smiled knowingly. "Of course chuck. And naturally you've worked out what's at the core?"

"Yes," Iris floundered. "Why wouldn't I have?"

"I do love helping the aged. At least tell me you know who I am."

"I've an inkling chuck. I've an inkling …"

Ida pulled her parasol out of the disinfected corpse. "Panda and I found the centre of the maze. It's a power source, much like you expected I imagine." Iris met her eyes with added frost. "If you'd care to follow me I can show you what all the fuss is about …"

She pivoted neatly on her heel and set off along a trench. Her Panda gave Iris's Panda the finger before waddling after her.

"Be careful baby!" called Shunt, jogging into her orbit.

Iris and Panda followed at a short distance. She bundled her emotions into a ball and held them in the pit of her stomach as Shunt fawned helplessly over her slender counterpart.

"She's me. Or at least a version of me."

"Another bodily renewal?"

Iris shook her head. "This is different love. Counterfeit's the word. She's got all my prowess, all my genius …"

Panda resisted a put down with some effort.

"But they're borrowed. Does anything strike you about the characters we've met here today?"

"They are characters, I'll give you that." Then it hit him. "Wait a minute. They really are characters."

"Fictional creations imported by whatever fiendish mind we're wandering in. That annoyingly attractive fembot up ahead … she's based on my exploits."

"How did you end up as a …?"

"Don't ask me chuck." She didn't have the gall to tell him her suspicions. A wild night at a sci-fi convention a few years back in her timeline with an untamed, curly-haired Scottish TV writer. Had that sordid dalliance borne fruit of the most unexpected kind …?

A stench mounted under Iris's nostrils. She had an unnerving sensation, as if while inhaling the smell, something large was behind, doing the same thing to her. A sting of resentment riled her system. Maybe she wasn't keeping herself in check like she thought. Her frustration at Ida bubbled over, and at her rear the walls were converging, getting set to envelope Iris and feast on her angst.

"Iris …" whimpered Panda over his shoulder.

"I know," she said. "Don't worry, I've just the job …"

She wrenched something red out of her pocket and slung it into the mass of ravenous fabric. The walls ceased their pursuit and formed a blob, satiating on the treat it had been offered.

"What was that?"

Iris wiped her hand on her skirt. "Tom Jones's jockstrap."

"If you two have finished messing about … we've reached our

destination!" Ida gestured upwards with her parasol.

Looming overhead, dreamlike but unhygienic, was a castle composed of old material. Instead of medieval brickwork, sheepskin and quilting. The fog hung thick about the spires and turrets.

"The mists of memory," the women remarked in unison.

"Ready to meet the King?" It was the only time a smug Ida bothered to turn round.

Passing through the oddly impressive archway, Iris blinked as she reached the interior.

They were in a small front room, nicotine on the walls, cluttered with ephemera. The accumulation of a lifetime's endeavours, both fulfilled and fruitless. Panda and his costumed counterpart were now scuffling, in a frantic bid to see who could locate the most revelatory item first.

Ida and Shunt stood by a recliner in front of an old TV set. Seated there was a diminutive man in a cardigan and flat cap, brim pulled over his face. He exuded stillness. He was quite dead.

As Iris went to the recliner she nearly tripped over a pile of DVDs. The top sleeve showed Peanut Head. She knew she'd find Shunt, Mr Soprendo and everyone else beneath. The closed curtains and sad bachelor trappings indicated the deceased sought refuge in the adventures of these characters. They'd come to personify who he was. The pedantic side, the aggressive … the self-loathing and doubt. The onesies homed in on these negatives. Perhaps instead of enemies they were like antibodies, purging bad blood.

She went to lift the cap, only to find no head. The skull had long since disintegrated, melted down into wax by the rapacious demands of the fabric. Strands of organic matter came away with the cap, and as Iris removed it completely they broke and the atmosphere changed.

Panda halted his battle, biffing his paws into thin air. Ida and Shunt had vanished and the icy breeze of the maze blew no more. Iris and her friend, the genuine articles, were all that remained.

She should have told Panda what had been going on right that moment. That this was Alan The Widower. The pensioner who collected the spoiled fabric from the Shopkeeper, absent for a long time and not missed. But a sadness prevented her from revealing this straightaway. He must have established quite a bond with all that dispossessed material, plugging the hole left by his wife when she departed. Unwittingly sowing the seeds for a bridge to be built between their world and his.

When he died in front of the telly he gave up his kingdom, etched as it was with the sorrow of his final years. The raft of emotions that cramped space had preserved in the concrete and carpets ... his home steeped in what he'd become through the brush strokes of time's cruel hand. The fabric seized this opportunity like subjects swarming across a moat. Alan now a battery, the embers of him helping to generate the energy for the warped realm that had worn him and everything he was like an old cloth cap.

Iris would tell Panda all this. Eventually. Though not right now. Not until she was ready to acknowledge that time affected her, just like everyone else.

"Best get back to the shop chuck," she said softly.

As she went to leave her foot disturbed something leaning against the leatherette of the recliner. It was Ida's parasol, the embossed initials glinting in the dim light. Iris picked it up, rested it on her shoulder and made for the exit.

THE OPERA OF SAMHAIN
DONALD MCCARTHY

Iris Wildthyme stepped out of 23rd Century Venus and into the Fancy Dress Costume Hire Shop, her companion, Panda, only a foot behind her. Without looking at him, Iris said, "You have no taste."

"I have no taste?" Panda said. "Anyone who could sit through that opera with a smile on their face is a questionable source of criticism in my book."

They'd come and gone through the shop who knew how many times, using the costume shop's mirrors to visit the strangest of places, from other planets to other time zones to other realities to one particularly disturbing incident with a large cat that viewed Panda as a chew toy. "A most unsophisticated adventure," he'd said afterwards. Upon returning to the costume shop, they arrived in a different time period. If they left in 1963, they could well return in 1887 or 1989. It'd be a disconcerting reality for most, but Iris and Panda had travelled in even stranger ways in the past and enjoyed the quality of randomness the shop offered.

Iris wasn't surprised Panda hadn't liked the opera. Venusian operas seldom attracted outside attention and Panda wasn't one for the finer things in life. He was a perfectly pleasant companion for her, of course, but sometimes she wondered what it'd be like to travel with a slightly less cynical person. The again, a less cynical person would probably be less amusing. Cock-eyed optimists rarely had anything to offer other than gasps of awe.

Iris pushed through costumes of clowns, pirates, Martians, ghouls, brides, grooms, and more, some of which were unrecognisable to her. One mask caught her eye, however, an all-white mask, one that could be worn by almost anyone thanks to its form. It had an adjustable string, a long and pointed chin, and large holes for a person's eyes. It was otherwise smooth. She touched it lightly. Plastic. Some amusing mask that related to who knew what, Iris surmised. Still, its large eyes seemed to stare at her, or maybe through her. What attracted people to it?

"Looks like death, doesn't it?" said a voice from behind her.

Iris turned and saw the costume shops' shopkeeper. He smiled at her, his hands clasped in front of him, his hair smoothed back, and his blue eyes wide. No matter when she returned to the costume shop, the shopkeeper was always the same.

"Can't say that I know what death looks like," said Iris.

"Of course, that's right," said the shopkeeper. "I suppose some lives are more, ah, what's the word? Ephemeral? Fleeting? You, though, are like a portrait, forever staring out at the world."

"You describing me or you?" she said, smiling.

He closed his eyes for a half a second. "Not me, no."

Iris flicked the white mask with her finger. "Seems a little darker than what you usually stock here."

"I haven't the foggiest idea how half this stuff ends up here." He smiled again, but there was a slight tightness to it, like he was forcing his mouth to move in a way it didn't care to.

Panda ambled up behind the shopkeeper. "Are we going to head out somewhere else?" he asked Iris.

"Hello to you, too," said the shopkeeper. He turned and looked down at Panda.

"Don't pat me on the head again like last time," said Panda, lifting his paw and pointing it towards the shopkeeper. "And, yes, hello."

This time the shopkeeper's smile seemed more relaxed. "All mirrors in here are available for you, as always. You may want to take a stroll through the rest of Samhain, though. Sometimes there's much to see. Our local church is of note. Second only to this place, if I do say so myself. If you haven't been there, you should go. And even if you have, you should go again."

"I could use a walk around town," said Iris. As fun as it was to pop off into an adventure, there was something to be said for a calmer environment on occasion. "What year is it now?"

"2004," said the shopkeeper.

"Oh, that sounds like a fascinating year to wander around a dull town," said Panda. "Let's rush to that."

It was autumn; that much was clear to Iris. The streets were sprinkled with dead leaves. Not the pretty kind, the orange and yellow ones that allowed one to romanticize the death of greenery, but rather the dull brown ones with shrivelled tips that disintegrated when touched. The clouds above were grey, the type that lingered for hours, perhaps even days.

The town was quieter than it'd been in the past, although there were still people out on the streets, friendly as always, but walking a little faster than would be expected in a small town. One passer-by, an older woman with red hair down to her waist, said to Iris, "There was a beautiful performance this morning. Bertolt Brecht's *Threepenny Opera*. It was put on by elephants. A lovely experience all around. They even stayed after to discuss staging. Never know what you might miss, huh?"

The woman went on her way, a smile on her face.

"Sounds more interesting than the opera we saw," said Panda.

Iris hadn't considered what Samhain had to offer in the past. The mirrors to other times and places offered so much that the town itself seemed to be something of a relic. Perhaps she'd been wrong. Perhaps there was something more here. Elephants performing Brecht wasn't a sight you saw every day, not even when travelling through the costume shop.

"Y'know, it's a shame we missed it," said Panda. "Brecht has always been right up my alley. You?"

"There's something about Chekov," said Iris. "When it comes to human plays, that is."

"Chekov?" Panda shrugged. "I suppose. Why don't we head over to the bar we passed earlier?"

"If we get you drinking then we'll never leave."

"True, but I can get a few in me and then I might be more sociable. I'll be dazzling the patrons with stories, no doubt. That's the benefit of arriving in a boring place; you can always entertain the dull folks. And you'd have to be a bit dull to hand around here, wouldn't you? I mean the Fancy Dress is right there. It's like living in Paris and never visiting the Eiffel Tower."

"I imagine the Eiffel Tower becomes background pretty quickly to the Parisians," said Iris. "We should go to the church like the shopkeeper mentioned."

"Ah, yes. A church. We'd fit in well there. Nothing says churchgoing like a vibrantly dressed woman who looks like she's ready to party."

"And you look like you're ready to be sent back to the zoo."

"Oh, touché, fair maiden."

A wind with a heavy bite rolled down the street, brushing up against Iris, slithering through her blond hair. There was more than a hint of a chill to it. "Something's off. It's small, but it's there."

"You're just sad you missed the elephant play. I know I am. They're one of my favourite animals. I mean, bears come first, obviously, but elephants are up there."

Iris stuck her hands in her pockets, wondering if his chatter was him trying to cover up that he noticed the edge in the air, too. "I feel like everyone here knows something we don't. Maybe it's even subconscious on their part. But we're out of the loop, Panda."

Panda stopped walking and put his paws on his hips. "Well, it's turning you into quite the bore. You've been melancholy since we arrived. Where's your sense of flair? You're going to be as bad as that opera soon."

"You need to let that opera go. You can pick our next cultural activity, I promise."

"Damn right," said Panda. "Now let's get this church visit over with."

The monument outside the church read *"In memory of Michael Drake who kept the war from Samhain"*. It had to be old, but someone had been keeping it in mint condition. It'd been freshly polished and the grass around it recently cut. Iris tried to recall if anyone in town had mentioned Drake to her, but she couldn't remember the name cropping up in conversation.

"He was probably a church donor," said Panda. "They always get the prime real estate. I should start donating somewhere so I can get a big statue when I go. How about you?"

"I'm not one to go anytime soon."

"Ah, yes. Our timeless Iris."

She touched the monument. It was cold. "Never understood graveyards."

"They're items only those cursed with mortality need worry about," said Panda. "I'll be popping off one day. I hope you'll be suitably sad."

"I'll make sure you get that statue and then some."

Iris and Panda headed inside the church. It was empty, but someone had been here recently. The floors were spotless and leaflets peppered the pews. Iris picked one up and perused it. There was a bunch of nonsense about believing in one's self and grappling with a changing world. She dropped it back down and wondered if stopping in here was the wrong call. Surely, if the town had changed, it'd be most noticeable here, in the centre of town?

Maybe she was growing paranoid. Or maybe she wanted the town to be more exciting than it really was. All that traveling could've ruined her for quieter places, much as she liked to think she was above such base influences. What type of cultured person couldn't enjoy some downtime?

The closing of a door brought her attention towards the front of the church. A man dressed in black pants and a grey button down shirt walked towards them, a smile on his face. He had blond hair, blues eyes and the face of someone fresh out of high
school, all warm and excited, as if the world had rolled out the red carpet for him. He'd come from a door towards the right, one that presumably led to an office.

"I hate him already," whispered Panda. "Do you think I should tell him? I think I should tell him."

Iris put her hand on her companion's shoulder. "Try and behave for now."

The newcomer stopped a few pews in front of them. He crossed his arms and his smile became wider. "Hello there. Is it your first time in this place? I know timelines can get rather wonky around here."

"We've been through Samhain more than a few times," said Iris. "Just taking a quick stroll around. Thought there might be something of note."

"Did you see the pictures on your way in?"

Iris turned around and noticed a line of photos on the wall near the entrance. "I hadn't."

"Go take a look," he said. "Town history."

Iris walked to the pictures. Each one was labelled with a year: 1700, 1854, 1932, 1999. One picture looked like something out of Mardi Gras, with people and creatures in masks and face paint. She thought she recognized a couple of them, perhaps one was even the shopkeeper, but it was tough to tell. Masks could grant an uncomfortable amount of anonymity.

"It's amazing to think how much has gone on here," said the man. "In day to day existence things can seem so dull, but when you take a step back there's a story that snaps into place."

"You've certainly chosen a hopping time to check in on this place," said Panda.

Iris turned back to the man. His smile had not wavered in the face of Panda's sarcasm. She wished it had. No one should trust a person that smiled for so long. "What's your name?" she asked.

He laughed. "I think it'd be polite if you introduced yourself and then asked me, no?"

He had a point, much as she hated to admit it. "I'm Iris. He's Panda."

Panda threw up his arms. "Hey! I wanted to remain nameless. The mysterious is always more attractive."

"I agree with your little friend," said the man. "But I'll ruin the moment. I'm George. Isn't that a letdown? I'm sure you wanted a better name. Something more revelatory. But the most interesting people are not always blessed with the most striking of names. Just think of this planet's history. George Washington? Bleh. King Louis? Not much. Even Alexander had to add the Great to the end of his name in order for him to catch on."

George moved as he spoke, walking in a semi-circle around them, never coming too close, reminding Iris of an animal scouting new territory.

"So are you here for the show?" asked George.

"What show is that?" asked Iris.

"Don't tell me you haven't noticed." His lips puckered, as if he'd tasted sour food. "Can't you tell? You must've or else why would you have come here."

Iris shrugged. "It's in the centre of town."

"And yet people rarely come in. What brought you in here, Iris?" He nodded towards Panda. "Doesn't seem like it was his idea."

"Damn straight," said Panda.

Iris sat down in one of the pews, putting her feet up on the one in front of her. She did her best to look relaxed. "I come to town from time to time and thought I'd get a read of the area. It's been a while, is all."

"I'm sure it has been," said George. He moved towards her, leaning up against the edge of the pew, his shadow falling across her. "You're an explorer, aren't you? Always on the move. I can tell that your friend is, too. He doesn't care for staying on one place for too long. And how about you?"

"I like to travel," said Iris. "It's the goal of any cultured person."

"And how long have you been traveling?"

"A long time."

"I thought as much. You've been alive for so long that you don't even realize you're living. How old are you?"

"What an unseemly question."

"Unseemly? Or uncomfortable?"

Iris stood. "I think it's time to get going."

"I just got interested," said Panda. "I don't know how old you are either. Now there's a mystery I would like solved."

George looked over to Panda and laughed gently. He turned back to Iris and stepped aside, putting out his arm. "You can leave. But at least tell me what brought you here."

There was no easy answer to his question. What could she say that didn't sound moronic? That she was driven by a gut instinct? That she sensed something was off? That there were more leaves on the ground than she'd expected? She'd sound mad. She settled on saying, "Melancholy."

George clapped his hands together once. "I love that word. It's the perfect definition of the human experience. We live in a state of mourning what has gone before because we know we won't experience it again and fearing that the future, whatever momentary pleasures it might hold, ends in our demise. It's a beautiful feeling. Like a surprising wine, really. Reminds you that you're living."

"You're very cute," said Iris. "I'm sure you could be a good preacher or something."

George came in very quickly. He grabbed her arm. His mouth went right to her left ear. "Don't you realize? The end is here for this town. All the people see it. The town itself sees it. Don't you? Isn't that what brought you here? Or have you forgotten what it is to contemplate an ending?"

Iris leaned in and brought her lips to his ear. "I'd highly recommend letting go of me. Like you've noticed, I've been around for a while. It hasn't gotten that way by being a pushover to young men who have no sense of boundaries."

Panda chuckled. George let go and stepped back, putting up his hands.

"I'm sure this town is fine," said Iris. "Samhain has been around a long while." She moved passed him, returning to the aisle.

"All the more reason you should suspect its death," said George. "Not everything is infinite, especially as it gets older. Except maybe you."

"You seem to be under the impression that you know a bit about me."

"You're Iris Wildthyme. You're eternal. Your reputation here precedes you. And your sense of fashion gave you away, I'm afraid."

"I've talked to her about that," said Panda. "To no avail."

Iris lifted an eyebrow. "If you think this town is really at the precipice then why don't you do anything to stop it?"

"It can't be stopped," said George.

"And why is that?"

He placed his forefinger to his mouth. "Shh. You might be heard. There are ears in here. You have no idea what slithers beneath the floor."

"Paranoia and an obsession with death. Are you some sort of philosophy student?"

"A quick wit to hide how uncomfortable you are, no doubt. I've heard tales of where you've been. Yet, for some reason, you're so curious as to why this place feels just the littlest bit off. Why?"

"I'm not in the habit of psychoanalysing myself," said Iris.

"Curiosity," said George, obviously happy to answer his own question. "We are all drawn to what we don't understand even if we're afraid. It's the nature of existence. Why do animals wander into towns even though they know that humans will harm them? Why do people reach for the stars even though they know that space is a vacuum that will kill them within milliseconds? Why does Iris Wildthyme come to investigate a town that's at the end of its existence? Does she realize how important endings can be? Perhaps you could analyse all of that. Perhaps then you'll understand."

"Perhaps," said Iris. "But I think my interest has run out for now."

George waved towards the back of the church. "Are you sure you don't want to explore here some more? Maybe get a real feel for what's happening?"

Iris looked behind him, towards the altar, towards the door he'd come out of. "No."

"Are you certain?" George stepped back a few paces. "I've looked into the eye of this church, of this town, and I understand what's to come." He walked back further, passing the altar, and opened the door. The room was dark and Iris couldn't see inside from so far away.

"C'mon," said George. "Take a peek. What do you have to be afraid of, right?"

"No, thanks." Iris turned to Panda. "Time for us to go." She started down the aisle, not looking back at George. Still, though, she heard him chuckle.

"So do you regret stopping in the church?" Panda asked.

On their way back to the costume shop, they'd gotten a little turned around. The roads were more mazelike than Iris remembered. "No regrets," said Iris. "Don't have the time for them."

Panda laughed.

"What?" said Iris. A raindrop hit her face.

"Oh, no," said Panda. "Let's get out of the rain. My hair will get all matted."

"I'm ready to leave," said Iris. "We're going back to the costume shop even if we have to walk through a monsoon." She tapped his head. "And what was the laugh about?"

The rain started to pick up. A wind arrived with it, sharper than earlier. A few bits of dust floated with the wind and Iris wiped them away from her face.

"Well, I don't mean to offend," said Panda. "It's just that, in terms of regrets and not having the time, uh, y'know, you sorta do have the time."

"You say it like it's a bad thing," said Iris. She didn't want to talk circles around this topic again, not after spending time with George.

"No, I didn't," said Panda. "Just an observation."

"Well, no regrets, sorry, but I can't say I'm eager to run into that idiot again. I think he thought a dragon was in the back of the church or something."

"Did you see anything through the door?" asked Panda.

"No. Did you?"

"No. No, I don't think so. A shadow perhaps. Maybe a movement. Could've just been a trick of the light."

Iris and Panda were soaked when they arrived at the costume shop. Iris was cold and Panda was complaining, saying his fur would smell musky for a while. She paid him little mind. Perhaps, for once, she'd actually buy a costume in the shop. Couldn't stay in these wet clothes, could she?

"Welcome back," said the shopkeeper. He spread his arms and came around the counter. "How was your stay in Samhain?"

"Wet," said Panda.

"I'm going to need something to wear," said Iris. "I don't know that I have any money on me. You might have to take credit."

"Oh, don't worry," said the shopkeeper. "It's on me. I have something that might fit you nicely." He turned and went into the back.

"I wonder if he has a blow dryer," said Panda.

Iris looked around the shop, noticing several more of the white masks that she'd spotted earlier. They hung around costumes that didn't match with them, almost as if they were advancing through the shop. And the costumes – something was different. They were darker. Blue, purple, black. "What is this?" she muttered. "Are funeral director costumes in style?"

The shopkeeper came out of the back and held up a black, lacy dress.

"Apparently they are," said Panda.

The duo walked into a room without a roof. The sun shone down on them. The floor was covered with a thin layer of sand. Iris glanced behind her to see a mirror, the mirror that would return them to the costume shop when they finished here. It'd probably be a while. She needed a break from Samhain and whatever was going on in it. When she returned, who knew what year it'd be? Maybe the town would be back to normal. Maybe not. An annoying uncertainty.

"I have sand in my fur already," said Panda. He walked towards the opposite end of the room where a staircase led to the surface. He ascended and Iris followed him, hoping there'd be items of interest above.

She first noticed the statue. It stood at least thirty stories high. She didn't recognize the species; perhaps it was one that never managed to reach the stars. Whatever the species, it was far from a humanoid, more birdlike. The statue had three wings, two on the side, and one in the front. A beak hung down, sharp at the end. Two webbed feet were almost entirely obscured by the shadow from the statue's body. Most striking were its eyes, shining emerald in comparison to the dull brown colour of the rest of the statue.

Other than the statue, the peaks of pyramids dotted the desert landscape, the main structure of them buried under the sand. Near a pyramid about a quarter of a kilometre away was a four wheel vehicle, definitely a product of humanity.

"Care to investigate?" asked Panda.

"How can we not?" said Iris.

The heat was a little much; Iris' black dress didn't help matters, although she managed to avoid sweating too much during her walk towards the vehicle.

A man knelt down near the truck, brushing at the ground in slow, gentle strokes. He looked up and waved. Iris recognized him.

It was George.

"Well look at this," said Panda.

"Oh, great," muttered Iris.

George walked over and Iris noticed his hair was a little longer than it'd been in the church. He looked even more baby-faced than before. Was it possible this was a younger George? What were the odds? Unless the shopkeeper, or the shop itself, sent them here on purpose. Could coincidence really be this cruel?

"You my new assistants?" asked George. He held his hand above his brow to block out the sun.

"You acting like you don't recognize us?" said Panda.

Iris put her hand on Panda's shoulder. "I don't think he does."

George pointed to Panda. "I think I'd remember this cute little fellow." He rose and stuck out his hand. "I'm George."

Iris shook his hand, keeping her grip weak. "Iris Wildthyme. This is Panda. We're not your new assistants. Sorry. Just having a peak around."

George nodded, turning towards the statue. "Marvellous, isn't it? I wonder what it was like in its heyday, eh? Probably brimming with spirit. And life. I'm sad I missed it. I guess it's my job, though. I'm an archaeologist. I always end up arriving at the end of things."

"Someone once told me endings are important," said Iris.

"I think that someone might be onto something. You sticking

around?"

"We'll be on our way," said Iris. She walked away, Panda a few feet behind her, silent. She turned back to George and raised her voice to make sure he could hear her. "There's a room in the sand about a quarter mile south of you. You might want to check it out. There's a mirror down there. Could be something interesting behind it."

"A mirror?" George replied. "Sounds unusual and the unusual always calls to me. Thanks for the advice, my new friends. Have a good one."

Iris resumed walking, deciding to head to the statue. Perhaps there'd be an adventure there. One seemed to always hone in on her.

"You okay?" Panda asked, catching up to her.

"Was that concern?"

"It happens from time to time. We all have moments of weakness. But you sure you're okay?"

Iris shrugged. "Sure. It's just …" She halted. "I don't know. The adventures never end and probably never will. I'll always be out there. I just never considered I might be missing out."

"Missing out on what?"

Iris looked around at the pyramid peeks, the remnants of an old civilization. The statue's shadow caught her eye, too, covering as much ground as it did, like a blanket slowly moving over the remains. "An ending. I've always considered myself knowledgeable, but maybe I'm missing out on the biggest part of existence there is."

Panda brushed his hand against hers. "Why don't we go and check out the statue?"

Iris nodded. "Sounds good. C'mon then."

A GROVE INVISIBLE
JULIET KEMP

"There you go."

Iris made a grandiose gesture as the bus shuddered to a stop. Panda ducked just in time for the largely-empty bottle she was clutching to pass over his head.

"There you go what?" said Panda.

"Time compression," Iris said.

In front of them, a bare, empty plain of blue-green dirt stretched away to a distant mountain range. They were parked right at the foot of a cliff, with the rear bumper of the bus nearly touching one of several large boulders, and to each side more blue-based mountains rose to purple tops. As Panda squinted his button eyes, he thought he saw something in the emptiness ahead. Was there perhaps a pale shimmer in the air?

"All I can see is heat haze," he said.

Iris tutted irritably. She tipped her head back to drain the bottle, and fumbled around under the dashboard. Panda shuffled backwards a little. There was a click, something under the seat began to hum, and the bus' headlights came on. Since it was daylight, they didn't do much, until Iris hit another switch, and the plain was no longer empty. The headlights showed row upon row of faint, slightly shimmering globes that looked like nothing so much as soap bubbles, each about the size of a small house.

"Time compression bubbles," Iris said, sitting back in satisfaction.

Panda had the sinking feeling that he was going to lose this bet after all. And that rotten woman had finished off the last of the booze.

"Bubbles, yes, fine, they're bubbles," he said. "Time compression I'm not seeing, and I still don't believe it."

"Fine," Iris huffed, sliding off the seat. "I'll prove it."

On her way to the door, she stopped to forage in one of the precariously stacked cupboards wedged under the stairs of the bus, and triumphantly pulled out a magnum of champagne. Panda's eyes brightened, but Iris shook her head at him and whisked it out of reach.

"For celebrating when I've won my bet, Panda my old chum. Now then …" She waved her hand around behind the driver's seat until she found the inexplicable cold patch that lived there, and wedged the bottle into it.

"There. That'll be just right when we get back. Now. Proof, you wanted." With a sigh, Panda followed her out of the bus.

They stopped just in front of the first row of the bubbles.

"Cerid," Iris announced, waving her arm again. "Suddenly came up with this lot, right here, no explanation provided to the galaxy at large. As far as I can tell, mostly because they didn't know where the hell the damn things came from either. Time compression bubbles. Time runs faster inside them, you see? Made the Cerideans' fortune for a while. Nice fertile soil, and they could grow at, ooh, a few thousand times the rate of anyone else. Biggest export economy in the sector."

"What happened?" Panda asked.

Iris shrugged. "Dunno. All went a bit wrong. No more export. No more population, come to that. Visitation interdict."

Panda frowned. "Visitation interdict? Should we even be here?"

Iris avoided his eyes.

"Well, that sort of thing doesn't apply to us, now, does it? Still, probably best to get a move on."

She dug into her handbag, and produced an acorn.

"Stand back," she said, and tossed the acorn, underarm, into the nearest bubble. There was a 'pock' sound as it passed through the film, still illuminated by the bus' headlights.

The acorn settled into the loose soil, and for a moment, nothing happened. Then Panda saw a tiny green shoot emerge from the ground. After that, it happened almost too fast to see.

Within seconds, the green shoot was a young tree, branches popping out of the trunk one after another as the trunk grew upwards towards the top of the bubble. For a moment it looked as if it might pop through, but then the brand new oak began to slow, growing outwards instead. After that first 'pock' the whole thing had happened in an eerie silence, any noise swallowed by the bubble.

Panda turned to stare at Iris.

"See," she said, smugly. "Just like I said. Time compression bubbles. Oaks live a good long while, so we could hang around to see it all the way through the lifecycle, but watching things die isn't my cup of tea, really. I win the bet, you pay up, and while I remember what it was we actually bet, let's get back to the bus and have that fizz."

Panda sighed. But just as he turned back towards the bus, Iris's eyes widened, and she started running.

"Oh strewth, the parking brake," she shrieked.

Then the bus rumbled past Iris' outstretched hands, and smack into the bubble two along from the oak tree. The 'POCK' was nearly a bang.

"MY BUS!"

Panda and Iris both stared, wide-eyed, at the bus, all but the last couple of feet of it stuck in the bubble. Despite the headlights no longer illuminating them, Panda's eyes had adjusted and he could see the edges of the bubble now without help, just on the edge of vision.

The bus sank to the ground almost immediately as the tyres deflated, lurching a little further into the bubble. Where the bottom of the bus was now touching the soil, corrosion began to creep upwards. The paint peeled off all over the bus in a blizzard of red flakes, settling to the ground then disappearing into it. First one, then the other wing-mirror fell off.

The metal around the wheel-arches was crumbling now, and rust raced up the sides of the bus, spreading in tendrils which then grew tendrils of their own. One side lurched as if caught in a high wind, then collapsed inwards, windows falling and shattering as it did. Metal corroded and folded in on itself in silence, and the rear of the bus collapsed into the bubble, the rust spreading to it almost immediately.

Something came flying out of the centre of the destruction just as the roof and the other side finally fell. Panda ducked. Iris stuck out a hand and caught it, without taking her horrified gaze off what was happening to the bus. It seemed like a very long time before all that was left was a pile of corroded metal and shattered glass. Even that seemed still, slowly, to be shrinking.

Iris was entirely, eerily silent as she walked slowly up to the bubble. There was just enough room for her to walk all the way around it. When she got back to where the back of the bus had been, she stood for a moment, looking down at the sand. Cautiously, Panda joined her. On the sand lay a single window of the bus, its metal frame miraculously unwarped, its glass uncracked.

"One window," Iris said. There was a tremor in her voice. "One window."

She sniffed, and raised her hand to her face to dab under her eyes. Then, as if she'd only just remembered, she looked down at the other hand.

What she'd caught, flying from the debris, was a magnum of champagne. The bottle Iris had put to cool. It was a good one, too, if Panda didn't miss his guess, and he considered himself moderately well-informed on the matter.

"One window and a bottle of champagne," Iris said. "Well, if you had to choose …" Her voice shook a bit, then she doubled over and began laughing. Panda caught her eye and soon both of them were hysterical. Iris collapsed onto her arse on the sandy ground.

"One window – and the booze!" she said, and set them both off again.

Once it had finally passed, Iris sighed, set the bottle down in front of her, and leant back on her hands, sticking her feet out in front of her.

"Trouble is, Panda, me old mate – I have to say, I don't know what we can do now. To get off this rock, I mean."

"Wait to see if we can hitch a lift?" Panda suggested. Iris was, after all, pretty good at that sort of thing.

Iris shook her head. "Interdict, remember? No visitors here." She stared at the bottle. "Still, I suppose at least we can drink this while we're waiting."

Panda preferred not to think about what they were waiting for. Then, just on the edge of hearing, he could have sworn there was a rumble. He looked over at Iris, but she didn't seem to have noticed it. Maybe it was just his overactive imagination, but … No, it was louder now, and it sounded a lot like, really very much like indeed, a spacecraft engine.

"Iris!" he said. "Listen!"

Iris's head came up, and she cocked it to one side. Then her eyes widened.

"A ship? Here?"

They could both see it now, a tiny speck coming slowly across the sky, getting very slightly bigger.

"Rescue!" Panda crowed.

"More importantly," Iris said, "what are they doing here?"

"What do you mean, what are they doing here?" Panda demanded.

"It's a ship. We can leave!"

"Interdict!" Iris said, and climbed to her feet. "Look, just because I might come visiting doesn't mean it's fine for any Jane, Ned, or Sally to just drop in here. Come on. Let's go take a look."

"And hitch a lift," Panda reminded her, but she was already on her way, skirting around the grove of bubbles towards where the trajectory of the ship suggested it would come down.

Behind them, the oak tree went through another cycle of leaf-flower-acorn. One of the acorns fell, with a tiny 'pock', straight through the bubble, and, in a slightly implausible trajectory, into the one next door.

Iris moved fast when she was riled. Panda, puffing along behind her, promised himself once again that this time, once they were off this planet (he gulped), he really would commit to some kind of fitness programme. Nevertheless, by the time they reached the other side of the valley, the ship had already come down and was settled some way away, dust from the valley floor puffing around its base. Iris ducked behind one of the helpful outcrops of rock that lay along the side of the valley, and peered out at the ship.

"So, now we can go and tell them we're travellers in distress, yes?" Panda said, doing his best to remind Iris of the realities of their situation.

Iris, of course, ignored him. In the middle distance, most of the side of the ship was opening out, and creatures of some sort were emerging. All he could make out from this distance was big round bodies and radiating spindly limbs.

"The Polumet," Iris said, sounding satisfied. "Well, at least that simplifies things a bit."

"They're known as Good Samaritans?" Panda hazarded.

"But what are they after here, anyway?" Iris asked.

"Do we care?"

Iris flapped a hand at him and continued to watch.

From the ship, the Polumet were followed by some kind of machines. Very large machines. As Iris and Panda watched, the machines trundled over to the nearest of the bubbles to their landing-site, and began … digging?

Iris, whose eyesight was evidently sharper than Panda's, let out a screech.

"Digging 'em up? Well there is absolutely no way that I'm standing around and letting them do that, or my name's not Iris Wildthyme. Which, as we all know, it is." She nodded sharply. "Right then. You stay here, I'll go sort this out. Shouldn't take a moment."

She ducked out from behind the boulder and was off towards the ship. Panda sighed deeply and followed her again, this time at a slightly more prudent distance. Whatever Iris might think, he had a sneaking suspicion that this might be a little more complicated than she hoped.

To his surprise, Iris marched straight up to the ship. Panda himself chose to hang back a little. Quite a bit, in fact. 'Hiding' might have been another accurate word to describe his behaviour, although he himself preferred something more like 'assessing the situation from a safe distance'.

Iris had perched herself on top of another rocky outcrop, this one quite close to the ship itself. She arranged herself comfortably, and from her capacious bag, pulled out – some knitting. Panda was ever more baffled. She put her chin up at an angle, and started to knit. Badly, Panda suspected.

She had the air of someone expecting to be noticed – and sure enough, within a few moments one of the Polumet walked up to her rock. It had a large, round, green body, which undulated a little as it moved, and seven legs arranged at regular intervals which held the body just slightly off the floor. It was hard not to think of spiders. It asked Iris something Panda couldn't quite hear. He could hear her reply, though.

"I am Metiset!" Iris proclaimed, in her best stage tones. "I am your Goddess! And I command you to desist!"

The Polumet backed up a few steps, and said something else.

"Well, get me the boss, then, and jump to it!" Iris said.

The Polumet scurried off. A few moments elapsed. Then a much larger, more self-important looking (Panda reflected briefly on how easy it was to identify self-importance even in a green space-spider) Polumet came up to the rock.

"I am Metiset!" Iris proclaimed again, this time waving her knitting-needles for emphasis. "I am your Goddess! And I command you to desist!"

"To desist?" This one spoke nearly as loudly as Iris, possibly for the benefit of the audience that had gathered around them at a respectful distance.

"To desist!" Iris agreed.

"Why?"

"What do you mean, why? I am your Goddess, chuck, and you should damn well do what I tell you, right? Now, off you go, and don't come back."

Panda couldn't quite see that this was likely to work.

"Ha! Superstition! Metiset is a myth, a myth from our past designed to trick and destroy us!"

A cheer went up from the audience. Iris began to look worried.

"Myth my arse. Here I am, large as life and all that."

"If you are a Goddess," the captain, or whoever it was, said, "you will be able to prevent us from seizing you, then?"

It waved forwards a few of the audience to do the seizing. Iris put up a fair fight – knitting needles can do quite some damage, skilfully wielded – but the Polumet's many limbs were impressively multi-function, and it wasn't long before she was being dragged away. After a very anxious moment, Panda concluded that they were at least stashing her away safely rather than, say, executing her on the spot.

Once the fuss had died down, he went to find Iris in what was, basically, a large and quite deep hole.

"What on earth was that about?" he asked, poking his head over the edge of the hole. The Polumet had all gone back to digging up bubbles, complete with the earth underneath them. They had quite the row already lined up by the ship, ready, Panda assumed, for loading.

"Oh, Panda, there you are." Iris sighed. "I have to say, I didn't expect that."

"Why on earth not?"

"Well, I've met up with them before. A few times, now I come to think of it. I found out the first time that I looked like one of their goddesses, and it was very handy. Saved me a lot of trouble. Saved me a lot of trouble the other times, too. Though, now I come to think of it, the last time around they did look a bit more sceptical."

"Maybe you overplayed your hand a bit?" Panda suggested, wondering what on earth a species that looked like the Polumet were doing with a humanoid goddess.

"But it was so convenient!" Iris complained. "Anyway. Apparently their religious phase has passed now, for whatever reason that might not actually be anything to do with me, and there we are. Or here I am, anyway. Any chance you could help me out?"

Panda gestured, indicating, he felt, quite neatly, the discrepancy between his size and the size of the large hole in the ground that Iris was sitting at the bottom of. Iris sighed again.

"But I'll see what I can do," he found himself saying.

Iris beamed up at him, then pulled a half-bottle of gin out of her bag, raised it to him, and took a generous swig. "That's my Panda!"

Muttering about being his own Panda, if it was all the same to her, Panda stumped off in search of a solution.

The solution to Iris' problem seemed obvious as soon as Panda looked once again at the large, efficient, big-toothed diggers that were busily chomping bubbles out of the ground a few hundred metres away. He got a bit closer to the spaceship, concealed himself again, and waited for the inevitable. Sure enough, after a little while, the diggers all stopped and their operators got out and congregated around the bottom of the spaceship, passing around some form of eatables and drinkables. With wistful thoughts of ginger snaps, Panda hurried over to the nearest digger.

The Polumet were, he had already noticed, quite a lot larger than him, and even getting into the cab was a bit of a challenge. But with a great deal of jumping and wriggling he was eventually successful. Hotwiring it was easier – Panda might not have had a misspent youth, exactly, but travelling with Iris had given him a misspent adulthood – and the Polumet chose to keep all their controls up high, which meant no need to worry about human-style pedals. Panda did have to sit on top of the dashboard and reach down to get at them, meaning that he was essentially driving backwards, but regular checks over his shoulder were good enough for what he was after, especially since the Polumet seemed oddly inclined to stay out of the way of an erratically-moving several-ton piece of heavy plant equipment with no apparent driver. Panda tutted to himself as he veered and bumped towards Iris' prison. Anyone would think they didn't expect stuffed animals to act on their own.

"Hang on a minute," he yelled to Iris as he got closer. "I'm pretty sure one of these controls the mouth bit …"

"Um, maybe stand back," he added as the digging part of the digger slammed into the ground and rocks scattered everywhere.

A couple more of those, and Iris herself appeared from the ground, perched on the top of the digger's mouth like – well, judging from the reaction of the Polumet over by their spaceship, very much like some kind of avenging goddess. Knitting and all.

"Stop it for a sec!" she shrieked over the machine's noise, and Panda banged at levers and buttons and brought the thing to a mostly-graceful halt before Iris got herself slammed right back into the ground. She hopped off, came round, and climbed up to the driver's cab.

"Thanks ever so," she said, beaming at him. "Now then. While we're here …"

"That bit turns it round," Panda said. "And that bit makes it go. No! The other bit!" Another chunk of the ground soared over their heads in a shower of pebbles.

"This other bit?"

The digger bucked and spun around. Panda could hear what sounded a lot like screams of terror coming from the Polumet.

Panda wasn't entirely sure that Iris had any more experience in the matter of driving diggers than he did, but she did have the advantage of being able to see out and operate it simultaneously. They bucketed back towards the Polumet ship, and the ranks of bubbles arrayed beside it, at an alarming pace. The Polumet, prudently, and with a few more screams, scattered.

"See!" Iris yelled out of the digger at them. "This is what happens when you lose your religion!"

She slammed on the brakes in front of the first of the dug-up bubbles.

"Panda love, which bit did you say makes the mouth bit move?" Panda pointed. With surprising dexterity, Iris scooped up the first bubble – with, to be sure, a certain amount of the ground underneath it – turned the digger, and trundled over to one of the holes. The bubble went back into the hole at a jaunty angle, and Iris turned for the next one.

Panda worried for a moment that some more robust-minded Polumet would try to stand against them. He was pretty sure that if it came right down to it Iris wouldn't run them over, although he had to admit, she did look quite annoyed. The Polumet, however, evidently valued prudence, and had all retreated back into their spaceship. The fact that by now Iris was swigging gin and cackling as she drove might have affected their decision. Fermented liquids: yet another of those universal constants, although their effects did vary by species. Panda was prepared to bet, on the available evidence, that alcohol wasn't a gentle soporific for this lot.

With a bang, Iris dumped the last of the bubbles back in its place.

"Now clear off!" she shouted.

The Polumet spaceship was, in fact, already in the process of leaving, having loaded all the diggers back in a hurry and abandoned the last one to its Iris-ish fate.

"And don't come back!" she added, shaking a fist after their retreating tail fins.

"They will, though," Panda said, once the engine was off. "Won't they? If they wanted the damn things in the first place?"

Iris scowled. "Possibly. It's not a permanent solution, I'll give you that. Best I could come up with in the circumstances."

"Mm," Panda said. "It has, however, scared off our potential escape route from this wretched rock. In case you had forgotten that minor point."

Iris climbed out of the digger, and Panda scrambled down after her.

"Come on," she said, with a sigh. "Let's go back to the bus."

"There is no bus," Panda said.

Iris ignored him, and started walking towards the distant blur that was the bubble containing the oak tree.

As they got closer, the blur began to look curiously large. Slowly, it separated out into what was undeniably not one, but multiple oak trees, in multiple barely-visible rippling bubbles. Closer still, and more saplings were beginning to sprout in yet more bubbles.

Not only that, but the first, the oldest, tree, the one that Iris had planted, now had no bubble at all, whatever angle you looked at it from. Iris and Panda stood in front of the small grove, and gawped.

"They don't," Panda said after a while, "look quite like oak trees any more."

The trees had taken on a bluish cast, and seemed somehow denser than his vague mental image of an oak tree.

There was a creaking, a muffled crack that reverberated under their feet, and one of the bubbles in front of them suddenly winked out of existence. The tree that had been inside it seemed almost to stretch itself out and shake its confinement off. Panda could have sworn he heard a satisfied, vegetal, sigh. A couple of trees further along, more acorns pattered down through hitherto empty bubbles, and bluish-green shoots began to poke up through the soil.

"The roots must be breaking up the mechanism," Iris said, staring down at the ground. "… Which is exactly what I hoped would happen!" she added, brightly, enthusiastically, and clearly untruthfully. "They'll deal with this whole dubious time bubble problem for us, no bother, given just a little while! Those Polumet will come back to a nice forested valley, and serve them right." She nodded. "Yes, no more interdict. Iris saves the day again."

Panda rolled his eyes and didn't bother to argue. But …

"They'll also come back to a pile of your bones, no? Since, as I keep reminding you, we are stuck here."

"Actually, I had a thought about that as well," Iris said. "We've still got that window, right?" She gestured at the bus's sole remaining window, wedged into the ground at an awkward angle. Panda had been trying not to look at it. It made him a little sad, and he didn't like feeling sad.

"What about it?"

"I reckon," Iris said, "that there might be just about enough power in it to take us somewhere."

"Where?"

"Well, that I don't know," she admitted. "But not here, so that's got to be an improvement, right?"

And if that wasn't a way to tempt fate, Panda didn't know what was. On the other hand, he really didn't fancy staying here indefinitely and watching trees grow. Even very fast-growing trees.

"So, what, we're going to crawl through it?"

"Ye-es," Iris said, then rallied. "Yes. Exactly that. And find out where we turn up, right?" She walked over to the window, looked at it for a moment, then picked up the bottle of champagne.

"But first of all, let's just have a little toast. For good luck."

"Well," Panda said. "That was on the bus too, right? If there's bus-power floating around, it might be," he waved a paw, "somehow in the fizz?"

"An excellent point," Iris agreed. "Bottoms up."

A few minutes later, she said, "Mind. We shouldn't have too much. If we don't go through at exactly the same time, we might get split up. We've got to get it right, right? Right."

"Right," Panda agreed. "Exactly the same time. Maybe just another couple, eh?" Underground, another deep crack indicated the demise of another bubble; above them, a blue-green not-quite-oak extended a branch a little further, and dropped an acorn, unseen, into Iris' handbag.

"Just … one … more … For good luck, right? Right. Mm. You know, Panda, this is nearly empty."

"Nearly time, then, Iris. Both of us together, right?"

"Ready … steady …"

Crack.

MICHAEL DRAKE
DALE SMITH, WITH IAN POTTER

The history of England is the history of the Church. Before the churches, the country was an ignorant, savage and godless place. Afterwards, it was much the same, but with churches. There were two ways it was decided whether a place needed a church: either it was so holy and virtuous that the inhabitants would need somewhere to congregate and praise the name of their Lord; or else it was the opposite, and God's servants would need somewhere to fortify themselves whilst they did their best to stop the corruption spreading. So the simple fact that Samhain has two churches can be considered most significant, one way or another.

By New Year's Eve 1799, the elder church was little more than a shell. It still loomed over the village, its graveyard filled with the weird dead of Samhain, but only its caretaker ever visited, and even then only begrudgingly. The villagers now mostly visited the new eight-sided chapel over the other side of the hill, still begrudgingly but without the pervading sense of dread they couldn't quite get accustomed to in the old church.

Not that the chapel had many visitors that night: everything in Samhain was celebrating the dawning of the new millennium by drinking wine in old Ned Pepper's westernmost field, having been assured that tomorrow marked the start of the Apocalypse. Even those inhabitants who had themselves moved to Samhain from times subsequent were standing in the snow waiting for the last trumpet to sound, on the understanding that you had to go where the party was at.

But the chapel wasn't empty, either. In the flickering light of an everlasting match, two figures huddled. It almost looked as though they were praying, except that they had missed the pews
and the alter by a good few feet and were instead kneeling at the farthest wall. The high *chink chink* of mallet striking chisel filled the air, but there was no-one else there to hear it. They could be sure of that, because Panda kept nervously starting and looking about him every other moment.

"You know, chuck," said Iris, her voice having a brazen disregard for the clandestine nature of their endeavour, "sometimes they found the bodies of cats plastered into the walls of old houses. They thought people in the seventeenth century put them there for luck."

That bought Panda's attention back in an instant.

"*Luck?*" he barked in disbelief. "Have they never heard of the Caterwaul?"

With one last thwack of the mallet a section of the wall fell away to the floor. The plaster turned to dust in an instant, and filled the air. Iris gave a less than demure cough, and waved the worst of it away. As the air cleared, both Iris and Panda stared into the hole that had been revealed.

They looked at each other.

"Did I ever tell you about the seventh Mrs Michael Drake?" Iris asked.

The first Mrs Drake was a Welsh woman. When her husband announced that he was going to go to England to fight for the King, her pragmatic response was to swipe him over the head with a ladle. It wasn't that she had any strong views either way about whether King or Parliament should decide the fate of the kingdom, you understand: it was more the thought of how much more difficult it would be to get a day's work done once her husband had been shot dead by a Roundhead. But when – after a few more blows and a considerable amount of sarcasm – Michael Drake remained adamant that his duty lay with the King, pragmatism once again came to the fore. She packed up everything she had that could be carried, and went with him.

She had, of course, more sense than to join the fight. But when her husband signed his life away to the Royalist Army, she was there to watch him sign. When he went through what scant training they decided to give him, she set up camp with some of the other wives and hangers-on and watched him scantly trained. When, in 1643, he was assigned to his first regiment and marched across the country to the bridge at Hebden, she said goodbye to the friends she'd made and marched a pragmatic number of yards behind him. The regiment met with Roundhead forces as they swept into the valley, and Mrs Drake pragmatically settled herself down on the lip of the valley to watch.

There was a lot of smoke, and loud shouting. She couldn't even make out individual figures in the confusion, and if she'd been particularly invested in any one side coming out victorious, would have been frustrated in any effort to find out the result. Then she saw a single figure come running out of the smoke, running frantically up the hill towards her. With a sigh, she lifted herself off of her stool and started packing up her belongings again. By the time the figure reached her, she was ready to move.

"Why didn't you tell me this was a bloody stupid idea?" her husband demanded.

Just for old time's sake, she hit him over the head with the ladle, pragmatically.

Then they set off over the hill.

By the time they reached the crest of the hill, the battle below seemed to have stopped raging. The valley floor was still obscured by a thick mist, but the sounds of musketshot and swearing no longer ghosted up to their ears. Mrs Drake wondered idly whether her husband's colleagues had been successful. Then she did a few calculations in her head, and started unpacking her things again.

"What are you doing?" her husband asked. "We need to be moving. They –"

"It'll be night soon," she answered in a patient voice that would take no arguing. "We'll camp here tonight. In the morning, we can see."

"But …" he started to argue, and then saw that she was setting up her second-best cooking pot.

"I'll need more wood for the fire," she told him, without looking up.

So Michael Drake went to collect wood.

On the long march to Hebden, the first Mrs Drake had been keeping her eyes open. Her parents – playing the long game – had given her the middle name Pragmatiaeth, unlike those Puritan families who called their daughters Chastity and Patience to make them unpopular at school. So wherever she'd seen something useful growing, she'd gathered up as much as she could as she passed. Three days back, she'd had the time to set a snare. Now there was a decent sized buck trussed up in her pocket, kept alive on dandelion, bay and hope. Once her second-best pot was hung securely, she snapped the rabbit's neck and started making a rudimentary stock from its bones. By the time she looked up to see her husband awkwardly approaching, she had everything ready for a quite serviceable rabbit stew. If only she had a little rosemary, but beggars …

"How many others are with you?" the lead horseman yelled.

Mrs Drake didn't respond. The roundheads were still some distance away, coming up the crest of the hill from the other side. There were six of them altogether, on horseback, but Mrs Drake supposed there might be any number more combing the area for survivors. The leader had his gaze fixed firmly on her. It was the horseman behind him who was dragging her husband, his wrists bound together with rope and then tied uncomfortably high on the saddle. His every step was a hop and a skip and a jump. He looked at her apologetically, whenever he wasn't being swung bodily into the horse's rump.

The leader drew a pistol and pointed it at her.

"Tell me true, old woman, and I'll give you a quick death."

The first Mrs Drake sighed.

"Listen, twll tin. You bring me some wood, there's some perfectly good rabbit stew here for us all. What d'you reckon?"

The leader stared at her for a good thirty seconds, but she didn't flinch. Then he put his pistol away and dismounted. The other five men all followed suit.

"There any dumplings?"

Over dinner, it had become clear that the roundheads weren't actually scouting the area looking for survivors. In truth, they hadn't even been involved in the battle in the valley below: they had become separated from their regiment just hours before the battle had begun, and had spent the following hours trying very hard to keep things that way. Their nominal leader – whose name, it turned out, was Kaye – was hopeful that with the due amount of care and attention, they could remain lost until the whole war was over, and possibly for some time after that as well. Fortunately, in their lost and hopeless wanderings, they had managed to ambush the regimental supply wagon and liberate three barrels of the local ale, before losing their bearings again.

For obvious reasons, when the next morning came, nobody was really in the mood for getting back in the saddle, and so they stayed put whilst Mrs Drake fixed them a breakfast of fried mushrooms. Lunchtime snuck up on them particularly unexpectedly, but by then Mrs Drake's makeshift larder was starting to look a little bare. She organised the men into teams and sent them out to scavenge what they could from the surrounding area.

As the teams started to return, bearing nuts, vegetables, and – in one case – a surprised dairy cow, it became clear that some of them had increased in number. People started appearing from nowhere, all wondering exactly what the strange group of diners were up to. History relates that it was Michael Drake who was the first to come up with an answer.

"We're claiming this land in the name of the people!" he yelled, standing tall on the back of the cow and sloshing a pint of milk excitedly around. "We don't need Kings or Parliaments or wars. We just want to live, and eat, and love as best we can. Any that want the same are welcome here. Together, we will build the finest town in all of England. Together, we will succeed. Together –"

At that point, he fell from the back of the cow, and a single half-drunk voice cheered sarcastically. But even so, it was that speech that got Michael Drake elected the first Lord Mayor of Samhain.

The second, and fifth, Mrs Michael Drake arrived in Samhain a few weeks afterwards, although none of the inhabitants could rightly swear to where she had come from. When she arrived, she already had the honour of being the fifth Mrs Michael Drake: time travel could play havoc with causality, but she always put a brave face on it. Since the first Mrs Drake was still alive, and the wedding wouldn't happen for another few years, she decided it best not to lay claim to the marital bed. Especially since at that point, the marital bed was a stained woollen blanket in a tent just off what would eventually become Festive Road.

So instead, she led her companion into the first building to be completed in the new village of Samhain: the local pub. She strode wearily up to the bar and ordered two gin and tonics. Then spent a good ten minutes explaining the process of making tonic water, before giving up and grabbing a bottle and two cups from the confused barkeep. She took them over to a table in a dark corner, where her companion was waiting for her.

"Drink up, Panda. Ah don't think we can do this sober."

Her companion gave her a bemused look, but she just returned it with aplomb. He pointedly rubbed his eyes with his fingers, and took the fez from his head so that he could run a hand through the wiry blond hair underneath. If he'd have thought it would make any real difference, he would have stood up to emphasise the fact that he was not actually a ten-inch tall cuddly toy. But instead, he just sighed and said:

"I don't drink, Iris."

She held up a warning finger and adopted a stern air. He knew what was coming, but there was no preempting it. He just had to brazen it out as best he could.

"No, pet. Ah don't have the right to that name no more," she attempted a haunted look and gazed off into the middle distance. It only made her appear half cut. "It's the war. Ah've done things, pet. Things ah cannae bear to live with, ye nar?"

It was true. He'd known her before the war and this latest incarnation, and she had done things. Nothing that he particularly thought any of the other Irises he'd met over the years wouldn't have done either, and certainly nothing so haunting that she wasn't happy to recount it with a gin and a wink whenever she got the chance. Whatever it had to do with the war he couldn't figure, but she had declared herself too tainted for her name at around the same time that the atemporal bailiffs had turned up at the bus after a Ms I Wildthyme. A petite young woman with the most amazing hair he had seen on anyone, this Iris affected a Geordie accent so strong that it was beyond pastiche and definitely beyond accuracy. He had taken to thinking of her as Wor Iris.

"Buy us a drink and ah'll tell yez all aboot it."

"You have a drink," her companion reminded her.

She squinted at him, then at the bottle.

"Alreet then," she said, downing her glass. "Drink up and let's get oot of here."

He sighed again, and gently pushed the bottle away.

"I don't drink," he said as firmly as he could. "And I'm leaving."

She blinked at him, and then loudly called him something scatological.

Eventually, the second – and fifth – Mrs Drake had been convinced by her companion that no, he didn't want a drink and yes, he was leaving. He would have been perfectly happy to leave matters at that, find out exactly where he was and put as much distance between himself and it as he could, but the second – and fifth – Mrs Drake was having none of it. If he was going, then it was probably at the end of a long and beautiful friendship: she could remember when she'd first met him all those years ago, and even then she'd known he would become a soul mate. She couldn't let him go without something to remember her by,

"You still think I'm Panda, don't you?" he said dryly.

She gazed at him a little surprised, but made no further comment. In fact, she'd remained oddly quiet as they'd gone back to the bus for him to collect his things, and had then disappeared for so long that he'd started to think she'd changed her mind about the memento and was just going to hide until he went. But then she'd reappeared with a heavy looking padded bag hung over one shoulder and a grim demeanour.

"Aye, well," she said. "Let's be 'avin you, pet."

She led him through the proto-village, where all around him were families from both sides of the Civil War involved in drunken, petty arguments about things completely unrelated to the running of the country. It was a wonder that they managed to get dressed in the morning without killing each other, and yet somehow they were pulling the beginnings of a home from nothing. No, from worse than nothing: from the chaos of the country around them. They'd decided that they wouldn't put up with lives lived at the whim of the seemingly mad, drunk and frankly bloody irritating and instead where going to walk away and take control of their own destinies. He had to admire them for that, if nothing else.

"This is it," the second – and fifth – Mrs Drake said.

Her companion looked around at the spot she had led him to. He could see nothing remarkable about it. It had a nice view of the valley below, but otherwise was just another bit of hillside. The idea that perhaps she meant to just push him down it and be done with it occurred to him. But if she did, it would still be worth it.

"This is what?" he ventured.

But she was already kneeling on the soft earth and flipping open the catches on her padded bag. She reached inside and pulled out a single pane of glass, gazing through it wistfully. It looked like it had been through the wars itself, having picked up a few hairline cracks and scratches and a fine covering of some kind of soot. When he looked at her face through it, she was distorted and distended. He also got the distinct impression that it was night behind her, even though the sun was blazing overhead.

"Yev bin ona amazin' joornee, pet," she said, looking at through it with eyes that drowned in sincerity. "Ah'm sorry. It's time fer that joornee to end."

He wasn't entirely sure whether she was speaking to him or the glass.

With a tear in her eye, she dropped the glass onto the soft earth and brought the heel of her palm firmly down into the centre of it. The glass shattered easily into six large pieces, each roughly the same size. She picked them up reverently, and then pushed them deep into the earth so that they formed a rough circle. Then she pushed them deeper, until they sank without a trace. With a sigh, she stood up, brushed her knees and shook out that amazing hair.

For a moment, neither of them said anything.

The moment stretched.

"Er, well," he said as jovially as he could. "I guess that's that, then?"

Suddenly, the ground shook around them. A blister of grass bubbled up, looking alarmingly ready to burst even as it kept growing. Soon there was the most enormous grass covered mound in front of them, the glass shards extending out of it like a crown. He looked to the second – and fifth – Mrs Drake, but she gave no reaction at all. For a moment, he wondered if she could even see the new-grown knoll. Then she reached into an inside pocket, and drew out a pin. It glistened in the sunlight. She gave a little smirk, and stuck the entire length of the pin into the grass.

There was an enormous *POP!*, and suddenly the knoll exploded.

In its place stood a large shop.

"Reet, pet," the second – and fifth – Mrs Drake said. "That's yer lot."

Her companion looked at the shop, and then prodded it with a cautious finger. The stonework felt like stonework. The glass in the one bay window looked like glass. It was cold to the touch, as if the shop had just come in from a snowy day and wanted to get warm. The sign said that it was a "Fancy Dress Costume Hire Shop", and its door was welcomingly ajar.

"What the hell am I supposed to do with *that?*" he shouted.

"What makes you think Ah give a hoot?"

And then the second – and fifth – Mrs Drake walked down the hill and away from the fledgling village of Samhain. Neither of them noticed Michael Drake, poking his head out of the battered old tent that currently served as the mayoral residence. He was looking at his new neighbour in open-mouthed wonder. But his new neighbour was busy looking at the shop, trying to work out whether it was safe to leave on its own.

It was a few weeks later that Mayor Drake was called upon to perform his first official function for the village. Samhain was starting to gain momentum, particularly once the villagers started hopping through the Shopkeeper's mirrors and bringing all kinds of exotic building materials – and, on some occasions, exotic builders – back with them. The mayoral residence mark two already had its foundations marked out, and a timber frame had been hauled up to mark the four corners. It was – at Michael Drake's insistence – a full storey taller than its immediate neighbour. The original residence was pitched inside the area earmarked as the second reception, and it was there that the delegation called, shaking the centre ridge in lieu of a door knocker.
"What?" snapped Michael Drake, his mouth still smeared with bits of breakfast.
The delegation lead him to the end of what would eventually be the main road down into Hebden. Drake went reluctantly, but with the air of a man who knows that the sooner the problem was identified, the sooner it could be delegated to somebody else to deal with. He spent a couple of moments kicking the ground in the hope that the problem was bad drainage, until the delegation directed his attention down into the valley.
Marching up the hill at a measured pace was a regiment of Roundheads.
"Bloody piss," decreed the Mayor of Samhain.
One of the delegation span Drake around to face the other direction. He blinked, and then saw a regiment of Cavaliers marching up from over there.
"Of course," Drake said. "Why ever not?"
The delegation gave him a supportive pat on the back.
"Let us know what you come up with," they said, and left him to it.

Michael Drake often thought of his failure of nerve during his first battle as a soldier of the King's Army. He knew that he had acted like a coward and fled, when the truly great man he always believed he could be would have stood firm and fought. He felt the bitter sting of regret, and knew that if he had his time all over again, he would do things differently. He would have deserted long before he got anywhere near the battlefield, and pawned his musket for a bottle of gin at the first town he came to.

It was with this in mind that he strode straight to the costume hire shop.

"So," he asked the Shopkeeper nonchalantly. "These mirrors ... I suppose that once you go through them, you eventually have to come back?"

The Shopkeeper gave an embarrassed shrug.

"Well I have to admit that I don't really know. I haven't figured out all the rules as yet. But old Catweazle went through last month and he still hasn't come back. None of my customers has described any particular pull back to the shop as yet. I can't see why it wouldn't be possible to remain on the other side indefinitely."

Drake nodded sagely.

"Fascinating," he mused.

Then he darted for the nearest mirror and dived through.

"Jings!" exclaimed the Shopkeeper in surprise.

There was a crash from one of the other changing rooms, and a loud burst of angry swearing. The Shopkeeper pulled the curtain aside just in time to see Drake diving straight back through the mirror. A second later, he popped out in one of the other changing rooms, still swearing and apparently not a moment older. Drake gave the Shopkeeper a despairing look, and then gave it one last go. When he appeared again back where he started, Drake slumped to the floor and started to cry.

"Well they've never done that before," the Shopkeeper assured him.

WE APOLOGISE FOR ANY INCONVENIENCE, an oddly mannered voice intoned, filling the air without need of any visible source. THIS AREA IS CURRENTLY TIME LOCKED. A REPLACEMENT BUS SERVICE HAS BEEN ARRANGED.

"A .. ?" the Shopkeeper echoed, before a thought occurred to him. "Oh no."

"Which one o' yez did that, ye bastards?" came a voice from outside.

The Shopkeeper hardly dared peer through the front window. But then how could he not? He had to confirm his worst nightmares were actual true. And so he looked, and – yes – there was the bus, its radiator grill poking jauntily through the scaffolding of the probably-going-fall-down-quite-soon future mayoral residence. Stumbling out of it was a young-looking woman with fantastic hair and a ludicrous accent.

She spotted him immediately and waved excitedly.

"Yoo-hoo! Panda! It's me! You-know-who!"

He did know who, God help him.

The first surprise was that Michael Drake seemed to be quite pleased to see her. For some reason – and the Shopkeeper couldn't really fathom why – the Mayor of Samhain seemed to think that Iris might be able to help them. The Shopkeeper had to concede that it wasn't absolutely impossible that she might, but experience had shown him that if she did it would most likely be by accident. The second surprise was therefore all the more surprising: the Shopkeeper realised that he was actually quite pleased to see her too. Perhaps he'd tied his bow-tie a little too vigorously that morning.

"Ah," the second – and fifth – Mrs Drake murmured to herself. "Ahl-reet then."

"What?" Drake asked rather too eagerly.

The three of them were standing at the crest of the hill, looking down at the two armies below them. Both forces seemed content at the moment just to make camp and glare menacingly at each other. It was as if they were waiting for some prearranged signal. Or perhaps for someone to come down and talk them out of it, like two drunks late on a Saturday night who didn't really have the balance for it.

"It's the war," she said gravely.

"Yes?" Drake replied, as if he'd managed to work out as much for himself.

She handed back a pair of opera glasses that were stamped "Royal Opera House. Do not remove". Drake took them and peered down into the enemy camps. Seeing nothing that struck him as out of the ordinary, he quickly passed the glasses back to the Shopkeeper. The Shopkeeper adjusted his own spectacles out of the way, and peered down into the Cavalier camp.

For a moment, he too saw nothing out of the ordinary. He was about to pass the glasses back when he noticed. A long-legged Cavalier came out of a tent with his hat pushed back to form a black halo around his head. His beard was black and neatly trimmed, his hair swept back. He greeted one of his comrades and reached out to take a skin of water that was offered. The other Cavalier had his hat pushed back to form a black halo around his head, and a neatly trimmed black beard. As did the third Cavalier who passed them both without even a nod.

"They all have the same face," the Shopkeeper remarked.

"Uniformity," she snorted, enjoying the way her accent bounced haphazardly off the vowels. "What d'yez expect from Chanticleers?"

"Well," the Shopkeeper said. He took a moment. "That explains the time lock."

"Prob'lees just the one," she continued, reaching back again for the opera glasses. "Warmeme, Ah reckon. Infected one o' them and then just got passed round like a dose of the clap."

"So the other army are –"

"Hornheads, aye," she confirmed.

The Shopkeeper looked again into the Roundhead camp. From this distance, they looked human, but that never really meant anything where the Hornheads were concerned.

Michael Drake held up a hand.

"I was just wondering: do you need me here?"

The second – and fifth – Mrs Drake looked him up and down.

"Oh aye," she told him.

"Only ... well, I haven't a bloody clue what you're talking about, and –"

She nodded as if Drake had asked her a small favour.

"Aye, ahl-reet," she said. "So there's this war, pet –"

"A warpet?"

"A war," she repeated firmly. "Pet."

She paused just in case there were any further interruptions. Drake said nothing.

"A War," she corrected herself, and then looked confused again. "Wait: the War. In Devon. Heaven. No, in time. Crime? Between the ... no, wait: I know this one."

She flapped her hands and blew a stray strand of perfect hair out of her eyes.

"Bugger it," she said sweetly. "You tell him, Panda."

"I'm not …" the Shopkeeper began automatically, then sighed. Fine. Whatever. "There's a war, between the know-it-alls and don't-care-at-alls. They've come here to fight it."

Drake blinked, and then swallowed hard.

"Should I be worried?" he asked hopefully.

The Shopkeeper considered.

"That depends very much," he answered eventually, "on your views on the afterlife."

"The important thing," she told them, "is the symbolism."

The gathered villagers had taken a moment to consider that, and after some consideration had declared quite loudly and with some throwing of objects that actually the important thing was the two armies down in the valley that were going to kill them. The Shopkeeper did his best to restore order, but to be honest order was a relative concept in Samhain. And there was always the chance that it might be quicker and easier to all kill each other and deny the armies the satisfaction.

"There's no time fer this!" the second – and fifth – Mrs Drake yelled over the sound of panicking Samhainians. "We've gotta cleanse the whole area, ritually like. Those things doon there won't just –"

"Iris!" the Shopkeeper yelled.

"How many times, pet? I'm …" she began, until she looked where he was pointing and her voice trailed off. "Knackers."

The Shopkeeper was looking down the lip of the hill that Samhain was being built on. Soldiers were starting to appear over it, marching up with that slow but assured pace that said they were in no hurry to start killing everybody, but they would get around to it eventually. The two armies marched side by side, and you would have been forgiven in thinking they were just two sides of the same force, not deadly enemies who could see no common ground.

The march stopped, and two soldiers stepped forward.

One Hornhead, one Chanticleer. Both holding standards.

"Cleanse the village," the second – and fifth – Mrs Drake yelled frantically. Most of the villagers weren't listening, being too busy running around in abject terror. "Claim it. Assert your right to –"

"This area has been designated a battleground." boomed the voice of the Chanticleer. He looked left and right at the panic all around him. "It will be cleared immediately."

"This is our home!" yelled one brave villager, throwing a stone that left a tiny dint in the Hornhead's helmet.

The soldiers didn't flinch.

"All time displaced inhabitants will be repatriated forthwith," barked the Chanticleer.

"Now just you –" hissed the second – and fifth – Mrs Drake.

And then, in a pop of yellow light, she disappeared. As did the Shopkeeper, and most of the villagers who had come to Samhain through his mirrors. The shock of seeing a third of the village vanish caused the rest to freeze, their panic-stricken cries dying on the wind. For a moment, there was utter peace and quiet throughout the Hain Valley.

"Now the extermination begins," said the Hornhead.

"Somebody has to go tell them to sling their hook."

The first Mrs Drake made no effort to hide herself. The Hornheads had made it quite clear that any such effort would be pointless. They were marching forwards, slow and relentless through the village. Anyone that drew level with them or passed within arm's length was dead at their feet within seconds. Those that tried to escape found themselves bouncing off an invisible wall that had sprung up around the village's furthest extent. The Chanticleers had not joined the slaughter: they stood where they had stopped, their heads turned diplomatically to one side, as if to make it clear that a blind eye was being turned. Everyone could see that within minutes the area would be "cleared".

"No, my love," Michael Drake said, cowering behind the scaffolding of his residence. "I won't let you. It's too dangerous."

"Can't be me. Has to be someone in authority."

She turned to look at her husband.

"I resign," he said, just a little too late.

"Now we need the egg."

The village of Samhain had grown quickly since that first pot of rabbit stew, bubbling merrily over an open fire. Some of the land on the top of the hill had been set aside for crops and livestock, with seed and cows generously donated by some of the neighbouring villages in the dead of night. The surrounding countryside was regularly harvested for the best that Mother Nature could provide: mushrooms and the tougher herbs could be found in abundance, and there were good signs that there would be brambles and crabapples when the spring properly bedded in. They were even building a baker's oven in anticipation of their first wheat harvest. But what nobody had been able to liberate so far was any chickens.

Michael Drake had suggested searching the bus, with the full intention of keeping searching it until the soldiers finished their battle. But the first Mrs Drake had not only agreed, but had also accompanied him. With her help, it was only a few moments later that they had found one down the back of a seat on the back row. It had a small square of luminous yellow parchment stuck to it, emblazoned with the legend DO <u>NOT</u> USE FOR OMELETTE. There was something odd about the surface of it: ice white, and cold to the touch. But it was an egg, and their options were limited.

"Maybe I should take my musket," Drake said as casually as he could manage. "You know. Just to really make myself look authoritative."

"Symbolism," the first Mrs Drake warned. "You go down there looking like a soldier, they'll treat you like one."

Drake had seen how the Hornheads were treating *civilians*.

He swallowed hard.

"No musket?" Drake echoed.

"No musket," his wife confirmed.

Michael Drake walked into the centre of the village on his own. He was dressed in a drab grey sweater, that his future wife could have told him was Fairisle but his current wife could only recognise as plain and unlike a uniform. The egg was in his left pocket, and with every step he took he didn't check that it was still intact. He could feel the slight bulge it made, and that would have to do.

All around him, his friends and neighbours were either running, screaming or else lying face down in the dirt, dead. The Hornheads paced relentlessly on behind them, reaching out with slab-like hands,

140

despite an array of strange and deadly looking weapons hanging at their sides. Apparently the villagers of Samhain weren't worth drawing arms for. They were more suited to having their necks snapped like chickens for the pot. So far, the Hornheads had ignored Drake – perhaps that was a sign that the sweater was working. The Chanticleers had seen him, though, and frowned their identical black eyebrows at him.

The idea that he could just pick up his pace with each step had occurred to him. By the time he reached the two armies, he could be running straight through and out the other side to start a new life somewhere else. But his wife had made it quite clear that he was now the symbolic representative of the entire village: if he fled, if he surrendered, then Samhain would surrender. And for some stupid reason, he had discovered he was quite attached to this stupid nearly village.

And so he kept walking, his steps slow and measured.

Suddenly, a Hornhead appeared in front of him. The soldier was nearly as wide as it was tall, and had skin that was almost as cold and as grey as a stone. The eyes burned red with hatred, however, and they fixed on Drake immediately.

The hand started to come up.

"Wait!" Drake said, his voice cracking.

For some reason, the Hornhead waited.

As one, the Chanticleers raised an eyebrow.

"This fight serves no one!" Michael Drake yelled, his voice squeaking as he turned his head up to avoid looking at the soldiers. "If you must battle over crowns, then do so over this!"

He reached into his pocket and drew out the egg. It felt like a shard of ice in his hand. As he held it aloft for the soldiers to see, the sunlight glinted off it and cast a strange reflection on the mud all around. Not one of them looked at the egg: all eyes were on him as they tried to work out exactly what he was planning to do next.

Drake swallowed hard.

He crushed the egg between both palms. He felt the shell shatter and send shards deep under his skin. His hands felt numb, so that he could no longer tell if he was holding the two halves of the egg or if they had vanished. Then he felt the white and yolk drip onto his face. As he went to wipe his face clean, he realised that his arms had locked above his head and were frozen solid. They would not budge, no matter how he urged them.

"There'll be no more blood than this shed," he said under his breath.

For a moment, there was silence.

Then the laughter started.

The Chanticleers smugly smiled to themselves and turned away, but the Hornheads guffawed like they had never seen anything so hilarious. Despite everything, Michael Drake found himself suddenly annoyed that they weren't taking him seriously enough. Then he felt the yolk slowly sliding down his face, and realised that they probably were. The thought occurred to him that either the young woman with the hair or his wife didn't have a clue what they were talking about. And he realised that any second now, the armies were going to stop laughing.

"Kill him," chuckled one of the Chanticleers softly.

"Wait!" screamed Drake.

But the Hornhead in front of him did not wait. It reached out with its slab-like hand, a smile still on its lips. Then its face exploded in a spray of purple blood, and it staggered backwards.

The first Mrs Drake appeared beside her husband, his musket in her hands and a look of intense disapproval on her face. Her eyes were fixed on the army in front of her, and didn't waver for a moment. Michael Drake could taste the yolk as it dripped into his mouth. It tasted of blood and ice-cream. Just what kind of an egg was this?

"Stay away from my husband," the first Mrs Drake was warning the soldiers.

And then he felt it. It was there – suddenly – in the back of his mind: for some reason, he could feel the Shopkeeper's shop behind him. Literally behind him – feel the space between him and it twisting and warping until it became irrelevant. He could feel the building behind him, knew he would see it if he could turn his head. But he was frozen. His heart beat in time to the pulse of the mirrors in the shop, and he could see the faces of the Shopkeeper and his friend with the hair pushing through them.

"Now!" they yelled in unison.

The mirrors warped and distorted, and so did Michael Drake.

His jaw dropped down to the floor, forming a cavernous opening the full length of his body. The soldiers had definitely stopped laughing now. Some tried to shoot, some tried to run. But Michael Drake opened his mouth wide and swallowed them all. As the last one slipped past Drake's tonsils, his mouth clamped shut again and the sound of their screaming was cut off in a moment. Michael Drake felt his limbs unlock and drop to his sides. For a moment he felt like the rest of him might follow them, but he managed to keep on his feet. Just.

It was a very long time until anybody said another word.

Michael Drake had to be carried from the battlefield by his first wife. He seemed unconscious, but he flailed weakly trying to keep her away. At first, she took him to their tent and tried to make him comfortable by wrapping him in their dirty woollen blanket. But when it became obvious that he wasn't going to wake any time soon, he was carried into the Shopkeeper's fancy dress shop and laid down in the Shopkeeper's bed. The Shopkeeper himself didn't return to the shop for two days, and
when he did the second – and fifth – Mrs Drake was with him.

"Aw, pet," she said softly, laying a hand on his chest, "y'look hanging."

It was clear to everyone that he wasn't going to get up again.

"Can you do anything?" the first Mrs Drake asked.

There was a moment of silence.

"Ah'm gonna need a white dress."

Within thirty minutes, Michael Drake had been manhandled into a 1930s dinner jacket and tie, while the second – and fifth – Mrs Drake poured herself into a white cocktail dress. Well-wishers had been persuaded to gather wildflowers and toss them casually around the bedroom. The Shopkeeper had brushed down his suit and picked out his smartest bow-tie. The first Mrs Drake sat beside her husband on the bed, a hand on his chest as it rattled and fluttered.

"Are you sure you want to do this?" the Shopkeeper asked the first Mrs Drake again.

The look on her face told everybody that she was less than happy with the idea of sharing her husband. But she was, above all, a practical woman: if there was any sin in this, it would be extremely short-lived. No marriage lasted beyond death, and Michael Drake was clearly not long for this world. She nodded.

"And you ..." the Shopkeeper caught himself, the name Iris dying on his lips, "... old friend. Are you sure about this?"

"Ah can share his burden," she answered firmly.

"No, *this*," the Shopkeeper indicated the white dress. "I mean – white? *You?*"

Michael Drake coughed. It sounded like he was tearing himself apart.

"Come on," the second – and fifth – Mrs Drake said firmly.

The Shopkeeper flicked through the sheaf of papers in front of him. It had been handed to him by the second – and fifth – Mrs Drake when he'd complained about not possessing a Bible nor knowing the wording of the marriage ceremony. On reading the
first page of the battered script, the Shopkeeper had suggested that it was actually worse than no Bible at all. He had been assured that symbolically it would do just fine, and he should just shut up and get on with it.

The Shopkeeper cleared his throat.

"Dave?" he intoned in a gravelly voice. "Dave?"

The second – and fifth – Mrs Drake pulled a ring from her finger. It was set with a sapphire the size of a duck egg. It caught the light in a way that suggested it would never again let it go. She slid it onto the cold hand of Michael Drake and bent down next to his ear.

"You're my wife now," she whispered softly, and kissed him.

Michael Drake let out a groan.

And then opened his eyes.

The celebration that followed went on for several days, and by the end of it Michael Drake was strong enough to stand on a table and raise a hand to the villagers. His first wife stayed close, but didn't get between her husband and his people. His second wife, however, was conspicuous by her absence: she had bundled herself into her bus almost the minute that her new husband's eyes had opened, telling anyone who asked that she needed to avoid a man named Roger Daltrey. Whenever anybody asked who he was, the second – and fifth – Mrs Drake laughed to herself as if she'd just been told the best joke in the world.

But the Shopkeeper stayed, despite everything. He stayed to see Michael Drake's strength gradually come back to him, and to see him settle into the role of Mayor. He developed a wisdom and an insight that surprised his first wife to her dying day. When his strength came back, it seemed to bring with it the wisdom of Solomon. He could see both sides of any argument, as if somewhere deep inside he held both opposing views in an eternal and delicate balance.

When the first Mrs Drake did eventually die, her husband told the story of how her rabbit stew had founded Samhain and
shed a tear. A few weeks afterwards, he took a third wife, and then – since he was already technically a bigamist – a fourth. The second – and fifth – Mrs Drake came to visit a few years later, although on this occasion she looked like a blonde sex astronaut and called herself Iris. She denied all knowledge of any previous encounter with Drake, but after a night of reminiscing and gin succumbed to his charms and married him all over again.

When Michael Drake finally died, the funeral was the biggest, most bittersweet party that Samhain ever saw. His third, fourth and sixth wives all spoke at the service. His second – and fifth – wife didn't attend. He was buried on the site of his greatest triumph, and the villagers promptly erected a church on the very spot. And they erected a memorial stone at the entrance to ensure that they never, ever forgot the debt they owed him.

In memory of Michael Drake who kept the war from Samhain.

"No hold on just a minute," Panda objected. "You said *seventh*."

"So?"

"You just said he'd had six wives when he died."

"I know what I said," Iris grumbled at him. "And then, after he was dead, he got married again. It's not that hard to understand, is it? He bound his soul to the concept of war and destruction. You don't really think a little thing like dying was going to stop that do you?"

"I," Panda said grandly, "don't believe a word of it."

"The seventh Mrs Drake came through the mirrors. No-one really knows where from. Somewhere in the future probably. You know what they're like. All bio-mechanical and resilient. Didn't come a moment too soon: things were already getting downright nasty at the church. That's why they built this place, as a counter-balance. But then she turns up, and Bob's your uncle. A few promises to love, honour and – above all – keep her husband well and truly dead, and everything quietens down again. Well, mostly."

"Absolute," Panda said pointedly, "tommyrot."

"You don't have to take my word for it. She's standing right behind you. That's why I brought it up."

There was a little yelp as Panda turned and saw a ten-foot tall exoskeleton attached to a few bits of what could quite possibly be an old lady. The legs looked sturdy enough to crush Panda without too much trouble, but that was by the by as the seventh Mrs Drake was also pointing a number of shiny looking weapons down at the two of them. One or two of them looked as though they might be nuclear.

Iris, of course, ignored her and reached into the hole in the plasterwork.

I CAN'T LET YOU TAKE IT, the seventh Mrs Drake warned.

Iris opened her hand. Inside lay two dusty halves of an ancient eggshell.

"Iris, let her have it!" whined Panda.

"Sorry lovey," said Iris. "Madame Blavoddy was most insistent. I was only meant to be borrowing the blessed thing anyway."

Iris Wildthyme slipped the eggshells into her pocket and stood up. She brushed down her knees and looked up into the heart of the far-future killing machine determined to not let her leave the area alive.

"Now then," she said with a smile. "What shall we do about you?"

But that was another story.

THE MIDNIGHT EMPIRE
JULIO ANGEL ORTIZ

If she had the choice between trying on one more costume or being consumed inch-by-inch by parasitic bloodwraiths, Iris would have begun to lean towards the latter.

"This isn't rocket science, you know," Panda muttered, a familiar edge creeping into his voice as he turned a page in his magazine. "Not that you'd excel at that either."

"Hush," Iris said, turning around for what felt like the millionth time to see the costume she had selected – a rather garish dress from an alternate Victorian England in which sabretooth tigers had risen to become the dominant life form – and sighed. The Shopkeeper's Fancy Dress Costume Shop really did have an insane assortment of outfits. But not every one was a keeper.

"Does this show –" Iris began.

"Too much brass? Yes," Panda said, not looking up from his magazine.

Iris sighed, the various ornaments on her outfit clanging in unison.

"This is impossible," she said, removing the russet costume in frustration. "At this rate, I'll never have a costume picked out in time for the Halloween party."

Panda looked up, eyebrow raised in an arch. "It's like, I don't know ... we don't have a time machine or anything if 'time' became a real issue."

"Remind me why I brought you with me?" Iris said, pulling on a costume that was much more to her liking. This one contained crimson and gold patterns interlaced with memetic highlights. Namely, the highlights would appear as different colours to different people based on their subconscious preferences. It was a bit of a cheat, Iris admitted to herself, but for the largest intra-dimensional Halloween party that occurred only once per multiversal reset, no expense could be spared. The last such party, before some cataclysmic event wound up re-writing large parts of multiverse history again, the hottest outfit was a tri-level affair made of silicon and closed time-loops. The word on the street was that only the originating race – similarly tall, quadruped, and who loved Nutella enough to import it from an alternate universe – were the only ones who could pull off wearing it at an event. Iris, Panda, and a few of her friends pulled it off in stunning fashion, even if said friends would later claim they were essentially press-ganged into it.

Iris was beginning to think that she wasn't going to be able to top it.

"Maybe I'll wear this and claim that I'm starting a minimalist trend?"

Panda half-heartedly opened his mouth, but then shook his head and went back to reading.

Iris allowed her arms to fall to her side, and stood for a moment, staring into the mirror. She stepped forward until she was almost nose-to-nose with her reflection. Iris raised a hand, tentative at first, and pressed her palm against the mirror.

"Have you ever looked into the mirror," Iris began, her eyes searching her reflection with all the eagerness of a stranger, "and felt like you were seeing yourself – really seeing yourself – for the first time? Like when you're writing a word and you know you've written it a thousand times before, but this time it looks foreign to you? As if that was the first time you've noticed how it's really spelled?"

Panda looked up at Iris. "So now you're a properly-spelled word?" Panda pondered that for a minute. "Wait, that might actually be an interesting outfit. You could show up as a shifting collection of letters and appear in menus and signs and what-not at the party. Except you would use words in Esperanto."

Iris turned to Panda, snapping her fingers and pointing at him in one swift gesture.

"I think you're onto something!" she said excitedly.

Panda nodded with a smile, but his pleasure was short-lived as the mirror before them rudely chose that moment to explode.

Panda never thought he could be annoyed at an explosion. But he was, and at the core of his befuddlement and surprise was the lingering question as to exactly what was going on. One moment, Iris and himself were talking, and the next the mirror was exploding outward. It was a glittering shockwave enveloping the space around them, but it had colour and shape, vermillion ripples that poisoned the air. Iris and Panda were airborne for a moment, time slowing down as if in one of those over-budgeted action movies. But just as quickly, the mirror began to implode, sucking them and a million particles through a malleable darkness.

Panda couldn't quite tell where the transition from 'falling through infinite darkness' and 'waking up on a heap of rubble' occurred, but it was no less annoying.

Panda sat up and found himself in an apocalyptic nightmare.

He was in the ruins of a city, on a street that was next to what Panda could only surmise had once been a park. Where once fountains and benches had entertained guests only cracked ruins remained, surrounded by the husks of buildings. The sky was a roiling sea of the now-familiar vermillion, laced with lightning orbs that drifted through the clouds like avian buoys. It took a moment for Panda to realize there was a suffused light emanating from these clouds that gave the area some fraction of lighting.

Iris' moaning immediately grounded Panda, and he looked over. Iris was lying face down, her arms slowly finding purchase as she began to lift herself. Iris settled on rolling over onto her back, then sitting up cross-legged on the ground.

Panda approached Iris. "You okay?"

Iris reached for her head, caressing her temple as she looked around.

"Oh no," she said, panic in her voice.

Panda looked around. "Yeah, who knows what mess we've gotten ourselves into now."

Iris shook her head. "I never paid for the dress," she said, wearily pointing at her clothing. "The Shopkeeper is going to kill me."

Panda shook his head and took a deep breath. "I think we have more pressing matters."

Iris nodded and stood. As she did, Panda saw her eyes glaze over for a moment, and her footing faltered. Panda reached out but Iris quickly steadied herself.

"Whoa, easy!" Panda said.

Iris shook her head. "No, I'm okay. I just got light-headed for a moment." Iris looked around. "Eh ... this place. Do you feel it?"

"Feel what?"

When Iris spoke, her words were muddled with a slight slur. "It feels wrong, somehow. Like this place is pulling at me, tearing at me."

"It could just be the Nyxian Nachos you had earlier."
Iris glared at Panda.
"What?" he said defensively. "I told you not to put on extra Sriracha!"
Iris shook her head.
"Anyway," Panda said as he looked around, "we should probably look for some shelter."
"Good idea."

"I think this is a horrible idea," Panda said, as he surveyed the humans they had just encountered.
They hadn't spent much time looking for shelter. Despite having a plethora of buildings around them, it was proving more difficult than expected to find a place to cower inside for a bit, away from the frenetic sky and dour surroundings. But every building they tried so far either looked like it would collapse if you so much as breathed on it or there were massive holes exposing them to the sky, and what would be the point then?
Panda had been ready to assail Iris with another round of sarcastic wit when they turned a corner and found them.
A man from ancient Egypt. Some guy in dirty overalls and wearing thick workman gloves. And a woman with slightly more refined tastes, even if her clothes did look a bit raggedy.
"Looks like they could use some help," Iris said.
Panda shook his head. "Because we're so on top of things?"
"Maybe they know what's going on."
"I highly doubt it." Panda reflexively rubbed his temples.
"I'm going to go ask," Iris said firmly, and began heading towards them.
"I think this is a horrible idea."

As Panda listened to their sorry tales, he began to pick up on a theme. Namely, it was *Don't ever use the Shopkeeper's changing room.*
"I'm impressed with the authenticity of your outfit," Iris exclaimed to the person in the Egyptian outfit, whose name he had given was Nakht.
"Thank you," he said bashfully, a blush engulfing the whole of his bald head. "It took quite a bit of research to get it right. I spent eight

hours alone pouring over the proper hex codes for the clothes' colours in the 3D printer."

Iris turned to Panda and whispered, "3D printer. Take note for the next party."

"Noted," Panda drolled.

"I was in the Shopkeeper's changing room, trying it on and making sure everything looked good for the party, when the mirror exploded and drew me in," Nakht said.

"Technically, it would have imploded if it drew you in," Panda said.

"Shh!" came Iris' rebuke.

Nakht smiled politely. "Yes, well ... and I woke up here." Nakht looked around wearily. "I just wandered around a bit before coming upon Marco and Souid here."

Panda looked over at Marco and Souid. Noting Marco's workman outfit, he asked, "Who goes to a costume party dressed as a millworker?"

Marco rubbed the back of his head, glancing downward and avoiding Panda's gaze. "It was supposed to be a retro 20th century party."

"You lost a bet, didn't you?"

"Yeah."

Iris interjected. "And you were changing as well when the mirror pulled you in?"

Marco nodded. "Pretty much."

Iris turned to Panda. "'We have to talk to the Shopkeeper about this epidemic of changing room disasters."

"Funny he didn't mention it to us," Panda said.

Iris swiftly turned towards Nakht. "Now that I think about it, I don't recall seeing you at the shop. Or any of you."

"I don't recall seeing you either," Nakht said dryly.

Marco shrugged. "I was too busy reading the results of the Inaugural."

Before Souid could respond, Iris perked up. "Inaugural?"

Marco looked back at Iris with a confused stare. "Everyone knows what the Inaugural is." When no reply came, Marco added, "Samhain's first football match? Against Beltane? Everyone was talking about it."

Nakht turned to Marco, skepticism etched into every line on his pale face. "First match? What are you talking about, that was 20 years ago." Nakht allowed a beat to pass. "In 1977."

Soudin spoke up at last. "A little longer, by my reckoning," she said quietly, her mind a thousand miles away as she brushed back her chestnut hair, revealing a small scar along the olive-coloured flesh of her cheek .

Marco scratched his chin, fingers smoothing out his reddish-brown, thin goatee. "No, no, that can't be right."

Iris nodded. "Actually, it would make sense. Sounds like we've all been drawn here across time, wherever 'here' is. Spread out across enough years, it would explain why no one thought to put up a warning sign in the changing rooms." She looked up at the sky, pensive. "It also explains why this place feels so wrong."

Souid looked at Iris intently. "What do you mean?"

"The problem is Time. It's somehow 'wrong' here. Like smog, there's this miasma that's getting to me."

"I still think it's the Sriracha," Panda said beneath his breath.

"What was that?" Iris asked.

"Zombies?" Panda asked.

"No," Iris said, annoyed. "I distinctly heard you once again criticizing my food choices."

Panda placed his hand on her arm. "No," he said very calmly, and pointed past them. "Are those zombies?"

Iris turned in time to see things shambling towards them.

They probably weren't zombies, Panda reasoned. There were too many reasons to doubt it, as any rational being would conclude. Sure, he thought, these humanoids that were coming towards them – about 20 or so, Panda figured – were walking with a distinct lack of urgency. Sure, their three arms were outstretched towards Panda and his companions. And yes, their flesh appeared rotted and scarred with a sickly blue hue. But how many had they seen that featured a strange vermillion (yes, there was that colour again) energy bleeding from their eyes and wounds on their bodies?

Panda decided to untick the mental checkbox for 'zombies', at least for the moment.

"Should we say hello?" Panda said at last.

Marco turned to him. "What the hell is wrong with you?"

"Just thinking outside the box," Panda said.

Iris began to back away, tugging on Panda's shoulder. "No, I'm pretty sure we should fallback for now."

Everyone broke off at a brisk run. Iris lead the way, and as Panda followed he hazarded a glance back, and saw the creatures had quickened the pace of their pursuit. It was around this time that Panda heard a male cry of 'Ugh!' followed by the sound of meat rolling on the ground.

Except that 'meat' was Nakht, who had tripped over either some unfortunately placed rubble or his exquisitely detailed robes.

Panda stopped and noticed the inevitable. The creatures were now coming at them at a full clip. Nakht's ornate Egyptian robes had gotten tangled up in his feet, making it difficult for him to stand quickly.

A moment of agony washed over Panda as Nakht reached out towards him. Panda looked at the bald man's eyes, noticing the fear and, for the first time, Nakht's black eyeliner.

"Please, help!" Nakht screamed.

Panda looked from Nakht to the mob almost upon him, and back at Nakht. Panda realized that there was only decision he could make.

"Nope!" Panda said, and turned to catch up with the others.

By the time he caught up with Iris and the rest, Panda wondered why he had been lagging so far behind.

Souid looked at him, her dark eyes betraying confusion. "What happened?"

Panda went to speak and found himself at a loss for words. Why had he been lagging behind? Those creatures were already uncomfortably close. He wouldn't just lazily try to escape from them.

"I ... don't know," Panda said at last.

"Where's Nakht?" Iris asked as her head darted left and right, looking for the next route to take.

"Who?" Panda and Marco asked simultaneously.

Iris looked back at them with skepticism. "I'm assuming the screams I heard were him meeting an unfortunate end?"

Panda stared at Iris blankly. "What do you mean? Who's 'Nakht'?"

Iris bit her lower lip, lost in thought. Looking between the three, she asked, "So none of you remember the gentleman dressed in Egyptian garb?" She pointed at Marco and Souid. "The one you two were traveling with?"

Marco and Souid looked at each other.

"I don't know who you're talking about," Souid said at length. "It was just Marco and I before we ran into you two."

Panda looked up at Iris. "Senility already? Getting old is a bitch."

Iris shook her head. "No. Well, yes it is. But no!" Iris looked back. "We … we'll just have to revisit it later." She looked back. "I can feel … for lack of a better word, something 'pulsating'. Over in that direction," she pointed. "It's sending ripples out through the air, like a stones in a pond. And I have a vaguely unsettling thought as to what it might be."

Before he could ask, Panda saw Iris take off. Muttering beneath his breath and feeling buoyed by the guttural sounds of the creatures coming up from behind, he followed.

It was like speed-running through hell.

The four of them were maintaining a good pace ahead of the creatures. But as they navigated the labyrinthine nightmare of shadows and rubble, they found that the creatures were relentless. While they began as slow and shambling, there was an urgency that their legs discovered. Panda imagined it was their hunger, their ecstatic desire to consume them that was giving these mobile cadavers their pace. As Iris would call out a new direction of where this 'beacon' lay, Panda would glance back and half-expect these creatures would be merely a breath away, ready to pounce and turn him into the poor nutritious lunch that Panda hoped he would become if caught.

Panda was grateful that they were maintaining a lead, however slim. So it seemed entirely appropriate when Marco chose that moment to trip and fall.

"Marco!" Souid cried, sliding to a halt and trying not to fall over herself.

Panda cursed under his breath and stopped as well. He called out to Iris, who turned back and saw Marco on the ground and stopped herself.

Panda briefly contemplated grabbing Souid, who was closest to him, and continuing to run while they held something of a lead. But Souid rushed to Marco before Panda could do anything, and realizing he was now committed to not leaving both of them behind, Panda cursed again under his breath.

He saw Souid frantically helping Marco up, and for a moment

Panda couldn't tell if the look on Marco's face was fear of the creatures overtaking them or the utter embarrassment he was feeling. Panda settled on the latter, but just barely.

In focusing on Marco, Panda almost didn't notice the creature throwing itself at him.

Everything happened in a rush. From the corner of his eye, Panda saw while helping Marco up, Souid was tackled from the side by one of the creatures. A horrified Marco reached down to grab something, but by then Panda was turning his attention to the creature that was in mid-air, arms outstretched, rotted gums and teeth and gristly jaw clattering with sick rhythmic desire.

Panda stood stock still, and continued to do so after the creature thumped right in front of him, having missed its mark by a good three feet.

I wonder if it feels stupid, Panda thought reflexively. But the thought melted away when Panda noticed the metal rod that was embedded in the creature's forehead and protruding out the back of its skull. Looking back, Panda saw Iris with her throwing arm outstretched, a glint of pride in her eyes.

"You okay?" she asked.

Panda nodded dumbly.

Souid's scream cut through the air and drew Panda's attention back. Marco was wrestling one of the creatures off of Souid, while she was keeping another one at bay with kicks. Looking down at the now-honestly-dead creature, Panda realized he was at an advantage. Reaching forward, he gripped the end of the metal rod and pulled it out of the skull. Rushing over to Marco, Panda whistled, and as soon as Marco looked over he tossed the rod towards him. In the same instance, Panda kicked the creature in the back of the leg, causing it to tumble backwards. Marco grabbed the rod and in one swoop brought it down through the creature's eye socket, disabling it permanently.

Panda proceeded to provide a similar distraction to the creatures harassing Souid, and between Iris and Marco, they were able to quickly incapacitate the creatures.

Iris helped Souid up. "Are you able to keep going?"

Souid nodded stiffly. Hearing the sounds of more creatures rushing their way, the group continued on into the unpromised safety of the shadows.

It was as if the eye of an ancient god were peeking in through the universe in corrupted glory.

Panda felt unease wash over him as they stood on the deck of what had once been a laboratory of some sort. It had not taken them long to find it, and blockading the door was a quick affair. The makeshift barrier was holding back the creatures for now, but they knew time was growing shorter with every bang and scratch from the feral natives.

But this rift before them was not only massive, it bled uneasiness that Panda could distinctly taste, like the copper of blood in his mouth. It was pallid, effusing a river of energy that was the same dreaded colour of the sky in this harsh realm as well as the one emanating from the creatures. It had a trance-like quality that Panda found himself being drawn to while simultaneously trying not to vomit in revulsion.

Panda's reverie was interrupted by Iris shuttering the silence between them.

"It's a hole in space-time," she said at last.

Panda looked at her. "I'm glad we had you here to tell us that."

Iris rolled her eyes at Panda and moved past him, over to where Souid stood, as she tried to work the touch interface of a computer system.

"I can help with that," Iris said.

Souid smiled. "Thanks. I'm pretty good with linguistics back home but I'm having trouble deciphering some of these UI elements."

Iris nodded and began assisting her. Before long, Iris was nodding vigorously.

"These people were running experiments in time travel," she said.

Panda pointed at the rift. "Explains the hole in space-time."

Iris ignored him. "But they got it all wrong." She harrumphed and began tapping away on the touchscreen keyboard. "They didn't even account for the variance in Chrono … oh, never mind." She waved a dismissive hand at the rift. "They obviously cocked it up. But in doing so, it unleashed a massive shockwave that not only engulfed this planet, but punched through time and space as well." She looked at Souid and Marco. "So even though you all were separated by centuries, it was the same event that dragged us here."

Marco looked down in thought. "Can we get back home?"

Iris favoured him with a smile. "Of course."

"But what about that man you said we were with? Nakht?"

Iris nodded, a hint of a frown creeping in. "This catastrophe changed them. Like radiation destroys flesh, this temporal fallout altered what they were. And gave them the desire to consume, not flesh, but Time."

Souid's eyebrows furrowed. "You're saying they consumed his timestream? So it was as if he never existed?"

Iris nodded solemnly, and Panda noticed Souid give Marco an uneasy look.

Iris tapped out several more commands and stepped away. "The device can be reprogrammed to snap us back to our native timelines, but because of the damage to the equipment, it would have to be done manually." Iris looked up. "So don't worry, I'll send you all home. That includes you too, Panda. I'm sure I can avoid this lot and subsequently rig something up."

"You won't have to do that," Panda said grimly.

Iris looked at him with concern. "Why do you say that?"

Panda pointed at Souid. "She's been bitten." Seeing Souid look back at him in shock, Panda said, "Haven't you?"

Souid nodded slowly. "Yes, it's true. Back when I was tackled," she said, turning aside and lifting up her shirt to reveal vermillion fissures in her flesh under her ribs.

"Damn it," Marco muttered.

Souid smiled grimly. Looking at Panda, she asked, "How did you know?"

"It's your face. Whenever I look away from you, I'm beginning to have trouble remembering what you look like."

Iris nodded sadly. "It's the temporal rot. It's already anchored into your timestream and will only get worse from here on out."

"It's okay," Souid said quietly. Looking aside, she continued. "Just show me what to do."

It only took a few moments for Iris to show Souid the appropriate commands, and then after saying their goodbyes, the remnant of the group stood by the rift.

Iris met Souid's gaze, and nodded. Souid held her gaze for a moment longer, and went to tap in the commands.

That was when the barrier gave way, and a flood of creatures came pouring in.

"Souid!" Iris said, stepping forward to help her.

"No!" Souid said, raising a hand as she frantically finished tapping in the remaining commands. "Don't! I've almost –"

One last triumphant tap.

"– got it!"

Iris, Panda, and Marco vanished in a vermillion flash as rotted flesh gripped Souid.

Reflexively, she pulled back, then swung an elbow to connect with a creature and give her some extra space. While one of the creatures stumbled back, another found purchase on her leg and tripped Souid. Reaching out to stop her fall, Souid's hands slapped against the touchscreen surface, haphazardly entering a number of alien commands.

Nothing happened.

Rolling on the ground, Souid allowed her momentum to take her forward and under, clipping the legs out from a few of the creatures. Another few crawled over the equipment, including the command console. In doing so, some of the towers of systems topped over, onto others, creating a small domino effect. Then the final large system fell, there was a spark.

Suddenly, that side of the room was engulfed in a fireball, the force scattering them like rag dolls across the room.

And throwing Souid up and over into a blazing white light …

Iris and Panda landed in a heap in the changing room. Panda was lying on his back, staring up at the ceiling, and then leaned forward. He could see the mirror shattered across the floor, but thankfully there was no longer a gateway occupying its space.

"That's a relief," Panda whispered.

"Yeah," Iris said, sitting up. She rubbed her eyes wearily, looking over at where the mirror had once been on the wall.

"We get up to some extraordinary things, don't we? In some of the most ordinary of places."

Panda shrugged. "I just think you're a magnet for bad luck."

Iris tutted. "It's not all bad." She continued to focus on where the mirror had been; only a busted frame remained.

Panda noticed this. "What is it? I'm sure the Shopkeeper won't be that upset. We'll replace the mirror."

Iris shook her head. "No, it's not that." She pointed to where the mirror had once been.

Panda looked over. In the corner of the frame a small remnant of the mirror remained. Upon closer inspection, Panda also noticed something odd. It was a logo, one he hadn't recalled seeing before. Which was even stranger, Panda mused, since the logo was faded, as if it had been there for a very long time.

It read Transport for London.

"I don't recall seeing that there before either," Panda said.

"Neither do I."

"Maybe our eyesight is failing in our old age."

Iris looked over at him with a smirk, her gaze lingering on him.

Panda immediately felt insecure. "What?" he asked at length.

She looked down. "The Halloween party."

Panda nodded, his eyes betraying his exhaustion. "That dress should be fine. Especially after everything we've been through."

"I think I'm going to skip it this time around."

Panda threw his magazine at Iris' head.

Every part of Souid ached.

She moaned involuntarily as she slowly rolled over, broken glass and wood crackling under her weight. Above her the sky was no longer a vermillion, but the pale blue she had expected. Leaning forward, she wondered if everything she had experienced had been a dream.

But soon, the reality came rushing back to her, as she took in the ruins around her.

Souid slowly stood, fighting a wave of nausea as she did. From within the destroyed shop, she could see the sky. Souid stumbled as she moved forward, trying to make sense of these recent events. Had she known what that mirror, the last surviving one in the shop, would have lead to, Souid would have left well enough alone. Her mother always warned her about her curiosity and her creativity, that neither would lead to a good end.

Go figure, mom, this had to be the one thing you were right about, Souid thought bitterly.

She made it to the door without incident, but upon stepping outside, Souid collapsed. She could feel herself fading fast, and she felt a lifetime of regret drowning her. Souid realized it wasn't anything major she regretted or wished that she could change.

It was all the small things.

It was not taking up Darren's offer for a walk that one night. Or having lunch with Clara before her trip to Perth. Or not being the one to drive her mom to the airport.

It was a tapestry of little mistakes that made Souid want to cry.

Souid crawled a little further, and then sat up on the ground, back against the brick remnants of the shop.

Arthur's End used to be so lovely. But look at it now. She just hadn't the heart to mention it to the other's. If they were really from the past, then it was for the best.

"Souid!" came a cry. Then another, from a different voice.

Souid recognized her friends' voices. They must have come looking for her when she didn't turn up.

"I'm over," Souid cried out, before feeling the burning pain in her side. Her hand slide down to feel under her ribcage, when she remembered the creatures. And the bite.

Souid dove headlong into a chasm of despair as she wished with every fibre of her remaining existence that she had never returned.

"She's over here!" came a voice, and the rush of feet moving over rubble and terrain to reach her.

Souid's despair was short-lived. Soon, her insides began to feel hollowed out, and with it went her regret and despair.

Souid's last memory was of her mother holding her hand beneath a crystal blue sky, asking Souid if she wanted to walk along the beach and maybe get some ice cream.

Then it was gone. And all that remained was hunger …

SELF POSSESSED
IAN POTTER

It's Saturday, March the 19th, 2005 and it's raining in Samhain.

Water splashes down a plastic Roundhead helmet and onto Kay's nose as she heads for the Hebden bus stop. She tries to look like she knows what she's doing as she splashes through the dark, imagining herself effortlessly cool and walking with a soundtrack. She fails. It's late, she's drunk in that way that mainly affects ankles and she's wearing a terrible outfit.

Samhain is a good place to dress up. Some nights it seems everyone has come kitted out as a dream. The pubs jostle with unlikely aliens, semi-retired deities and refugees from children's fiction, drunkenly weaving themselves into each other's mythologies and getting in each other's ways. It's a great place to come if you want to be something more than yourself for a while. Kay really wants to be more than herself.

She takes a left down Magdalene Street onto Festive Road. It wouldn't look like a shortcut on a map but Samhain's tricky to navigate. Even though the town's two main directions are 'up' and 'down' it's easy to get lost in, even in daylight. The roads wind unexpectedly about, looping back on themselves eccentrically and taking surprising detours. It's as if they're wrapping themselves around the town so they don't just slide off the hillside entirely.

The bus stop is just beyond the amazing costume hire shop that clothes most of the town's revellers. There are lights on inside, even now. Kay glimpses the leather-faced old assistant downstairs as she passes. He's busying himself fussing around the costume displays with a ridiculous feather duster.

Kay slides herself onto a seat at the bus shelter. It's an impressively engineered thing – too hard and narrow for comfort, and angled to make it impossible to stay on long. There's a Cavalier perched awkwardly on the next one along, felt hat all soggy, false moustache drooping to half past five. Kay remembers her from the party, when her moustache was ten to three.

"What you doing here?" Kay asks.

"Missed bus," the Cavalier mumbles.

"Story of my life," says a voice from the ground. There's an old lady huddled in the corner of the shelter. Neither Roundhead nor Cavalier had noticed her before.

"Be another soon," says Kay lightly.

"Life, chuck?" asks the old lady. It's hard to tell if she's a huge shapeless thing or a tiny one wrapped in layers of coats.

"Bus," says Kay. She sidles closer to the bedraggled Cavalier. The old lady is strange even by Samhain's standards. She smells of camphor and juniper and old cigarettes.

"Did the party get any better?" the Cavalier asks.

"Not really," says Kay. "Kind-of-offensive Al Jolson was sick on rugby-club Marilyn, and bad people got in charge of the music. It went downhill from there."

The Cavalier becomes animated. "He was kind-of-offensive, wasn't he?"

Kay nods. "Mind, when they cleaned him up it turned out he really was black, so I guess it was all kind-of-layered and re-appropriating really."

There's a noise from the old lady. It might be a laugh, it might be her stomach. It doesn't quite sound like her.

"Still creepy though," says the Cavalier.

"Yep, creepy and covered in puke."

"I like your clothes," says the old lady suddenly. Her eyes are green, wild and rolling. "You go well together."

"They're not clothes, they're costumes," snaps Kay. She surprises herself with her vehemence.

"And what, pray, is the difference?" asks an unexpectedly posh voice. It seems to come from under the old lady's coat.

"Clark Kent wears clothes, Superman wears a costume," says the Cavalier.

In another time and place, Kay might have quibbled over this, but not here and now. She feels an odd kinship towards this floppy-hatted girl with bits of glue-on beard in her mouth.

"Neat," says Kay, "Where do disguises fit in?"

"Everywhere," says the Cavalier, and for the first time Kay really sees her. Her eyes sparkle like Christmas.

Kay flicks her head back and raindrops fly from her Roundhead helmet. "Are you normally sort-of-sassy gnomic or have you just watched a lot of telly?" she asks.

"Yes," says the Cavalier.

Twin beams of light peek over the brow of the hill. It's the Hebden bus. Kay stands.

"It was nice meeting you," she says, turning to the Cavalier.

The Cavalier holds Kay's gaze. "We should keep doing it," she says. "Be nice to see you undisguised." Framed by strands of fake hair, her shy smile has Duchamp and Leonardo beaten.

The bus pulls up, and, as casually as she can, the Cavalier asks Kay to come back to hers.

"But, I don't even know your name," says Kay in mock-outrage.

"Did I not say before? It's Sara."

As Kay and Sara board the bus, the driver calls to the old lady on the ground.

"You not getting on, missus?"

"Not as well as some, but we get by," she sighs.

"No! On the bus."

"Not our bus."

"But, it's the last one!"

"No, love, there's another coming. I can smell it!" The old lady chuckles and it turns into a cough.

As the bus pulls away something moves under the old lady's coat.

"Was that her then, Iris?" it says. "The one we need?"

She nods as the toy Panda comes up for air.

"And the other one?" he asks, straightening his cravat.

"Maybe." Iris pulls an odd device from a pocket. It's mainly bits of old radios. "My demon detector seemed to think so, anyway."

"So what do we do now?"

"Panda – there's a party somewhere out there, with dreadful music being played. We go where we're needed."

The shopkeeper's assistant puts down his duster, switches off the lights and says good night to his favourite costume. As he shuts the front door behind him, the building creaks.

Inside the shop, the costumes whisper to each other. They rattle on their metal hangers, rustling and sighing their secrets in strange breezes. They tell of the people who've worn them and the people they've ridden. The clown costume recalls a shy teenager she made bold and a hundred more she's terrified. The saggy-kneed gorilla suit speaks softly of fiftieth birthdays and bosses who hate their jobs. Only the shiny wipe-clean nurse's uniform says nothing. It has seen too much.

Somehow, they know something remarkable is happening with the Civil War costumes that have gone out tonight. There's a crackle of electricity in the air that makes Medusas of cheap nylon wigs and makes fun fur spark like fireflies. A knot is tightening and reality groans.

Upstairs, the Shopkeeper senses it in his sleep. He dreams of other times and places, impossible people and intoxicating landscapes. He dreams of Iris and longs for nothing.

Tonight Sara and Kay will stay up late with a bottle of Kahlúa in Sara's ridiculous, scruffy flat. Kay will talk about poetry and they'll start watching a video of some Francis Bacon thing Sara's taped and end up kissing instead. They'll watch the video another time. Videos can always be rewound, kisses you have to grab.

"Love the costume," says a serial killer from a film who hasn't worked out why no one's talking to him. He's drinking with a straw because his right hand is a joke-shop murder weapon.

"I'm not wearing a costume," says Panda.

"Oh, I thought you were an Ewok."

Panda isn't sure how Iris managed to find the party. It's some kind of gift she has. Samhain is a jumble of streets and she seems to have no plan, yet somehow she always does it.

They're mingling now, which means he's been exploring the fridge and she's somehow come back from the toilet with boot polish on her lips.

Someone has put on an old Tony Christie record. A motley mob of pirates, nuns and serving wenches whoop in pleasure as they recognise the intro and begin to stomp around the room. One of them might be Catweazle.

"This is ghastly," bellows Panda, after he's fought his way through to Iris. "Why are they dancing?"

"Because it's expected of them," she replies, scooping anything that looks strong and unopened under her coat.

"Do they like this, then?"

"Oh no, it's just a bit fun, and it's for charity, so they're all being ironic."

"All of them?"

Iris nods soberly, a bottle of Thunderbird wine in hand. She'll not be nodding soberly much longer. Things are coming to a head.

It is a drizzly morning in 1764 and John Wesley is soberer than Iris can ever imagine being. He is looking at the old Samhain church and, for all his famous abstinence, he feels a sickness rising in him and a terrible pounding in his head.

'Can a building make you drunk?' he wonders.

The church is still intact in 1764. It's tall and imposing and dedicated to a heathen martyr. It troubles Wesley. It embraces sedition, and the aesthetics of it are wrong to his eye. It's full of galleries and grotesques and secret corners. It seems to cast a long misshapen shadow on the village that Wesley fancies shelters unpleasant things.

"This is not a true home of Christ," he pronounces. Someone nearby is writing his words down. "It's a nest of hierarchies and conflicts." As the echoes of his declamations fade he hears the scratching of his words being transcribed. He can feel himself becoming history.

His gaze rests for a moment on the moss-encrusted monument by the church entrance. The inscription on it reads 'In memory of Michael Drake who kept the war from Samhain'. Wesley shivers. The roughly carved image of Drake is a wild thing, almost pagan.

"This is not the church these people need," Wesley dictates. "It is full of old poison." Slowly, making sure all his words are faithfully set down, Wesley asserts that a new place of worship must be built in Samhain to supersede this monstrous, cruel building. "Just as the New Testament supersedes the Old," he declares and is rather pleased to see the words recorded.

He doesn't even know about the immured thing in the rafters.

"Is the bus really coming back?" asks Panda, as he and Iris stumble out into the early morning, her coat rattling like a milk-float. "Our bus, I mean."

"Oh yes, lovey," Iris rhapsodises, "I can hear it on the wind – decanters and lampshades tinkling, gramophone needle skipping." She flings her arms out like she's imagining a camera pulling back from her, taking in the old grey stone of the village, and dawn pinkening the sky behind them. "It's on a bumpy old road, but it's coming alright."

Panda thinks the tinkling is mainly the bottles in Iris' coat, but he doesn't argue.

On the 20th of March 2005 Sara and Kay get up late. They awkwardly defer to each other about who needs the bathroom more and spend an almost pleasant hour doing nothing they want because they don't want to impose.

Kay puts her Roundhead outfit back on, because asking to borrow some of Sara's clothes seems harder somehow. She just carries the helmet though. She doesn't want to look odd. Out of politeness Sara dresses up as a Cavalier again.

Eventually, they manage to discover both of them are hungry and head out for breakfast in a pub that serves lunch until tea time.

They head for a pub in Samhain where their costumes will seem less odd, and both order eggs Benedict, even though they want sausage and mash. While they sit together waiting for their food, they talk as casually as they can – trying to work out what they have in common and what sets them apart.

"If you had to be a bit of Velcro®," says Kay, "would you rather be the loopy bit or the wiry, hooky bit?"

"What is this – that bit in Spartacus about eating molluscs?"

"I don't know what you mean."

That's one of the things that sets them apart. Sara has seen a lot more films.

"I'd be the loopy bit," says Kay. "The hooks are too messy looking."

"Like pubes."

"I can take them or leave them."

Iris and Panda watch discreetly from a nearby table, spying through holes in a baroque tower of Jenga bricks that shields them from view. Neither of them seem particularly bothered by how very unlikely the tower's construction is. The normal laws of Physics are a bit squiffy here.

"So, what's happening, Iris?" Panda hisses.

"Banter."

Panda sighs impatiently. "No – what's happening in the bigger picture. Why are we stalking these girls?"

Iris rolls her eyes wearily, as if it's all far too obvious to spell out.

"Imagine reality in Samhain is a cat's cradle in eight dimensions, Panda, a cat's cradle made entirely of living worms …"

"You've no idea have you?" says Panda.

"I chuffing well do have! Have you imagined the cat's cradle?"

"Most of it."

"Right. Well now imagine there's a sticky bit at the middle, a sticky bit the worms really like."

"All right," Panda sighs.

"That's what's happening – the worms are clumping up there," says Iris, "and now everything 'round about here's going to go and get knotted."

"So, what's the clump, then?"

"It's the bus, or what's left of it, any road. Those mirrors we've been hopping about in. They're the bus windows, remember?"

"So?"

"Well, you know how sometimes a thing can get so massive it collapses under its own weight?"

Panda nods.

"It can happen with time too. Those mirrors mean time's a bit mixed up here – lots of future piling up in the past and so on. Samhain's looped and tangled its way through the same moments so many times it's in danger of collapsing under the weight of it all."

"Samhain's done that?"

"More or less," says Iris, suddenly becoming fascinated with the glacé cherry in her glass.

"Fine, so, what's that got to do with these two Civil War girls and Madame Blavoddy's demon detector?" asks Panda.

"I don't know. Maybe they're the Sealed Knot that holds the cats' cradle together."

Madame Blavoddy has a shop that sells incense sticks, fairy memorabilia and intensely spiritual music in tune with the rhythms of Nature. The music is composed, recorded and played on synthesiser keyboards mass-produced by children on starvation wages in a faraway country and it gives you a migraine if you listen to it for more than five minutes. Madame Blavoddy plays it in her shop all day. Few of her customers browse for long.

Madame Blavoddy also tells fortunes for the especially lucky. She says she has a gift. She also claims she hasn't been born yet and that she never lies. Iris quite likes her.

On the 18th of March, 2005 she is reading Panda's paw.

"I see the skeins tangling," she intones sonorously. She has all the lingo.

Panda tries to tell Madame Blavoddy what she sees as life line is actually a bit of not very invisible mending where his fabric once snagged on a bottle top. She waves his protest away.

"It's still a life line, I assure you – the future lays out its clues however it can."

Panda lets her carry on.

"Change is coming. The war is ending. It will be happening soon, or recently, or always has," Madame Blavoddy moans. She has the gall to charge for this.

Iris has a little dance to the shop's intensely spiritual bleeps while she waits for her turn in the consultation booth. It's ridiculously hard to keep time with.

At the muddy heart of Samhain stands Michael Drake, between two armies. The pale stones of the village are not yet laid, cart paths are still uncobbled ground. It is the 14th of April, 1643.

Michael Drake is a man of cunning and charm, who still knows what that means. He has dressed himself carefully in grey that neither army may call him theirs and he holds a hen's egg in his hands.

"This fight serves no one!" he yells to the heavens. His voice is disappointingly high. "If you must battle over crowns, then do so over this!" He raises the egg above his head and crushes it between his palms until its raw meat drips out between his fingers and onto his face.

"There'll be no more blood than this shed," he says quietly, and his voice will brook no disagreement.

As the opposing armies look on Drake opens his mouth wide and lets war pour into him. He'll be a difficult man, hereafter, as all his wives will attest.

On Monday the 21st of March 2005, the shopkeeper's assistant is cleaning the fancy dress shop on Festive Road. There's a thin layer of dust on the counter that wasn't there yesterday. It's not unusual. The nights have been stormy lately, and a lot of fine stone powder seems to have found a way in as the shop sways and flexes in the wind.

The shopkeeper's assistant has taken to keeping his favourite costume in a clear polythene bag to protect it. It's a rhinestone encrusted jumpsuit that reminds him of an old friend in Las Vegas. The shopkeeper's assistant knows he never truly knew Elvis, but he's been programmed to act as if he did and remember him fondly at every opportunity. He loves his fictional friend like a brother and guards his costume loyally. No one gets to wear it unless they too love the King.

The shop door sticks when Sara and Kay return their Cavalier and Roundhead costumes. In the Welsh mining village where the shopkeeper's assistant falsely remembers growing up, you'd have put that down to subsidence, but Samhain is a town built on weaving not coal.

As Sara and Kay leave they slam the door behind them, dislodging even more brick dust. The shopkeeper's assistant's quite impressed a building can shed so much stone and still stay standing. If only his non-existent Vegas friend had been built to last so well.

Wesley has requested the new chapel be a simple, towerless structure, or as simple as an octagonal building can be. The shape, he has explained, is perfect for public speaking and helps bring a congregation close to its minister.

Naturally, the masons know Wesley's plan for the new chapel is that it be free of the old church's superstition and ornamentation. They haven't just heard him say that, they've heard a man write it down behind him too. These are the 1780s, they've agreed. This is not an age to be hampered by tradition, they've nodded.

What the masons haven't told Wesley is that they have traditions of their own. They know a holy building needs protection even when it's unrequested.

When, on the 29th of March, 1782, they are given two empty egg shell halves to plaster into the chapel walls they do so willingly, even though it's Good Friday and they'd rather be elsewhere. It will keep conflict at bay.

Iris trots quickly over the cobbles with Panda stumbling behind her.

"I think somehow those two girls embody a kind of tension in this place," she says, "a force that can either sustain or destroy it."

"Yes, yes, it'll be love I expect," pants Panda. "It usually is. But what's that got to do with demons?"

Iris stops sharply. "Eh?"

"You mentioned something about a demon detector at the bus stop."

"That was Saturday night, Panda! Why have you waited 'til Tuesday to pick me up on it?"

Panda looks around. "Is it really Tuesday already?"

"Yes," says Iris.

It doesn't even seem to be early on Tuesday. Night is falling.

"But the last I remember, it was Sunday lunch time!"

"And you only had a shandy. I know."

"Why am I finding it so hard to keep track of time?"

"I think Time's slipping into some sort of messy, thematically-linked doodah instead of behaving orderly. We need to get to that fancy dress shop, sharpish. If we hurry we might be there by Wednesday."

She starts walking again, her ridiculous heels somehow always finding the right places to land on the uneven road.

"Hang on," says Panda, "this is just you avoiding answering the 'demons' question, isn't it?"

It's the 18th of April 1783 and, as they do every Good Friday, Samhain's mummers are performing the Pace Egg play. It's a tradition that goes back so far, no one quite believes it was invented.

It's a poor play – rough and crude and a lot longer than it should be and every year everyone pretends it used to be better in the old days. That's another tradition.

This year it's unexpectedly different. This is the first year St George and the Black Prince of Paradine find the words they bark out are not those they've rehearsed.

"There was a time when Angels warred. Nowadays it's people," says George.

"And we enact that endless war beneath the martyr's steeple," the Prince replies.

They look at each other in alarm.

"In the great Heavenly War, the Loyalists were God's servants," the words pour from George's mouth against his will.

"They fought the Argumentalists, the creatures of the serpent," responds the Prince unwillingly. Sweat beads on his forehead, making his Moorish make up run.

"The angels wished to keep God's plan as had been aforesaid," says George, terror on his face.

"They were the noble Chanticleers, opponents of the Hornheads," The Black Prince responds.

Even the dullest onlookers can see the men inside their costumes are now possessed by forces greater than themselves and that something has changed in Samhain.

When the play finally ends everyone applauds as usual. They pretend everything went smoothly, and no one ever mentions it again. It's a new tradition.

Kay's flat in Hebden is smaller than Sara's. It's tidier too. Right angles jump at you from everywhere. Old pants moulder in a basket not on the bathroom floor. Cutlery 'lives' in a specific part of a specific drawer rather than being found either in or near the sink. Books sit together alphabetised or in thematic groups not jammed together anywhere they'll fit. A lot of them are troublingly slim too – modern poetry collections, 20th Century plays, that Hare Krishna cookbook they hand out. Not many laughs and lots of white space. There's nothing you'd want to take with you to the loo. Sara doesn't really notice any of that on her first visit. What surprises her is Kay's pyjamas. They're tucked under the right hand pillow of her double bed. At Sara's, Kay has slept on the left.

As he looks down on Samhain, the Shopkeeper feels his skin tingling. He can see so many days outside his window now – days dressed as each other, days desperately keen to appear different, seasons rolling like clouds over the hills.

"My unbreaking approaches," he whispers, "my never having been."

He imagines himself younger, his hairline sliding forward over his temples again, flecks of grey vanishing as his skin tightens and loses its lines. He remembers who he was before Iris changed him as he looks for her slipping between the days up towards Festive Road.

Madame Blavoddy is telling Iris' fortune.

"There are opposing forces you must balance, dear. Forces within Samhain."

Iris has been hoping for a nicer reading, perhaps something about a tall man with nice teeth who's not fussy.

"Forces? What blumming forces? No chance of the navy is there? I like a sailor."

"This village is possessed."

"What by?"

"By you, of course. It's your most prized possession."

"No, you've lost me, love."

"You are governed by warring forces, Iris. The laws of Gravity and Levity – pushing and pulling you out of shape. One wants to make you a hero, one wants to make you a fool."

"And I have to choose which, do I?" asks Iris, as heroically as she can.

"No, don't be a fool," says Madame Blavoddy. "Samhain is built on that dynamic tension within you."

"Like Charles Atlas?"

"Well, I'd have said Yin and Yang myself," Madam Blavoddy sighs, "but close enough. You've leaked into it, seeped into its stones. It feeds on the sparks of conflict in you. Samhain has turned you into a war, Iris. A war between heaven and hell played out on its streets."

"Blimey."

"That'll be five pounds, please."

"Bit steep."

"Not really. I'm throwing in a free demon detector. You'll need someone with a bit of devilment in them if you want to get out of here."

Sara and Kay trace a path through the old churchyard in Samhain, weaving through long grass and untended graves. It's dusk, but there's something odd about the light, shadows seem to curve unexpectedly, congregating strangely between the headstones making it easy to lose your bearings. Kay's trying to show Sara to the grave of a poet, an author who meant a lot to her growing up, but all they're really doing is getting lost. Sara doesn't mind, she just wants to make Kay happy, even if she's not sure hunting dead poets will do that.

When they finally find the grave, in a spot they must have traipsed past a dozen times before, Kay puts a biro in the little pot by the headstone like hundreds before her. Sara finds it uncomfortable somehow. She's not sure the gesture is really about Kay or even the poet. It seems to be more about fitting in.

"You think I'm being stupid, don't you?" says Kay.

Sara doesn't answer quickly enough. Now no answer will help.

The doorbell tinkles as Iris and Panda crash into the fancy dress shop on Thursday morning in a cloud of glittering stone dust. They cast crazy-angled, strobe-dancing, shadows as the sun shifts unpredictably in the sky behind them. The shopkeeper's assistant can't help being impressed by their stagecraft.

"What's new –" he begins.

"Don't!" says Iris.

Footsteps descend from the room above the shop and, with a huge smile on his face, the shopkeeper appears.

"Finally, the moment approaches," he says, "the history of Iris Wildthyme is about to devour itself."

The shop begins to rumble.

"It'd better be chuffin' hungry."

"No, that's not what I said!" Sara protests.

Sara and Kay feel like they've been together forever. It's not always good.

"But it's what you were thinking!" says Kay as she strides off through the churchyard.

Reluctantly, Sara follows. "No, it's what you were thinking I was thinking!"

"That's just you projecting your over-thinking!"

"No, that's you protecting your under-thinking!" says Sara. She knows how stupid it sounds the second she says.

"That's not as clever as you think it is, actually!" Kay calls back.

"You've no bloody idea how clever I think it is, actually!"

Kay finds herself standing by the monument to Michael Drake. His ugly wide-open mouth leers at her. "I'm scared, Sara. How did we get here?"

"I don't know."

"I don't even know why we're fighting."

"Are we fighting?" Sara asks.

"If we are it's your fault."

It's meant to be a joke. It convinces neither of them.

"I just want us to be happy and everything stay the same," Sara starts, "but the second we stop still –"

"– it all falls apart. I know."

Someone is crying.

"I just want to give you what you want, Kay."

"I just want you."

"I don't. I want you."

An awkward silence descends that only awkward words can fill.

"I'm sorry."

"I didn't mean –"

"Me neither."

"I wish we could have today all over."

"What so you could win the argument this time?"

"No, so we could avoid it."

"By not finding out we disagree?"

"No, that's not what I said!" Kay protests.

"But it's what you were thinking!" says Sara as she strides off through the churchyard.

It is happening again. R D Laing could write a book on the strangling knot holding Sara and Kay together.

Something enormous creaks. A huge shadow falls over Kay, a shadow that isn't where it should be.

"Demon detector?" asks Iris.

"Oh yes, demons are real enough here," says Madame Blavoddy. "Samhain has turned the conflict inside you into symbols. We all try our best to make them other things but they keep ending up as angels and devils."

"Get away! How do you know all this?"

"I'm from the future, Iris, aren't I?"

"Are you?"

"Yes."

"Oh. Does it end well?"
"Well, it ends."

The whole shop is quivering. Coat hangers bounce excitedly on their racks. Musty costume sleeves flail, threads flying from frayed cuffs. Dust motes dance a frenzied gavotte. The very bricks of the building are bouncing rhythmically, grinding like a huge stone engine revving up.

At the centre of it all stands the Shopkeeper, beatific and still.

"What's going on?" bellows Panda. He's raised himself to his full height. It's not much but it's a lovely gesture.

"We've finally hit the critical mass. Pumpkin O'Clock. Samhain is unmasking itself," the Shopkeeper smiles. "It's only ever been a series of disguises, you see."

Panda doesn't see.

"Jings, it's all Iris in stupid hats, really." The Shopkeeper sighs, and raises his own hat. Panda braces himself to see Iris underneath it – for a disguise to fall and for the Shopkeeper to reveal his fez has been some kind of cloaking chapeau.

"Except for me, of course." The Shopkeeper adds. He's thinning quite badly on top and Panda finally understands why he wears that ridiculous felt plant pot.

"You fiend!" snarls Iris.

The Shopkeeper chuckles. It's expected in these situations. "Oh no, the fiend is you, dear lady. Don't you see? You're the devil in the detail and the god of the gaps. You've made this place in your own image, and now it's closing in on you."

The shopkeeper's assistant can't believe his ears. "You're the devil in disguise?" he asks.

Metal pings across the shop as its vibration increases – the stair carpet untacking itself as it shakes itself loose and thrashes like an angry snake. Underneath the underlay Panda glimpses familiar metal steps.

"Iris has spread herself across the whole history of Samhain," explains the Shopkeeper. "She's written herself into the place without realising. She's become such a part of its history and psyche the whole town depends on her presence to survive, and now she's finally got too big. Every move she makes pulls strings across time and draws the town tighter around her. Her continuity is so tangled she's disappearing under her own weight."

The shopkeeper's assistant frowns and turns to Panda. "Can that happen?" he asks.

Iris nods. "Aye," she says, "happened to a friend of mine once. I'd explain properly but it'd need a pen."

There's a horrible creaking sound. Cracks scurry like lightning across the ceiling and great flakes of plaster fall away like icebergs calving. They spin down onto the racks of clothing below.

The shopkeeper's assistant instinctively darts towards the polythene bagged Vegas suit to protect it from harm. As he scoops it under his arm a huge section of ceiling unexpectedly gives way and crashes down on top of him. He and his beloved costume disappear under a mound of rubble.

For a second Panda thinks about trying to dig him out but then thinks better of it. It's almost certainly too late and it looks like more of the ceiling could give way at any minute.

"Iris!" he shouts over the rattle of shaking stone.

"I know, love." she replies. Through clouds of dust, Iris makes out short leather straps swinging down from above – looped bands for commuters to cling to that she's hardly ever used for any other purpose.

Her bus is coming back.

The spire of the old church is warping, twisting like it was made by amateurs or craftsmen from Derbyshire. Slates are feathering and splintering as it turns to point in unexpected directions. Then from within it a huge talon emerges, a long thin yellow stained claw of a finger. Something is hatching out.

"Run!" shouts Sara grabbing Kay by the arm and tugging her out of the shadow that should not by rights be there.

The shop is shrinking, becoming thinner. Chairs are organising themselves into rows and plumping themselves up. The changing room mirrors are sneaking out from behind their curtained cubicles and arranging themselves neatly on the walls. The brickwork outside is pinkening, turning red.

"Iris, the bus is regrowing itself!" whispers Panda.

"Yes, chuck. I can see, you know."

"So, we can just drive it away!"

Iris shakes her head. "We've been through too many time mirrors, Panda. When all those windows are back in place they'll be wanting to short out the time difference business and balance the books."

"So what'll happen then?"

"Iris will finally do what I always said she would," explains the Shopkeeper. "She's going to disappear up her own arse, isn't she?"

"You engineered this, didn't you?" yells Iris.

The Shopkeeper tuts. "I'd say 'oversaw'. Engineering sounds rather more blue-collar to my mind."

Iris opens her mouth and then stops as a thought occurs. "Hang on, hang on," she says, "roll back a bit there, matey. When did you ever say I'd disappear up my own arse?"

"When we travelled together –" says the Shopkeeper. "In your future, Iris."

"I never did!" Iris protests. "I'd remember." She struts towards the Shopkeeper jabbing her finger. A metal pole sprouts up from the rubble on the floor by her side, very nearly unbalancing her.

"Well, you wouldn't, would you?" the Shopkeeper says witheringly. "It hasn't happened to you yet!"

"Oh," says Iris, thinking on her feet and then attempting a sweet smile. "Did we not get on, chuck?"

"Oh, we got on famously for a while, until I realised why you had to travel, that is."

"Enlighten me," says Iris.

Sara and Kay run, but the ground beneath them is misbehaving – balling and bunching and playing tricks. Suddenly everywhere in Samhain seems to be uphill. Thin passageways that were once reliable shortcuts through the tangle of houses emerge in unexpected locations, bootlacing around in bows and spirals, always looping back towards Festive Road.

As Sara and Kay flee the churchyard and the great strutting thing that is pulling itself from the church spire, Wesley's octagonal chapel rises up ahead even though it really shouldn't. Its huge walls seem to be opening out now, unfolding like a grey stone flower. The roof cracks like an egg and black matted fur pushes itself up above the petal walls.

The rumble of the shop's shaking sounds increasingly like an engine as the shop's fittings crash away to reveal familiar London Transport fixtures beneath.

The Shopkeeper walks towards Iris. He sounds almost tender as he takes her hand. "Iris, you only travel because if you stayed in the one place you'd have to interact with other people properly, and you don't know how to. You'd have to remember yesterday and work to make tomorrow better. You'd have to learn and grow and give and take and all those other things you find scary. You'd rather stay drunk and keep moving instead – stay the same."

"Sounds good to me," says Iris defensively. "That's how you get to have adventures."

"Oh, it does sound good at first, I know. I remember. Except one day you wake up and find everyone you ever knew has grown up and turned into someone else, and all you've done is shrivelled. You think you're living in the present but really you're just dressing up as your past. You end up hollow, Iris."

"So, is that why you wanted me to stay in one place? So I'd grow up?"

"Grow up until it killed you. Yes. It's for your own good, really. You'll get to mean something. Samhain's time and space is so bent around you now it fits you like a glove. As your bus pulls all its pieces into the present, it'll feed off that temporal curvature and tighten it further. You'll swell in importance as your world shrinks around you, until you're so full of yourself you'll collapse into a singularity, reduced to nothing but a point.

"Well, I say reduced. You having a point will be progress."

"Hang on a moment!" says Panda triumphantly. "You can't just blink Iris out of existence, can you? You come from her future! If you did that your future-past would stop happening!"

"I know," says the Shopkeeper. "But unlike you two, I can imagine a world without me. To be honest, I'm quite looking forward to it."

"But a future can't stop itself. Can it?"

"No one knows," says Iris quietly. "After all, who'd notice? It'd be like it never happened. It wouldn't have from most angles."

"Ah," says Panda. "So, is there anything we can do? It's usually about now you have a clever idea or a ridiculous stroke of luck or something."

The Shopkeeper checks his watch. "I rather afraid you're powerless. Any action either of you take will create causal ripples that simply tighten the trap further."

"But, we can't just stay here staring out a shop window for eternity! That'd be a rubbish ending."

"I know," says Iris grimly. "There's not even a customers' loo."

Samhain is tightening, spiralling in on itself. Days slide into each other as the bus windows slink back towards their true homes and the shop becomes ever more vehicular. The views through all those windows, the times beyond the mirrors, concertina into each other, crumpling and buckling as they collide.

Sara and Kay run through contrary geography, jostling past Michael Drake, mouth agape, as he tries to trap the forces of Civil War in a metaphor, slipping by a lady poet who feels the weight of these mixed up times harder than most, sidestepping a man dressed as Al Jolson reciting the Black Prince doggerel from the Pace Egg play. They feel they've always been running. Space and Time swirl, dark and light dance, good and evil war and order and chaos quibble over terms. Only Sara and Kay's clasped hands are constant as Samhain waxes and wanes about them.

The things that were trapped in the church and chapel loom over all of Samhain, as they somehow always have. They're monstrous, destructive creatures, devouring the town, and pulling it into themselves, fighting over scraps. Neither quite angel, nor quite devil, they both wear fake fur, though only one has a bippity-boppity hat.

The stones of Samhain are glowing now, even in those blinks of confused time that are night. The houses are steaming and melting, streets candle-dripping in swirls down the hill. Smoke curls backwards and forwards through the stories of the town.

Old men who are sometimes babies and briefly young men stagger/crawl in search of freedom through this chaos of burning days, but they too are melting as Samhain boils away.

Madame Blavoddy walks backwards through it all on her way from her shop. ".uoy dloT" she says.

Sara and Kay stop running as the hillside erupts like a volcano behind them and undifferentiated times and places rain down like hot snow.

Inside the shop, Iris and Panda look out at the town they've come to think of as home, as the bus reasserts itself around them. They see the molten roads, the creatures destroying Samhain, they smell burning hair and frying fat. Even though they can't hear them over the noise of the shop destroying itself they know there are people screaming.

"Can't we stop this, Shopkeeper?" yells Iris. "Can't we just die in a way that'll let this place live?"

The Shopkeeper gasps. "Is that you growing up, Iris?"

"Would it be enough, you bloody idiot? If Panda and I just stopped now?"

"You know, I really haven't a clue."

"Only one way to find out," says Iris. She's heading for the shop door, ready to face her demons and angels outside. It's almost a bus door now.

"Don't!" says a commanding baritone voice from behind her. She turns to see who it belongs to.

It's the shopkeeper's assistant, newly emerged from under a pile of broken stone. He has put on a costume. It's the only one he ever wanted to wear.

He straightens his quiff. "Seems to me, ma'am. I'm the only person here can resolve this. You're all a little tied up in time stuff and all, but me – I'm a free agent."

The Shopkeeper laughs. "Come on, you're not even a person, are you! You're a robotic parody of some ridiculous entertainer!"

His assistant curls his lip in a sneer. "Yeah, well that's as maybe, but that's not all I can be. I got me a disguise!"

He grabs hold of the metal pole that's grown up in the middle of the shop, and presses a red button that's appeared halfway up it. 'REQUEST STOP' it reads.

The shop/bus stops rumbling and shaking. There's a silence. Then there is a whiteness.

As the bubbling, fluid days of Samhain descend on Sara and Kay, they close their eyes, waiting for oblivion, hoping it's pain-free. They can still see red, glowing through their skin. Then they hear the horn.

Opening their eyes, there's more red. It's a bus. Not the normal

Hebden bus, a double decker, one they've never seen before. It's surfing down white hot rivers of time, smashing its way through liquefied walls. At the wheel is an old man with skin like worn shoes and a smile broader than Norfolk. The rhinestones on his jumpsuit are shining like diamonds.

As the bus passes by they see the old lady from the bus shelter standing in the footwell at the back.

"Hop on!" she cackles and they do, nearly trampling a tatty soft toy underfoot as they leap aboard. Together, they tear down the hill towards home.

"Thanks for picking us up!" says Kay.

"Think nothing of it," says the old lady. "The more passengers who don't live here the more chance we have of breaking free!"

"Can we do it?" asks the soft toy unexpectedly, from somewhere near Sara's shoe.

"Uh huh!" says the driver in the jumpsuit. "With a bit of luck."

"Oh, we'll be fine then," Sara laughs nervously. "I've the luck of the devil!"

The bus strains, then slows, labouring as if up to its wheel arches in mud. For a moment that might well be a lifetime it seems to stand still. Then suddenly, something gives. Tiny holes in causality pop into being for the bus to nose its way through. The shopkeeper's assistant puts his foot to the floor and the bus accelerates away, snapping ties to the past as it flies straight and true towards Hebden.

A twisted tangle of events rip themselves apart and a tunnel of almost working Time and Space opens up in the bus' wake. It's not much, a handful of seconds and feet, but it's just enough to let a few people slip through to safety. Dazed and distressed, Samhain residents stumble away from the flaming ruins of their histories. They stagger down the hill in rags together, faces blackened like mummers with the soot of burning ages. Then the tunnel collapses behind them.

Loose flapping fronds of boiling history and geography pang back like elastic. Events wrap themselves around each other as they rebound back up the hill. They start to congeal in clumps, collapsing in on themselves. Sticky strands of old stories rain down on the town, tying everything in knots. They get caught up in the fur of the great stalking monsters that have made Samhain their battleground, pulling them together. As the creatures come together they shrivel and fuse. A fight, a dance, a hug, and suddenly they're one. Soon Samhain itself starts to deflate about them, folding in on itself until it's nothing but a hard ball of shiny heat – a coal compressed to diamond, no bigger than an egg.

You can still see what's left of Samhain if you ask politely in the right circles. Madame Blavoddy keeps it on a shelf in her caravan. Now it's cooled down it looks like a tiny glass ornament – a little town in an egg-shaped bubble somewhere it's always snowing. Sometimes it's so snowy the whole village is covered in a shell of solid white.

Iris and Panda visit Madame Blavoddy now and again, now they're back on the bus. More again than now, to be truthful. They don't see much of the shopkeeper's assistant, at all. He has a lot of tour dates with his tribute act. The Shopkeeper they don't even remember these days. It's as if by some magic, he's disappeared. Kay and Sara they leave alone, to face futures as yet unwritten.

"What'll we do now?" Sara will ask when she and Kay are safely back in Hebden.

"Let's kiss and see what happens." Kay will answer. "Then what will be, will be."

CLOSURE
PAUL CASTLE

Working in a pub you see so many people that thoughts and conversations often roll into one big blur, but I can clearly remember what I thought when meeting Iris Wildthyme for the first time. I still think it every time I see her – "Good God, what is that woman wearing?!" – but, because I'm a good host, and also still remember my upbringing, I politely compliment her outfit as I serve her and her little furry companion, Panda, their first round of drinks. As I pour the generously proportioned gin and tonics, and regard once more the lady's figure hugging zebra print leather pants, thigh-length scarlet silk blouse held in with a silver studded biker's belt with death's head buckle, a presumably Wonderbra supported cleavage revealed by perhaps one too many unfastened buttons, a glitzy silver and black waistcoat, and a pink feather boa, all topped off with a battered suede-green felt hat, jammed down over a mop of blond curls, the thought pops into my head that the advice my mother gave me when I was very young to always be polite and always be truthful really was terribly contradictory.

"Oh please, don't encourage the old biddy, she's been up on the top deck of the bus for simply hours throwing all that together" Panda snorts as he takes his first sip, "we're only staying here, not popping downtown to Leeds or anywhere."

"Panda lovey," replies Iris, putting down her drained glass, "This may be just a village pub, nothing special in the grand scheme of things, but Danny here mixes the best G&T's in West Yorkshire, if not indeed the whole of The North, and I like to look my best. Now get the next round in as I grab a suitable table".

I watch her totter over to a bench seat by the window where my first customers of the evening – Erik and Sheila – were finishing off their pudding, and proudly poured with a shameless grin another couple of my highly praised drinks for Panda. I've not been a barman that long, you see, and no-one's ever commented on my work, aside from maybe my late uncle's father-in-law, who passed the property onto me – his only living relative – on my second day before buggering off to Spain with the barmaid and the proceeds from the sale of his recently deceased wife's house. He simply said after my first day "Aye, you'll be fine". Two weeks in and I'm starting to think he might not be too wrong.

I'm brought back to the moment when Panda calls out "Iris, give us a hand with these, will you!" She comes back over, flashes me a grin and a wink, her face momentarily all teeth and curls, scoops up the ten inch tall cuddly art critic (who should never be called a toy, or a bear, unless you wish to incite all the hell and fury that you'd barely imagine a few pounds of cloth and stuffing can produce) and puts him under her arm, seizing the two glasses with her long fingers with their sparkly purple painted nails.

On the way back to Erik and Sheila's table she cheerily greets Dave and Dave, who're just coming through the door and shaking off their heavy winter coats, which believe you me, are an essential part of pretty much everyone's wardrobe as 2004 breezes into its final quarter. A couple of whiskeys precede these gentlemen's usual Guinnesses, a couple shots of Jameson's, which beardy Dave informs me are from the same factory as the Guinness, and curly Dave adds that not only that, share an identical process in the brewing, up to a certain point. They move to the pool table, through the alcove in the next room, as Petula Clark suddenly bursts out from the jukebox.

Startled, as so far that evening there'd just been the hubbub of more recent oldies-in-the-making such as Blur and the Stereophonics, I look over, to see Iris intently perusing the CD track listings, bopping a little to the beat. I like her. She reminds me of a lady who looked after me sometimes when I was a kid, a sort of honorary aunty. She was called Iris too, Iris de Lacy Lacy, a name that might make you picture someone exotic from a distant shore, but was English, had a raucous laugh, and a kindly nature.

Not thought of her for years. Long dead now, as are most people from my childhood, but yeah, watching Iris now, there's a definite resemblance.

The pub is filling up nicely now, the inhabitants of Arthur's End braving the chilly October evening. It's quiz night tonight, as it is every Tuesday, and as it's my third quiz I'm just starting to get into the swing of things. There's usually enough freebies from the brewery to keep us in prizes, and Old Harry's supply of wooden toys that line the shelves around the room, brightening the place up, is frequent enough to bulk that out with a model or two each week. The winners tonight turn out to be the team who don't generally fare too well, the Summer Wines, whose name seems chosen purely to make their last place in the scoreboard get a bit of a laugh, but who had the advantage of Iris and Panda at their table tonight. As well as a Wychwood promotional t-shirt and some Halloween themed glasses, I let the team choose a couple of the models. Young Vince selects Darth Vader's Tie Fighter, and Denise goes for a Windmill that was probably based on the one from *Trumpton*, or *Chigley*, or whatever series it was. Old Harry may like to make wooden toys, but he's far from traditional in his approach.

I pour myself a ginger beer, filling a pint glass with a couple of bottles. It's thirsty work watching people slowly slipping into gentle inebriation. I'm no teetotaller, but in my long fifteen day career as a barman I've insisted on remaining totally sober. Rarely do people get out and out drunk here, but tonight seems to be a bit louder than usual. Iris seems to have dominated the jukebox, with Cilla Black, Dolly Parton, Tom Jones, and Shirley Bassey belting out number after number, and Iris and Panda have been working the company, moving from table to table through the evening, talking and laughing and, seemingly, getting people to divulge their closest secrets and darkest fears.

Waves of intensity seem to ebb and flow across the room as they join each group, reaching a peak as the next round is due, and their hosts come to the bar to buy the next round. I feel as if I could map out the room on a graph so that it resembles a Mexican wave of heightened emotion as they make their rounds, if only I had the time. Something is happening tonight, something unusual. I shoo the thought from my mind as I pull pints of Arthur's Ale and Stella Artois for Phil and Sandy, deciding to ask Iris and Panda to remain behind after hours for a nightcap, the only occasion of late when I let my hair down and have a few beers.

I always thought that being a barman would be like it always was on old American telly shows, be it 'where everybody knows your name' from *Cheers*, or Moe's Bar from *The Simpsons*. You know, places where people came in and plonked themselves on the barstool, and poured out their every trouble to the unruffled barman, who would rise to the challenge and deliver words of wisdom that would solve their troubles. Come to think of it, *Cheers* and *The Simpsons* are probably bad examples, but I'm sure you remember the sort of thing. Maybe Captain Pike's doctor-cum-bartender in the pilot episode of *Star Trek*, or the barman from the last episode of *Quantum Leap*. Yeah, that works better. But life's not like that, it would seem. Shame.

Curly Dave is the first to plonk himself down on the stool in front of me, buying another Guinness and another bottle of ginger beer to top up my glass. I leave him to contemplate the settling clouds in his glass as I pop to the gents, squeezing past the pool table, where Panda is playing beardy Dave, and Iris is rummaging in her bag for twenty pence pieces for the next few games. On my return I top up curly Dave's drink, and pour my ginger beer. He looks me in the eye, and starts to explain what's been troubling him. It's his job, it seems, and he's quite happy with it. However …

"It's a dead end, never going to go anywhere. I mean, I love it, but my mother keeps on asking when I'm due for promotion. Every phone call, every visit, she asks me how I'm getting on, and whether I'm running the firm or not. I work at DIY Homestores for goodness sake, not an accountancy firm. I know about mixing paint, working out measurements for how much wallpaper you'd need, can cut carpets and advise on curtains and drapes and all the sort of stuff Blair Tweeney goes on about in Freshen Up Your Gaff on the telly show that advertises us."

He looks really glum, and not the sort of person who'll gladly get up at 6am in the morning to freshen up anyone's gaff. A vein throbs on his forehead, and I remember another of my mother's pieces of advice; "be careful what you wish for."

What can I do? I'm no wise sage with years of experience, just a bloke in his twenties who's watched too much telly and is suddenly, by a series of weird quirks of fate, the sole inheritor of an old man's pub. I look at Dave, and just start talking. I talk about the rat race, and how it chews up and spits out people, all those young managers who pass through the company, climbing up through the ranks, passing from department to department, getting more stressed and less likeable as the months pass, before they leave the store, one way or another. Like I say, I know nothing really, but Dave fleshes out the story with his observations and anecdotes, and the vein on his forehead calms. I start to get an inkling of a headache, just a stab above my right eye, but it's been a busy evening. Anyway, next time Dave talks to his elderly mother, he's going to emphasis the joys of working in the position he does, and his sorrow for the lost souls who are, fleetingly, his immediate bosses.

No sooner than he's gone young Vince is at the bar. Well, I say young, but he was probably only a few years my junior. It's the hair, all fashionable and floppy over the eyes, not like my receding crop, that does it. The Tie Fighter he won at the quiz has been bothering him. It's bringing up memories of all the *Star Wars* toys he inherited from older brothers as a kid – brothers my age from the sounds of things – but sold for beer money when he was seventeen. All the figures and spaceships and playsets, gone to something you piss away after half an hour. "No offence" he adds to that. Now though, he wants them back.

The movies are popular again, with the last of the prequels due out in the summer. But all gone. Not only the toys, but the Weeklies, duvet covers, novels like Han Solo's Revenge and Splinter of the Mind's Eye. All gone.

Well, with my success with curly Dave, the answer came to me easy. Young Vince was a successful up and coming manager type, dead young and keen, and had a decent pay packet. I told him to type 'vintage star wars figures' into eBay, and buy anything he wanted. He looked a bit astonished at this, having been drummed into him over the last ten or so years, by both parents and brothers, that toys were for kids and had to be let go of. I asked if his parents collected anything – his dad liked die-cast vintage cars and his mother cheery pottery pigs – and he made the mental adjustment. None of us really let go of our childhood, not completely, and *Star Wars* toys are only different from a generational perspective.

Another satisfied customer, but with it, another stab of pain above the eye. I look at the time; only ten past nine. About two hours to go.

Over the next hour, it seemed that everyone who came to the bar had concerns about this, or worries about that. Kate, Denise's sister and fiancée of Vince, was starting to wonder if she was right to marry someone who was looking like turning into a collector of *Star Wars* toys, so I reassured her that most people had a similar comfort blanket. I revealed that I collected *Transformers* from the 1980s, and had a growing collection of cartoons on DVD which I had watched as a kid. Denise herself was worried about climate change and rising sea levels, so I pointed out that we lived far from the coast and quite high up. Beardy

Dave was concerned about also becoming baldy Dave, but as it turns out, curly Dave quite likes Patrick Stewart, so that reassured him. Erik and Sheila weren't convinced that they were suited for each other, they explained quite separately and with some shockingly personal details, but when I pointed out that Erik hadn't even noticed the last couple of really rather attractive girls that I served whilst talking to him, or that Sheila hadn't paid any heed to the two tall blokes with movie star looks who were playing darts in direct line of sight of their table, both were somewhat reassured, and looked happier the rest of the night.

I, however, was feeling rougher and rougher with each tale, and more and more drained with each reassurance. The funny thing was, it was only after each conversation that I felt it, that stabbing pain above my right eye, and the general feeling that I was going a murky green in colour. When I was talking to people, or listening, or indeed interacting with anyone, I felt fine. It was just those moments in between. Was I becoming a conversation junkie?

Iris Wildthyme caught my eye again. She and Panda were talking with yet another group of people, playing some sort of card game, pontoon or twenty-one, or something. I swear that they've chatted with everyone in the place. Just as I have. Looks like they're having more fun though, whilst I should be pulling in a wage from the West Yorkshire County Council as a Citizen's Advice Bureau clerk. I look around everyone I've spoken with, all look relaxed and cheerful, with nary a care in the world. My head throbbed, the stabbing pain above my right eye having grown to an area the size of my outstretched hand. I wanted to die, or at least, to get into bed. Twenty to eleven. Not long now ...

I felt Iris looking at me, all her cheer and noise quietened for a moment. It seemed as if she had a direct window into my soul. I thought of the Iris I knew as a child, this time though the memory was painful. I remember how I was when I was older, when you didn't need to be babysat when Mum and Dad went out, when instead you just watched horror or action movies all night at a mate's. I remember –

I remember that it's time to call last orders, to do another round of collecting glasses, to pop them in the dishwasher in the back. I rang the bell, served a last few people, solved a few more of their life problems (miss your old Lego, just buy some more, feel disturbed by all the violence and gore in the blockbusters of today, just start to get the movies you remember your parents enjoyed when you were a kid on

DVD, can't bear being reminded of your ex with all the love songs on the radio, just change stations and listen to some jazz, or club classics, or hardcore dance, anything without much in the way of lyrics) and eventually everyone was gone, leaving me exhausted, face down on the bar, feeling like death.

Everyone, that is, apart from Iris and Panda, who now sat on the stool, or simply propped up against one of the pumps.

"So pet, what's troubling you?" she asks.

I just want to cry. I don't know why. The pain in my head is there for no reason, I should have had a great night, for despite having no staff I've managed to run one of the busiest nights that the pub has ever seen, and lived up to my preconception of what a good barkeep should be like, pouring out oodles and noodles of great advice to people who need it like some agony uncle from the papers, remembering people's regular orders and those who like to sample a bit of everything, mixing cocktails like Tom bloody Cruise, and wiping glasses like – I don't know …

"I don't know! I've had a great night. It's been a couple of bumpy weeks, but tonight I feel like I'm really coming into my own, you know, learning how to run a pub. But my head's killing, it's been getting worse and worse all through the night, and all I can think about right now is someone who's been dead for a decade, longer maybe, and I've not seen since a kid. Watching you all night I've just been reminded of her. You go around being Aunty Iris for everyone, making everyone better, happy and laughing, well she was my Aunty Iris all those years ago, except she wasn't really my aunty, I don't think I ever even called her that, but that's who she was."

Iris and Panda, against all expectation, just sit and listen to me talk. After a while they put some money into the till, a whole wad of notes, and fetch a few bottles of Bombay Sapphire from
the back, and a whole load of tonic, the bottles still bound neatly together in that thick and sturdy plastic wrap. They pour three glasses, in measures even more generous than my own, and we drink. It makes me shudder a little at first.

"You know," I say, "I was really disappointed when I first poured you Bombay Sapphire a couple of weeks ago, that first night of mine here. I thought that it would be –"

"Blue" interjected Panda, "I thought the very same. It's just the colour of the bottle. After a couple of glasses you don't mind so much though."

"Danny, love, tell us more about your aunty Iris" pressed Iris Wildthyme gently, like some practiced therapist, adding "and drink up, sweetie."

I gulped back the drink, letting the booze soothe me with its almost disinfectant aroma, and let Panda pour another, before taking a sip. I carried on talking, supping at the drink like it was lemonade, paying no heed to further refills, just supping away at the bottomless glass. "She was just someone at my parent's church. There were dozens of old people who Mum and Dad chatted to after the service, over their cups of tea in the hall, whilst I ran around with the other kids. But it was only really Iris and her neighbour, Irene, we used to socialise with, video nights in and barbecues and all that. It probably wasn't like that at all, you know, memories from childhood are very selective, and I've not even thought about this at all until tonight. But Iris became that everyday aunty that my actual family aunties, who lived all over the country, hundreds of miles away, couldn't become.

"When Mum and Dad went out for an evening, which wasn't that often really, or had to pop up country to a funeral of a great uncle or someone, it was Iris who looked after me. I loved staying over. She had a whole wardrobe filled with video tapes with movies recorded off the telly. Loved comedies, she did. I probably saw all of the Abbott and Costello movies round hers, and she used to watch all of my *Star Trek* and *Blakes 7* videos with me. She helped me see them with a sense of humour. I was an over-earnest fanboy and though they were Serious Science Fiction, but I learned to appreciate them on different levels, with her cackling away at lines which I never even knew were jokes. Lots of the fanboys I've met still take those stories too seriously, and don't get why I find them funny, or love the ones they think are crap. Is this down to me having an aunty Iris? She laughed a lot, and a mean a lot! It was all from the heart, and from the belly too. She never had any children, so never learned to censor movies. I remember there being some sex scene in a movie, I think that one where Sean Connery is a medieval monk investigating a murder, if such a film even exists, and her laughing and telling me to avert my eyes. But I was twelve years old, and you know, very interested in the boobies and bottom of some actress.

"And this was one of my last memories of her. I think I stayed over one night when Mum had to get a nasty crack on the head from a cupboard checked out at the hospital. We watched a comedy like *Brewster's Millions*, or maybe *Home Alone*, but I was getting too old to be baby-sat. I was becoming a teenager.

"That was one of the worst times of my life. Looking back, most of it really doesn't seem like it was me living in my body. I'd cleared out most of my childhood so quickly, getting rid of toys and comics, wanting so desperately to not be a kid any more, and have girlfriends and stuff. I just wasn't me anymore. I don't know how I looked from the outside, but to me it feels that I became selfish, unlikeable, unattractive. I didn't want to do anything aside from play on the computer, read my sci-fi books, or do my paper-round. Everything else was out. My schoolwork suffered, but as I was well-behaved and always had my head stuck in a book, or quietly struggling with maths or English and not making a fuss, no-one really noticed. I never let anyone notice."

I took a sip of my G&T, recently refreshed by Panda, and felt the alcohol course through my system, making everywhere feel fuzzy and warm, aside from the hot patch on my head, which felt massive. I clutched my glass, and gulped down the liquid, glass after glass, refill after refill. I couldn't shake off the feeling that, should I feel my head with my hands, or glance in a mirror, that I'd resemble the elephant man.

"I suppose everyone suffers as a teen, but it's the quiet ones, the unathletic, unsociable ones who get it the worst, I think. It's those kids who become introverted, and have no outlet. I withdrew into myself, and people like Iris got pretty much forgotten. Well, not forgotten, but neglected. Loved, but as a memory, rather than as the person they still were.

"I went to university a few years later, and on one of my visits home Mum asked me to visit Iris, as she was getting old and less mobile, and would appreciate seeing me. But I was still rather scrunched up inside the protective shell I grew as a teen, and promised that I would, but I didn't. Visits home after visits home, Christmas and Easter and the Summer, and the request from Mum came to visit Iris again and again and again. I promised, but never did.

"Eventually though, a girl at Uni got inside my shell, and broke it open. I only knew her for a couple of weeks, but she was who I needed to finally grow up. I changed suddenly, and started to socialise, to become the me who I have been ever since, happy and, well, normal. Well adjusted, and adult.

"Too late for my old aunty Iris though. On my next trip home, Mum told me that she'd died."

My head felt like it was going to explode, my vision swam, my ears felt like they'd each grown a heart, pumping and pumping all the blood around my now engorged head. I looked at Iris, and simply said "I know it's not you, but please, would you accept my apology on her behalf?"

She nodded, and behind her in a mirror on the wall I saw my head. Elephant man. I raised my hands and felt my engorged cranium, and screamed. A cracked, pathetic whine, too terrified to let anything past my lips. Panda grabbed the bottle and poured it down my throat, and I passed out.

I woke, feeling surprisingly light and fresh. In a bucket on the bar in front of me was a soggy wet mass, a thing resembling a bladder, but with faintly gesticulating feelers and slurping suckers. I felt my head. That, at least, was normal. I tried to speak, but only croaked.

Iris gently placed a steaming cup of black coffee in front of me. "Drink up lovey. As for that thing, well, better out than in."

Panda was sitting in the corner, doing the Times crossword. The papers had been delivered, sun was streaming through the windows, and in the distance, the gentle whine of the milk float and the clink of its calcium rich payload attested to the fact that I'd been out for the count for hours. "Better tell the poor lad what's happened, Iris", he bellowed.

She looked at the thing in the bucket, and then at me. "It's a parasite from an alien planet. It lives on fear and guilt and suffering."

I stared at her, and then at it. I gulped down the black, bitter brew, and felt my ability to speak start to return. "How did that get into my head? How did you get it out?"

"Before you moved up here, just a few weeks ago, I threw a massive party on my bus, practically everyone in Arthur's End came along. It went on for days and nights, and they ate me out of house and home. The avocado dip was very popular, but the avocados came from an alien marketplace far in the future –"

"Your avocados came from another planet?" I asked, incredulously, then looked at the thing in the bucket, simpering to itself, gently sweating gin from every orifice, and realised that alien avocados weren't so all that far-fetched.

"No, they were imported from Israel" she admitted, "but they'd been contaminated by some alien spores, a gestalt entity that infects other creatures with fragments of itself, and something or other, I don't know how it works, but it really does not like alcohol, once the spores germinate. Tonight I invited everyone who was infected to the pub, and plied them with so much booze that the creatures went into a germination cycle –"

"Iris," warned Panda from behind the crossword, "Stop making this sciencey bollocks up. We don't know how it works, we just know that alcohol affects it, makes people worry too much, and it somehow passes from them when they're comforted. We got it out of them, and into you, my boy. And when you had the lot it sort of became whole, and manifested itself fully into that thing in the bucket."

"We just needed you to ply you with several bottles of gin and an inordinate amount of tonic first, and get what's been troubling you for years off your chest." she finished.

"But it's not been troubling me. I've not thought about Iris for years." I objected.

"She was there, a tiny splinter of guilt in your heart. When I accepted your apology on her behalf, your soul was cleansed, and this proved too much for that thing in the bucket."

"But how did it get out of my head, and into the bucket?"

"Kiddo," said Panda, "you really do not want to know."

"Right then, Danny my love, time for you to do something for me." And she plonked a fez on my head, one of those funny red hats from the Middle East that Tommy Cooper used to wear.

"Look. I'm sorry I was so annoying. Alright?" she begrudgingly tells me.

I'm speechless, and my face must have been quite a picture. She reaches forward and grabs the fez, and chucks it over the thing in the bucket, which gurgled gently. "Not you, duck, just someone I used to know."

"What was all that about?"

She cracks one of her enormous teeth-and-curls grins.

"Closure, love, closure."

THE END